In The End, Love

Rod Hacking

Copyright © 2022 Rod Hacking

All rights reserved.

ISBN: 9798433388048

To the memory of my close friend and Bishop

Peter K Walker

Olim Eliensis

1

Lifelong marriage was the means whereby from earliest times, men kept control of their women, and adultery was always the fault of women who, in times past, and times present, could be stoned for it, though rarely the man. Relationships, once the product of intense love, could also falter and fail for many other reasons. Those advocating arranged marriages justify the practice on the grounds that feelings of love towards another are an unreliable basis for life together, and that it is better for people to grow in love than depend on transitory feelings.

Darcey, one of Jo's detective team, and for whom she had long held special affection and whom she had known since her earliest days as head of CID in Norfolk, had warned her against taking up with Judith (as she was initially known before shortening it to Jude – a move Darcey mistrusted) so soon after Marie had left for America.

Jo trusted Darcey's judgement and began to have doubts herself about the relationship but was also aware that Jude had given up the Church and her Vicarage to come and live with Jo. That made ending the relationship difficult. They had met during a previous investigation and one night Jo called on her and spent the night with her. That had been playing with fire, and only as unacceptable to the Bishop of Ely as it would have been to her own Chief Constable.

Jo's great guru was Sigmund Freud and as she drove home on the following morning she could picture him sitting alongside her chastising her for forgetting the force of sex and reminding her that she would not be the first person in a prominent position to fall from grace. Jo had been relieved when she let him get out!

It was ludicrous. Here she was, the most senior detective leading her own team, and the holder of a DBE for previous work, but profoundly uneasy about saying to Judith that it had been nothing more than a one night stand. She just might have been able to put a stop to it had Judith not announced her departure from the Church and clearly expecting to move in with Jo, to help look after the children, and do the household chores.

And what starts small has an odd habit of expanding, and it had. Jo liked

Jude and she had appreciated her taking of the funerals both of Karen, Marie's mother-in-law, and Marie's own.

Then came the matter of the baby. Ollie, Jo's son was born from Jo's womb using IVF from an egg provided by Marie, and fertilised by an unknown male. Stupidly, because she thought that would be what Judith wanted, even though she herself did not, she agreed to what is known as reciprocal in vitro fertilisation, provided it was Judith who carried the baby.

They did this through Addenbrookes, as had been the case with Ollie, and they were extremely kind, but it took two goes, which was expensive and demanded two periods of preparation by Jo, involving repeated injections to stimulate the ovaries.

The pregnancy had not been easy for Jude and she had mostly hated what was happening both to her body and her mind as the months went by. In retrospect Jo wondered whether her own ambivalence about the relationship was being experienced by Jude, who could hardly wait for the end of pregnancy, scheduled for ten weeks time.

On this day Jude should never have come to St Albans with the others. Josie was always pleased to be visiting her dad who worked there, and Ollie still enjoyed being his half-sister on these visits, glad to see her so happy with him. They had in common the fact of their genetic mother's suicide in America, and although a number of years apart in age, they remained close.

Nathan, a senior registrar gynaecologist, had the whole day free and was not on call, so nothing could disturb their day, a thought which he knew was tempting providence, but he had plans for them all to enjoy. Until Jude arrived, that was.

Nathan opened the door and he and Josie greeted one another effusively, as did he and Ollie (Nathan being the nearest thing to a dad). Next came Jo, someone he loved deeply, not least because once having got him into prison, she went not quite to the ends of the earth, but almost, to get him released. And then Jude came. It had often been said in Cambridge that Nathan was an outstanding doctor, that nurses claimed he had the best eyesight, when it came to diagnosis, of all the staff.

'Keep your coat on Jude. You and I need to pop up the road. We'll see the others again before too long.'

In a matter of seconds he had in his own car.

'Remind me how far you're gone,' he said.

'30 -31 weeks.'

'I want to give you a good look over as you're obviously feeling pretty grotty. When did you last see a medical professional?'

'The community midwife came two weeks ago.'

'Did she do your blood pressure?'

'She said it was a bit high but told me not to worry.'

'She didn't suggest you saw your GP?'

'No.'

'Are you in pain?'

'A dull nagging pain under my ribs on the right. Also I've got a horrible headache, and I feel totally exhausted.'

'Sickness?'

'Yes.'

'We're nearly there. Tell me your ethnicity?'

'Mum is from the North of England and my dad Nigerian. Is that a problem?'

'Ethnicity can change all sorts of things in medicine but I would have been more concerned if your mum had been West African. All the same I have to take it into account, and do you know the ethnicity of the baby's father?'

'He is a Nigerian PhD student at Cambridge though we know no more than other that his medical report, which declared him fit and healthy.'

'You and Jo no doubt gave this a lot of thought and it seems to me a wise decision for you to be the mother of a baby that will look like you.'

'It was Jo who made the decision in the end. I would have happily used a white donor, but you know how wonderfully, or is it annoyingly, principled she is?'

'Yes, I've had no shortage of evidence of that.'

Even Jude laughed at that.

'I bet she hasn't told you that she has now twice turned down requests to be a Chief Constable.'

'No, but it doesn't surprise me. Now, here we are. This is my workplace and you're about to ruin my day off.'

'Nathan, I'm so sorry.'

He parked the car and asked Jude to remain where she was. He went inside and a man with a wheelchair came to the car and instructed Jude to get in. He then pushed her to the entrance and along a corridor into a room with a bed, where a midwife/nurse was waiting for her.

'Hello, Ms Bartram.'

'Please call me Jude.'

'I'm going to take your blood pressure and one or two other tests including listening to baby's heartbeat. Then we'll give you a scan and Dr Coddington, an obstetrician will come and see you.'

'Where's Nathan, I mean Dr Vickery, disappeared to?'

'He's gone to call your partner and the children, so they know what's happening..'

A few minutes later, as the scan was taking place, a man clearly of West Indian origin (a real give away as he was wearing a West Indian cricket motif on his sweater) came into the room. He was warm (including his hands) and friendly, and with a lightness of touch asked Jude all about what she had been experiencing.

'Did you mention these things to your community midwife?'

'Mostly not. I've never been been pregnant before and I just assumed they were normal.'

He looked at the scan and also at the charts given him by the midwife. At that moment he was joined by Nathan who also looked at the scan and other test results.

'I'm so sorry, Jude,' said Nathan, 'but your baby has died. Normally we would move you to the labour ward and induce the baby by vaginal delivery but I regret to say that you are suffering from a condition called pre-eclampsia. Your blood pressure is 230/170 though we shall immediately put you on an intravenous infusion of drugs to get it down. Then, we are going to remove the baby by means of a c-section. If we are to do the best for you we shall have to act today and we need to keep you in a for a while.'

Jo arrived.

'The baby has died, Jo.'

'Yes, Nathan warned me on the phone that he thought that was the case. He's changing for the operating theatre now. You know you will be in the best of possible hands – literally.'

'Oh, Jo, I'm so sorry.'

'There's nothing to be sorry about. Sharon told me a story of a suspected Irish terrorist who was arrested in a house in Devon and although under guard, suddenly realised that one of the women there was having an obstetric emergency, bleeding extensively. He leapt towards her risking being shot, and then made everyone obey his instructions to enable him to get her to hospital. He saved her life because unknown to everyone he was an obstetrics and gynaecology doctor, and he is now a consultant at the Royal Devon and Exeter Hospital. So what a good job we came to St Albans, and that Nathan is a medical class act.

A woman came into the room.

'I'm Helen, your anaesthetist. Can I just listen to your chest, please?' She did so.

Right, we'll get you to the anaesthetist's room straight away. You'll be ok, Jude. You'll have the country's greatest gynaecologist, the country's greatest anaesthetist (I award that title to myself, by the way) and, I believe, the country's greatest detective with you. What's not to like?'

As Jude was wheeled towards the theatre, Nathan came out to see Jo.

'What happens afterwards, Nathan?'

'All being well, and provided she responds to treatment, we'll keep her in for some days.'

Jo entered the anaesthetist's room with Jude and was holding her hand as Helen sent Jude to sleep.

Afterwards, in the Recovery Room there was something of a hiatus when Jude was overwhelmed with nausea and Helen had to come and inject her with an anti-emetic. She was taken into a single room in the maternity wing and it was there that Jude and Jo were able to see and hold their deceased baby.

'Oh, she is so beautiful, looking just like you,' said Jo.'

'No, she looks more like you,'

In The End, Love

* * *

Jude was crying. 'Oh Jo, I've failed you and I'm truly sorry. Forgive me, please.'

'There's nothing to forgive and Nathan pointed out to me that it might even have been some sort of defect in my egg, not seen at the time of the IVF, which brought this about, so it might be the fault of my egg. We shall never know, but the important thing is for us to live with this together, and then, in the fulness of time make a decision about whether we want to try again. Neither of us is in a position to know that today. The most important thing for both of us is to concentrate on each other.'

'What a good job I came today. I dread to think what might have happened if I'd stayed at home.'

'Well you didn't and how fabulous Nathan was whisking you away as soon as he saw you. As men go, he's pretty impressive.'

'Please don't make me laugh. But now I need some time alone and the children need you. Will you stay the night?'

'Yes, and Nathan has said that when you come out of here you can stay with him if it seems a good idea.'

'Oh thank him. However did you arrest him and put him into prison – he's such a brilliant doctor?'

'You know the reason, which goes by the name of Marie. The important thing is that I got him out at the first opportunity. I will go home first thing and my mum and dad are coming to care for the children, as will also Katia. Then I'll come straight back to be with you.

'Thank you.'

Nathan came and joined the two women.

'We're not completely sure what causes pre-eclampsia and research goes on all the time. But there are certainly factors which increase the risk. Black women tend to get it more often than white and your genetic inheritance from your father as well at that from the donor may have played a part.

'We know too that IVF increases the risk, possibly because the process of conceiving takes place outside the womb, but we don't really know why. What happens is that the placenta fails to develop properly due to the failure of theblood vessels supplying it. I'm not here in the morning but one of my colleagues will come and see you. Tonight get some sleep and use your bell if you need anything. I'll head off now.'

As the door closed behind Nathan

'You arrested him once, Jo. Yes, I know Marie set him up, but he must have made himself susceptible to what she did. I know he didn't in fact commit the murder which she actually did, but is he truly as white as driven snow?'

'He should know better than allow a detective the freedom to wander round his department, chatting to nurses and midwives. I spoke about how brilliant Nathan was and at first they agreed that medically he was the best. I said I had known him a long time, since his time in Cambridge at Addenbrookes. This produced a series of smiles and knowing looks, which fully alerted me to listen attentively. Our great surgeon, and that bit is not in doubt, is coupled with a number of ladies on his staff, and not least his boss, his consultant, married with three children, though I was told he prefers junior members of staff who are flattered to be asked into his bed.'

'God Almighty, no wonder you were suspicious of him before.'

'It was worse because we found filming equipment concealed in the bedroom of his house and I left a couple of my people to look through the films he made. They reported that they quickly grew bored and thought it odd that a gynaecologist should want to spend his time off looking at what he looked at day in day out!'

'The reality, my love, is that I've been feeling worse and worse in recent weeks and suddenly I feel as if I'm coming alive again. I know how awful it is for us both and facing the loss is not going to be easy, but to be with you here and now and for the first time in ages my body is not hurting and with no headaches, is such a relief.'

'Of course. I want you to have a good night's sleep. Call me if you need me to come, at any time, and I am happy to come again tomorrow morning.'

They kissed and Jo left for the night.

The night staff could not have been kinder, having brought her medication for the muscle pain where she had been cut open. Finding her still awake later on, one of the nurses asked if she could come and sit with her for a while.

Jude had a feeling that she knew what was coming and was proved right.

'I was so sorry you lost your baby and I gather your pregnancy came about through IVF using a donor and the egg of your partner. When you first recognised that you were gay, how did it come about?'

'At school and at university, I didn't know I was a lesbian, but I did know I wasn't interested in men, and I've never had a boyfriend not least because when I overheard men talking about sex I was put off completely. Then I became a priest, believe it or not. I did notice that in the course of my work I was far happier in the presence of women than men, but that's not difficult in a church, though as yet I wasn't putting two and two together and getting four. And then, out of the blue a fellow woman priest suggested I join her for an evening at a night club. That took me to a regular Saturday night in the AAA Club in Cambridge, which turned out to be a lesbian club. Not at first, but I can recall the very moment when my enjoyment of the dance floor suddenly became something more – a powerful longing for another girl, and she for me. Now I knew I was a lesbian and delighted about it. I suddenly felt fulfilled and then I met Jo, and knew what fulfilment and joy really was. I left the Church and here I am.'

'Wow, what a story. Did you meet Jo at the club?'

'No. There was a murder of a woman, a journalist in fact, which Jo was investigating, and in the course of which she called to see me at my home. Am I to assume that there may be a heart-felt reason for asking?', asked Jude gently.

'I'm finding it all very scary. I know I shouldn't but I do. I like working here because I work with women and I know what you say about enjoying being with women but the next step feels enormous. How could I tell my parents, for example?'

'I don't know your name.'

'Abby Clarke.'

'Well, Abby, I had to tell the Bishop of Ely and all the members of my church, so why not use a day off or two to come and visit and talk it through.. I'm hardly at my best right now. Jo has always known about her sexuality, even from when she was small, as did her mum and dad, and she hides it from no one.'

'I should be letting you sleep, but I would love to come. Saxmundham is near Aldeburgh on the Suffolk coast. I've been to the Festival.'

'Look in my notes and copy down our address and phone number.'

'I can't do that. They would cut my head off.'

'In which case, before you go off duty in the morning pop in and I'll give them to you and let's be in touch. At least you will be safe from the clutches of Mr Vickery.'

Abby laughed.

'I know, but he's a lovely man and a great doctor. His wife committed suicide and I think he gets lonely.'

'I am sure he does.'

2

The junior registrar called on Jude shortly after breakfast.

'Hello', she said, introducing herself. 'How does the world appear this morning?'

'I won't pretend that the loss of our baby isn't extremely painful and I cried in the night more than I have ever cried before. But at the same time the pains and wretched illness that has characterised the past months has gone, and that is such a profound relief, so it's rather paradoxical to say the least.'

'Yes, it must be confusing. There's no reason to assume that this will happen the next time, you know.'

'I understand that, but now is not the best time to make that sort of decision.'

'You're right there. However any help you need can always be had from Nathan. He owes your Jo a great deal, getting him out of prison.'

'She was also the one who put him in there.'

'Ah well, at least in a men's prison the virgins would have been safe.'

Jude laughed.

'But is it true that Jo is a Dame of the British Empire?'

'Yes,' said Jude proudly. 'She makes light of it but it was awarded for extreme courage in the face of a major terrorist attack. She really would never mention it to anyone, but I know how proud she is of it, and rightly so. She has a forensic mind and I could never lie to her because she would know straight away.'

'Oh my goodness that's terrible. How do you manage when you go shopping for new clothes? I have to lie to my husband every time I shop.'

'You're forgetting that we are two women and we like to shop together.'

'Surely that has to be the best reason for being lesbians!'

They laughed again.

'Now back to business. We need to do some tests today and again tomorrow, to check your kidney and liver functions which can be affected by pre-eclampsia. A nurse will check your wound. We no longer dress wounds but use metal clips with an over sprayed plastic coating. Later you may find that massage with Aloe Vera will help. We still do not know a great deal about the causes of pre-eclampsia so I'll ask you a couple of questions.

'How much do you drink, Jude, and more especially, how much have you been drinking during your pregnancy?'

'None at all during my pregnancy. I live with a Detective Chief Superintendent and believe you me, she would know if I was a secret drinker.

'What about smoking?'

'Never have, even once.'

'Ah, that's because you were a priest and not a doctor. You'd be surprised just how many doctors smoke and even more who drink too much.'

'Yes, but just consider the sort of life and death decisions you are sometimes called to make.'

'How do they compare with those taken by Jo?'

'Not too long ago a potential assassin was stopped by one of her team and it was clear she was going to be the target. The team member, a woman, hunted him down through a small wood and stopped him with an extremely well-aimed use of her boot which he had the cheek to complain about in court, which, after seven months on remand, he maintained was still hurting.'

'My patients don't have those appendages, which is probably a good thing.'

They laughed.

'I must get on as Nathan is not here this morning. You can get out of bed if you wish but no further than the chair. It will be difficult to stand upright and I recommend you call for a bedpan if you need the loo. I'll see you again.'

'Thank you. Bye.'

Ollie was overjoyed to see Jude when they came in to see her but both Jo and Jude noticed that Josie was quiet.

'Ok, Josie, my dearest darling,' said Jo, 'You're with the three people who love you most in all the world. You can tell us anything and we'll always be here for you, so tell us now what it is.'

There was a short silence.

'I've sometimes overheard you, Mummy, talking about Dad, and why it was that you arrested him all that time ago. I know now that it was his wife, Marie...'

'Your mum, remember.'

'...who murdered the police officer and not dad at all. But I also know that when he worked at Addenbrookes he had a reputation for having lots of girlfriends and affairs, especially with young nurses. I know Marie did too with men, but she's not here any more and he is. I kept hoping that after prison he would change but he hasn't, has he? And then I discovered that he wasn't around this morning not because of a meeting he said he was going to but because he is out with another girlfriend. I sneaked a look at his diary and saw names of women. He's not married, so he's entitled to a girlfriend and he's a clever doctor, but he preferred her to me, his daughter, and to us. I think he's sex mad and I don't want to have anything more to do with him.'

Jo decided not to try and brush away the question and in any case Josie was far too sharp for that.

'It's true what you, say, darling, and what's also true is that your dad saved Jude's life yesterday and that's not an exaggeration, and he does it all the time. I have noticed that many doctors drink to excess, or even use drugs to cope with the pressures such things place upon them – and not just doctors, even police officers. The other way in which some cope is sex and not always with the same woman, and perhaps that is the price we pay for having doctors and others living with such pressures.'

'But you don't do that,'

'People know about your dad at the hospital but nobody minds because they know how superb he is as a doctor and accept it as his way of coping,' added Jude. 'We weren't intending to stay overnight and he had something arranged for today. I know you feel hurt, and that all this sex business is a bit bewildering if you don't feel what he does, but without him, I would possibly be dead this morning, and I'm happy about him cavorting in bed with anyone he chooses today.'

Josie laughed.

'Cavorting?'

'There are worse names.'

'Oh, I know. Thank you for saying these things, and perhaps when I see him next I should tease him about his girlfriends.'

'That,' said Jo, 'sounds to me like a very good idea.'

'I couldn't tease Marie though, not after she lied and cheated you. In fact I feel ashamed that I am her daughter.'

'Darling, you are *my* daughter. I brought you up and have always cared for you, together with your grandma Karen, who died. Your mum loved you but she wasn't really equipped to be a mum which is why trusted me with that. But never doubt that she loved you.'

Ollie, who had been quiet throughout, suddenly said, 'I think I would quite like to be a girl, Mummy. Can I change?'

Jo and Jude looked at one another in quiet horror!

When they arrived home they found that Marian and Sidney were already there, talking to Katia who lived in the self-contained flat which was part of the house.

Almost as soon as she arrived, Jo's phone rang and she could see it was Nathan.

'How was your morning?' asked Jo, with a trace of sarcasm she had caught from Josie.

'I got the job.'

'The job?'

'Yes, it was an interview for Consultant, and I got it.'

'Brilliant, ex-con Vickery. May I tell Josie because she's convinced that rather being with her this morning, you were cavorting with one of your girl friends.'

In The End, Love

Please tell her that she's my number one girl friend, one above you.'

'I've missed out there, Nathan.'

'There are not many 100% lesbians, Jo, but you are by far and away the best, and whilst I know many women love you, so do many men.'

'That's quite enough flattery, Mr Consultant.'

'Listen Jo, what Josie thinks matters to me hugely. Can I come and tell her the good news myself?'

'It's a long way.'

'She's my daughter. I'll pop in and see Jude first and then I'll come.'

'That will be great, Nathan.'

Jo put the phone down and said to her dad who was sitting on the nearby sofa, 'I'm not proving lucky as a partner or a wife, am I?'

'Jude's not Ellie, darling, and there's every reason to think that she'll make a full recovery.'

'Nathan is on his way. He's going to see Jude first. As from today he's a consultant and wants to celebrate that with us. Also he needs to have a chat with Josie who was hurt that he went off this morning to an event and didn't stay with her.'

Later a car pulled up outside. Jo went to the door and let Nathan in.

'Nathan, this is Marian and Sidney, my mum and dad.'

'I'm so pleased to meet you and what a daughter you've given to the world..'

'She's alright, I suppose,' said Sidney with a grin, 'when she's not locking up innocent men.'

'I can assure you that was not her fault, but getting me out was all her own work and I shall owe her forever.'

'And congratulations are very much in order, I believe,' added Marian.

'Thank you.'

'Nathan, do you see that door down there. That's a self-contained flat belonging to Katia, and if you knock on the door, you'll find Josie inside. Tell her your good news and why it was you had to go out this morning.'

He did so.

'I'll get on with supper, Jo,' said Marian. 'He's such a nice man and obviously good at his job. What went wrong with his marriage to Marie?'

'Every marriage is different, so who knows? But my own marriage to Marie was not exactly perfect.'

Nathan did not reappear for almost 20 minutes but came back with Josie, hand in hand, into the sitting room, chattering together.

Josie, I'll call you, Katia and Ollie when supper's ready. Your dad and I have some business to attend to in my study. Is that ok?

'Yes. I trust you with Jo! See you at supper, dad.'

'You bet.'

Once they were in the study, Jo said,' Yes, I can see how easily you sweet-talk the ladies, Nathan. But please tell me about Jude.'

'I have every reason to expect her to make a full recovery, Jo, but I would advise you not to try again. Pre-eclampsia is more common in black women and pregnancy has really taken it out of Jude. Perhaps you think you could do it again yourself but I would ask you to consider whether you want to go through a pregnancy again and even more through IVF to bring it about.'

'Thank you for saying that, Nathan. I had already made up my mind, and I don't think Jude would want go through this again.

'But it's my turn now, Nathan. Please, please, for Josie's sake as much as your own, be discrete in your relationships with women, especially young women. Josie heard about it in the hospital and you just about get away with it because of your undoubted skills as a doctor. But Consultants can't behave like this. I know you enjoy the company of women, as I do, but I don't feel obliged to fuck them all. Please, Nathan, be careful.'

'I can only say, thank you Jo, for that. I was shocked when Josie told me what she'd heard about me, and I promised her that I would change. I guess it's just that I'm lonely and still hankering after Marie. Forgive me for saying that but it's true.'

'I don't mind. I still long for my dearest Ellie and in her suicide note, Marie apologised for not being able to be her for me. But you need someone with whom you can overcome the power of those longings and provide you with the settled love we all need. For me Ellie was my coming-out love and therefore both precious and a fantasy. I could not foresee how my marriage to Marie would end, but I knew it was inevitable because, to be frank, it had no foundations. You know how beautiful she was, and unbelievably able in everything she did, but it was always doomed. The time has finally come for me to change my life.'

'But you're at the top and still young. The sky's the limit, Jo.'

'No, becoming a Chief Constable is the limit and I would hate every moment. My close friend Dani hated it, and I would.'

'And what would you want to change to?'

'I need time to think but I'm determined to do it.'

'When?'

'Soon. When I get back to work tomorrow I shall begin the process by setting up the team I need to feel can best carry on the work.'

'Isn't there a chance that without you they will wind it up? After all it's very much "Jo's Unit".

'I know it's harsh of me to say so, and I might be expected to go on for a good many years, but I've only got one life and whilst I have greatly enjoyed detecting, I want to live a different sort of life now. I might train to be a plumber or become a delivery driver for Amazon, or a farmer, but I need difference.'

'Can I ask you as uncomfortable question as you asked me?'

'Go on.'

'Does your future include Jude?'

'The weather forecast says we're in for a cold spell.'

'I thought as much.'

In The End, Love

3

The smell of supper greeted them as soon as they opened the sudy door. Josie was sitting, eagerly awaiting their appearance.

'Mummy,' she said to Jo, 'did you know dad is now a Consultant.'

'Yes, isn't he clever?'

'You need to get married again, dad.'

'Give me time, darling. I only became a Consultant this morning!'

Amidst the laughter, Jo noticed Ollie holding himself back. Later, before bed she broached the question she knew he was asking.

'We've spoken lots of times about the extremely special way in which you were born, how an egg from mum, was mixed with a sperm given by a kind and generous man, whom we don't know, and he doesn't know us, but which he wanted us to have to produce the very special you, and then doctors placed it in me and after nine months I became your mummy, and have never stopped loving you ever since. I know tonight you must have looked at Josie and thought she has something you don't have, but never forget how much unhappiness Nathan has also brought her, and mum before that. And I'm not sure either, that Nathan even now is a happy man.'

'Are *you* happy, mummy.'

'Yes, I am, but how could I not be with you and Josie at the heart of my life.'

'And Jude, and Nanny and Grandad, and Katia, and aunty Dani, and Darcey.'

Definitely, my darling, but only one of all these people I love was inside my tummy for nine months – you. That makes you the most special of all.'

With Nathan on his way back to St Albans, the children asleep, and Marian and Sidney also off to bed, Jo sat with Katia.

'Ollie said something surprising to me earlier. He was naming those we especially love and who love us – including you, because I do so very much – but he stunned me by mentioning the name of Darcey, the only one of my team he mentioned.'

'"Out of the mouths of babes and sucklings!",' said Katia. 'Oh Jo, with a fearsome reputation like yours as a detective, what's under your nose you often can't see. Ollie knows, and I think we all know, and that includes Jude because she's mentioned it to me, that whilst you may love Jude, you are totally *in* love with Darcey.'

'Oh! And apart from you, Ollie and Jude, does anyone else think this?'

'Not here, because most of us don't get to meet your team, but I would imagine all your team will have twigged. It's so obvious from your way of looking at her and I'm not surprised. I feel the same.'

'Katia?'

'O come on, detective chief idiot. How many boys have you known me bring back to the flat?'

Jo smiled.

'I love you too, Katia.'

Katia grinned.

'No you can't come to bed with me, but for what it's worth, Jo, I will never forget what you did for mum and for me, releasing us from the prison house of hell. I would love you always for that, if for nothing else, but my love for you is ever so deep, but you're still not coming to bed with me, I'm sorry to say.'

'All that dross showered on you and your mum across the years has been nothing more than the finest fertiliser to produce an exceptional young woman. If I was you I'd get back into your flat and lock the door more or less immediately.'

Each leaned forward and gave the other a chaste kiss though their eyes communicated more.

After Katia had departed, Jo poured herself a gin and tonic. She didn't as a rule drink much but this had been one hell of a day and she was back at work in the morning after a three-month sabbatical insisted on by her superiors, the very people who had almost certainly wanted her to take the break and use it to prepare becoming for becoming a Chief Constable.

She woke early and telephoned the hospital first. Jude was awake and apparently hungry which sounded like good news. Jo prepared breakfast for Ollie and Josie and went to join them. They still chose to share a room despite the difference in their ages though how much longer Josie would want that, remained to be seen. Today was the first day of the autumn term for both, and Grandad would be taking them to school, allowing Jo herself to leave early for work. At least, not being a Chief Constable, she didn't have to wear a uniform.

She had an awkward moment as she drove towards her HQ in Stowmarket, when she realised how much she was longing to see Darcey, now Detective Chief Inspector, married to Belinda Gorham, now herself a Detective Inspector. She recalled Katia's words of the previous night and felt her face redden, mainly because she knew it was true.

She parked her car, greeted the officers in the village police station and then climbed the stairs to her own offices, only to find a total absence, a veritable Marie Celeste, which was baffling, unless of course they had all been called out on an urgent matter. Then her phone rang.

'Call yourself a detective,' said the familiar voice of Jodie, her deputy.

'Surely you saw the cars parked as normal. You're out of practice, Chief Superintendent, so you'd better come and join us across the road in the regular coffee shop who kindly have opened early to welcome you back.'

'Sounds like I might have to start my return by demoting you all for being wicked! I'm coming.'

There was a great cheer as she opened the door and saw the familiar faces she loved and trusted as outstanding cops. There were of course, questions about how Jude and the pregnancy was proceeding.

'I'm sorry to say we lost the baby, probably on Friday. Jude developed pre-eclampsia and had to have immediate surgery, a C-section, and the baby had probably been dead for 24 hours. Those of you who were involved in the original business in Norfolk, which I guess now is only Darcey, though you will all know we got him out of prison, might be surprised to know that the person who saved Jude's life was Nathan Vickery. He was astonishing, and has now been appointed Consultant in St Albans.'

'Oh Jo, I'm so sorry about the loss of the baby,' said Darcey, others echoing her words. 'Will Jude make a full recovery?'

'Nathan thinks she will, but our baby-making days are ended.'

'And now things go from bad to worse', said DI Frankie Wawszyczk, whom Jo knew to be the finest detective per se in the unit, 'after a weekend like that you have to return to work with us!'

'I've missed you, and I shall continue to miss Ed. How is your boyfriend doing, Kelly?'

'He's enjoying it even though he's quite a bit older than the other students. The demonstrator in the anatomy class usually defers to him given how many post-mortems he's been present at, and if he gets the chance, he accompanies Dr Colville in the mortuary. She says he has an amazing eye for anything abnormal.'

'Yeah, well that's why he chose you.'

Everyone, including Kelly, laughed.

'But welcome from me to the two newest members of the troop, Ahmed and Warren. I'm so pleased that you've joined us, guys, and I'm looking forward to working with you. Jodie has told me good things about you.'

'Thank you, ma'am,' said Ahmed.

'Oh no! Fallen at the first hurdle.'

Everyone laughed and Ahmed looked puzzled.

'Ahmed, the essence of this team is mutual trust. We are all equal in the tasks we are given or undertake and therefore we only use ranks and titles when identifying ourselves, when engages in investigation and when the Chief Constables pay a visit. For the rest of the time we use names. Warren knows this because he recently bumped into Bonnie, who used to be here and is now heading the police in Barbados and trying to poison the cricket team so that England might just win when next they play. Bonnie would have told you how we operate.'

'She did, Jo, and what she told me made want to come and join you.'

In The End, Love

'She's a lovely lady, but people, we should go and do some work, but thank you especially to Howard and Jean for opening up early. We'll be back for the coffee break soon.'

Arriving back in the office, Jodie, Kelly and Jo met for a short time together.

'It's been very quiet,' said Jodie. 'Criminals, it seems, enjoy a summer holiday too. The biggest thing was a request from Devon and Cornwall to investigate a string of robberies from minor royals, well, very minor royals, with which we managed successfully to deal. It was very minor criminals. While I was on holiday, Darcey was in charge and dealt with a couple of matters to the satisfaction of our superiors.'

'It was like having you here, Jo,' said Kelly. 'You've been her model ever since she joined the force, so functions exactly as you would, even adopts your tone of voice when speaking to the team. Imitation, they say, is the sincerest form of flattery.'

'Frankie was a bloodhound in her previous life – that's certain', said Jodie. 'Give her a sniff and she never lets go. A natural sleuth and a lovely personality even if she doesn't smile a great deal.'

'Belinda is the person who should be appointed to take over after you and in some ways should have been in charge whilst you have been away, and not me. She has the most wonderfully organised mind and way of working, an ability to de-clutter information at a speed that even leaves Kelly amazed.'

'It's true,' added Kelly. 'I suspect she is not the natural investigator Frankie is, but she handles what we know much like like a forensic pathologist does a body. She's also generous to a fault in being willing to help and support.'

'As yet we haven't seen either Ahmed or Warren in action, but they come with good records.'

'Good, and what about you, Kelly? Are you seeing Ed enough or will you soon be wanting to leave us?'

'Whilst you are here, Jo, there is no way I will ever leave. I don't just owe something to you, I owe everything. I know MI5 think I'm wasted here and I could do a great deal there, but here I stay, though I should tell you that when we are quiet they do incorporate me into their network and I help out. Also I'm doing some writing with and for your friend Sharon, contributing to a forthcoming book on women in prison.'

'Excellent, Kelly and what a wonderful person to work with.'

'And did you know that her wife, Kim, is now a colonel?'

'Yes. She says she will not become the next Head of the Service, but when the present Director stands down, efforts will be made to persuade her.' Jo turned to Jodie. 'And so to you, my darling Jodie. How has it been in charge?'

'Not that there has been much, but I miss the cut and thrust of direct action. I didn't want an office job which is why I joined the police and I hadn't anticipated how much paperwork there is even during a quiet time, most of which I have no interest in. There is no adrenaline rush doing quarterly returns and although everyone assumes that of course you want to get the top where you are safe, that's not the sort of copper I want to be.

'Asking me to take charge of the unit as Acting Super was typically generous of you, and we miss Esther very much because she made light of some of the administrative work, but I am more than happy to ask for the demotion you spoke of earlier, and to accept the workload of a DCI, if that accords with your plans.'

'I understand what you saying Jodie, and please you two, say nothing about this, but during my sabbatical I was offered two different Chief Constableships, if that's the right word, making three in total so far, and so far I have turned them all down, for the reasons you have spoken of, Jodie. Plus I couldn't stand wearing a uniform all the time. And just imagine, if they wanted eventually to send me to the Met, well obviously they couldn't appoint a lesbian in charge, could they?'

'Oh no,' said Jodie and Kelly together, laughing.

'I therefore accept your return as DCI, but thank you so much, Jodie for everything, and not least, saving my life with a well placed use of your boot!'

'My pleasure,' she said with a large smile.

They went out and joined the rest of the team, and Jo informed them that fully in accordance with her own wishes, Jodie was delighted to be returning to the rank of DCI. Jodie confirmed this.

'My plan for the rest of the morning is to see each one of you individually. Nothing heavy, but so I can remember who you are. After lunch, I shall go to St Albans to be with Jude. Jodie will stay in charge until a new Super is appointed.'

Jo noticed a knowing look and wry smile on a couple of faces but ignored them when Darcey rose and followed her into Jo's office.

'The slight giggles that are present when I am present with you, my darling Darcey, don't trouble me at all. What about you?'

'I don't think they are intended to hurt or be nasty. They suggest only that they know how close I am to you.'

'I do love you, Darcey, so much that it hurts, and apparently even Katia who has our live-in flat at home, says that she notices that whenever I'm with you, I look at you in ways I never do at anyone else.'

'But we also have an extremely important job to do and you are a key member of the team. When Jodie was away, you led the team. How was that?'

'Nothing special in terms of operations though I didn't enjoy not being in the front line, and the paperwork was simply awful.'

'Would you want to take over from Jodie and be responsible for a great more paperwork? Esther applied herself to it and didn't mind being in the office.'

'And she was good at it. The only advantage of the job would be a greater proximity to you.'

'DCI Bussell, control yourself!'

They laughed.

Following Darcey came Belinda.

'How are things, Belinda. I've been hearing great things about you from the senior members of the team?'

'I think you know that from the very first, that is, when you were able to bring me back into the Force because you were able to perceive it was what I was made for, from that moment I have grown to love my work more and more, and apply myself to it with renewed energy day by day, in the process driving Darcey crackers.'

Jo smiled.

'I have gathered an amazing team of women, and the odd man, around me who are very attractive, including you. But I know full well that there are those in the Force who hope for my downfall and would love the lesbian detective to be caught in bed with one of you. And it isn't going to happen and has never happened, even with Darcey, in case you had anxieties in that direction.

'When I announce the appointment of the new Detective Superintendent later on, an important part of whose job will be to tell me how things are, and when I am getting things wrong to tell me straight. The job demands considerable integrity and profound understanding of the role of the police service, and has the trust of colleagues. So I'll tell you who it is – I didn't even tell Darcey. It's someone called Detective Superintendent Belinda Gorham!'

'What?'

'Congratulations, Belinda. I have no doubts that you are the right person for the job and equipped with everything needful. And I am overjoyed at the thought of working extremely closely with you.'

Belinda's mouth was wide open.

'Need to see a dentist?'

'Jo. What can I say? That's amazing. It's ... I don't know.'

'The word you're looking for is "Yes"'

'Yes, thank you. Am I allowed to kiss you?'

'Not every morning, otherwise people will talk, but you can now.'

After a hug and kiss, Jo asked Belinda to sit down again.

'I haven't completely finished. During my sabbatical, attempts were made to tempt me to accept the office of Chief Constable of two different Constabularies and for the second I was "invited" if you take meaning to visit the Home Office in London and have coffee with the Home Secretary. Eventually she accepted my refusal but brought up another job, which she knew was not intended for me, but which because of our experience in the West Midlands of sexual exploitation by police officers, she wanted some advice about someone who could lead the task force into sexual predation by male officers on women both in and out of the force. It would be at Commander level, based at the Yard and answerable to the Commissioner. The new Commander would appoint her own team and more or less have carte blanche to investigate everywhere.

'I said that there would be many experienced officers across the country who could do this, though I only knew one who having herself been sexually assaulted by a police officer, would have the great abilities required plus a remembrance of the pain.

'That Belinda is you, and I have been told by the Home Office that you are on a shortlist of three and will be called for an Interview to be held at the Police College.'

'Jo, this conversation is going from the sublime to the ridiculous.'

'There is nothing ridiculous about it, Belinda. You are outstanding in your work, as I knew you would be. We can talk together about how you handle the interview, but the other two women will have to very good indeed for them not to appoint you. I am not expecting you not to tell Darcey, but until the appointment is publicly ratified it must remain top secret. In the meantime you begin your new position tomorrow morning, and I fear it's a uniform position.'

'I don't mind that, ma'am.'

Jo led Belinda out of the office, and everyone turned.

'Ladies and gentlemen, allow me to introduce to you Detective Superintendent Gorham, or as she will be at 8:00 in the morning when it is ratified.'

There was a stunned silence, eventually broken by Kelly with a handclap in which others then joined. Darcey came forward and kissed her.

'Is it alright to do that ma'am?' she asked Belinda with a grin.

'Until 8:00 in the morning you're still my superior, so make the most of anything you want.'

'That's an offer I can hardly refuse.'

'Belinda,' said Jo, 'you need to spend the rest of the day with Jodie.'

'Yes, Jo.'

'Next I need a visit from DI Francesca Wawszyczk,' who followed her into Jo's office.

'Isn't the team one member light?' asked Frankie.

'Ed has gone off to study to be a doctor, which is wonderful for the patients he will treat but is still looking eventually to study to be a pathologist. Sadly he won't be coming back. As you know, Willie came off his motorbike and broke most of his bones but they are expected to be working again by Christmas and he wants to return. The good news is that Steph wants to return too, and leave parish life to her husband. I saw them briefly in the summer and they seem so happy together with their infant and Fergal now in his own parish, but she's bored out of her mind, so will rejoin us before the end of the month. And now we have Ahmed and Warren who both come well recommended, but I want you to be responsible for their continuing training and be their mentor. Would you be willing to take that on?'

'I would love to do that, Jo. Thank you very much.'

I'd like you to stay but could you bring Ahmed in, and then Warren, and I'll tell them the good news.'

The team, minus Kelly and Jo, retreated once again to the coffee shop. In the afternoon they were due at the shooting range in Ipswich for their regular

In The End, Love

check-up, and would allow Frankie to begin her supervision work with Ahmed and Warren.

'It looks like you took notice of Jodie and me, boss. Who might you have chosen had we not said what we did?' asked Kelly.

'Jodie is the best officer we have in just about every way but head of ops is what she's best at, not a paper pusher behind a desk. Next in line would be Frankie, who's the best detective in the team, but putting her in the no.2 position would be a dreadful waste of talent and she would hate it, as would I. So Belinda more or less appointed herself with the references from you and Jodie. And I need you to let know whoever it is you need to let know.'

'It has to come from you with your signature.'

'Can you do it before I leave for St Albans?'

'I've already done it, or that is I've done 5 letters: one for the Home Office and one each for the four Chiefs.'

'Tell me, Kelly, did you do it before I announced the appointment?'

'Might have!'

'It's no wonder you ended up in prison.'

'Aw, boss, that's the nicest thing you've ever said.'

4

Jude was looking much more alive than she had over the previous few days. On her part that was because of her "night visitor" Abby Clarke who coming each night to spend time with her, a time of gossip and laughter, not something Jo specialised in, to which Jude increasingly looked forward.

'I received special dispensation to come and see you outside visiting – it just shows that being a top police officer means nothing, but the title Dame opens all sorts of locked doors.'

'I wondered what it was for. Perhaps it's compensation for my letting you down.'

'We need to agree something, Jude, that we never speak of this again. You let no one down and certainly not me and the only thing that matters is that you get fully well again, which will be soon. But then we have to give thought to the rest of our life together. I'm ready to give up the police.'

'You're serious, aren't you?'

'Completely so. If you had died, what could possibly have been the point of my life? I've spent the morning reorganising things at work so that they could continue without me and I want us to go and discover an unexpected life together somewhere else. I'm sick of crime and criminals. It's not that long since only Jodie's boot and foresight saved me from a bullet. I don't want that any more.'

'Have you any thoughts as to what and where?'

'Something is forming deep inside my brain, but let's wait until you're home. Whatever we decide has to be ours together, so you need to give thought to this too. After all, you've nothing better to do than lie here until they throw you out.'

'Never thought of that!'

'They all send their love and I'm sure Frankie would ask you to make sure the chaplain doesn't say anything offensive or she'll come and arrest him.'

'It's alright, the chaplain is a *her*.'

'Did you know her in your previous existence?'

'No, and I feigned extreme sleepiness when she came. The last thing I need is a theological conversation.'

In The End, Love

'Has Nathan been in to see you?'

'I'm not his patient now, though his colleague, Mrs McAndrew, did come in. She says I still need further kidney and liver function tests, but all being well, I might be able to return home in a day or two, though standing and walking are still both very painful, as they stretch my wound.'

'Would you mind if I went to see Mrs McAndrew and find out her thoughts for when you might come home.'

'No, do, but please come back.'

The staff at the nurses station directed Jo to where they thought the Consultant might be and arriving at the door with her name on it, Jo knocked and a voice asked her in.'

'Hello, I'm sorry to interrupt you, but I'm Jo Enright, the partner of Jude.'

'I think you mean you're Detective Chief Superintendent Dame ...,'

'Jo.'

'Come in and sit down, Jo. I'm Julia. I am so pleased to meet you. I've known about you by repute ever since Nathan came to work here, and he and I and lots of staff and patients owe you a considerable debt for getting him released and his conviction overthrown in the Appeal Court.

Jo laughed.

'That's very kind, but don't overlook the fact that I also arrested him and got him into prison in the first place, and I only discovered the fact that he, and I, had been set up in the first place, by means of a suicide note in Los Angeles.'

'You have a difficult job.'

'Whereas obs and gynae are a piece of cake? I think not, and I am grateful more than I can say for the skill and care that has been taken with Jude.'

'That, as you know, was Nathan's doing. You will know that on Sunday morning those important people who make decisions gathered at my house and decided we need another consultant in the department and he was unanimously selected.'

'Yes, and I am overjoyed. I always thought Addenbrookes missed out there though he didn't help his own cause.'

'I imagine you are the only one, other than Nathan himself, who knows all about it, though he has told me that he was promiscuous to a considerable degree.'

'I won't make excuses for him nor can I possibly reveal to another person what was the subject of a police investigation, but I will say his wife, Marie, made him look an amateur. She had a thing about doctors and set about seducing as many as possible, especially consultants. Sadly she continued this in my own marriage to her though she concealed it. Marie was extremely attractive and could draw men to her with ease. Nathan was aware of this and I think decided to let go the constraints upon him as a doctor, almost in retaliation. Please do not judge him too harshly. As a lesbian I also love the company of young pretty women, so I understand how it is for him, though I'm not given to seducing them.'

'Last night two things happened, Jo. The first was that he reported to me that you had given him a call to reform his life with regard to spending time with nurses and the like and that this had been reinforced by his daughter Josie.'

'She's also my daughter, having lived with me for the best part of her life.'

'Jo, I'm sorry I said that. I know it is true and Nathan always speaks of you as Josie's mother.'

'Whilst she was with us, Marie was mum and I was mummy. It's the sort of arrangement single-sex parents work with.'

'I've sometimes wondered how that might work.'

'And the second thing from last night?'

'Nathan asked me to marry him.'

Jo smiled.

'And your reply?'

She smiled back.

'That is simply wonderful news and makes me feel so very happy.'

'I would urge you to keep it a secret until next Saturday when we shall announce it at a party. Nathan has said that he would like to Zoom Josie tonight and let her know, if that's ok with you.'

'She will be so excited. Do you have any idea when it might happen?'

'Soon, but I know no more than that. I do know however that both Nathan and I want you and the children, to be with us.'

'Thank you, that would be wonderful, especially for Josie who has a lot to come to terms with as she grows up, not least being as stunning a young woman as her birth mother was. A father in prison for a while, and then a mother who murdered and then took her own life is a heavy burden and may lead to complexity alongside her beauty. She may need therapy at some stage, I suppose, but for now I give her all the love I can manage, and she is especially close to her brother Ollie, with whom she shares Marie's genes even though I carried him.'

'I imagine that can get quite confusing in your mind.'

'When a lesbian or gay relationship breaks up it certainly can. But now, tell me how Jude is doing.'

'She is getting frustrated but I wish to keep her in a little longer. She has been very poorly indeed, more perhaps than she realises, and I'm far from sure she has even begun to come to terms with the loss of your baby. I don't want her leaving here with any risk factors. Fortunately she has a lot of muscular pain and therefore cannot walk very far.'

'Fortunately?'

'Yes, because it will mean Dr Brodie, the psychiatrist and psychotherapist who works with us in this department will have the chance to call in and see her a couple of times at least. You would not, I'm sure, want us to be any less than thorough.'

'By no means and I'm relieved by what you've told me. As a priest I know she used to store things up inside her and she might with this.'

'And what about you? It's your loss too.'

'I don't underestimate what you are saying but I have only just recovered from the suicide of Marie and trust me when I say that the work of a detective, whether a constable or a chief superintendent is often fast moving and dealing with distressing circumstances. I have to build up a measure of protection.'

'I do understand that, for as you can imagine not every day in maternity is a happy one, but nevertheless please attend to your own needs and not just those of others.'

'Thank you, Julia. I'm so happy for you.'

Jo stayed with Jude for another half an hour when her phone rang. It was Kelly.

'Something big, boss. Call Essex CC.'

'Something big, Kelly said. I have to go.'

'Of course you must.'

A quick kiss and Jo was gone. Outside she made the call.

'Adam, she said, using his name, it's Jo.'

'Chelmsford Station. How soon can you get here, Jo?'

'I'm in St Albans but with blue lights and siren I will be with you in less than half an hour, but I can send Jodie and Darcey and they can be with you in a very short time.'

'It's awful, Jo. A child murdered and the chief suspects are the parents, one of whom is one of our officers. I've told our people that you will take it on. The parents are being held.'

'Adam, I'm leaving now, and Jodie and Darcey will be with you very soon. Can they be briefed and then they can brief me?'

'Of course.'

Blue lights and a siren cleared the streets of St Albans and she was quickly on to the motorway where she drove at little less than 100mph. Soon after she began, she called Jodie.

'Suspicious child death in Chelmsford, one of the parents is a police officer. The CC wants us. Take the whole team to the Police Station now. I'll be there soon but you and Darcey go to the house, and permit entry to Forensics asap.'

The afternoon traffic into Chelmsford was heavy, but she made it to the station before the team. Inside she saw the Chief Constable looking agitated and talking to an officer who nudged him.'

'Oh Jo, I am so pleased to see you.'

'The rest of the team are on their way, sir.'

'I've asked Inspector Holly to brief you. The paediatric pathologist, Dr Israel, is on her way.'

At that moment Jodie and Darcey came in through the front door and flashed their warrant cards to the desk sergeant.

'The rest of the team are still in the cars, ma'am', said Jodie to Jo.

'Inspector Holly,' said Jo, 'would you prefer to brief just three or will you be happy with four more?'

'I don't normally get asked, ma'am but I'm happy with the larger group.'

Darcey was already on her way out to bring the others in.

'PC Peter Delaney and his partner, Susanne Day, have a six month old baby, Martha. I hardly know Susanne and she has part-time work in Greggs, the bakers. Pete says they're happy and considering marriage. However a neighbour expressed concern about bruising on the face of Martha, and Pete told her to mind her own business. The woman reported the bruising to the social services.

'Someone from social services visited and reported that there were no grounds for concern and she has visited regularly. She is called Amanda Stone.

'At about 9:00 pm last night, Susanne dialled 999 and reported that the baby had fallen whilst having its nappy changed and was clearly far from well. The paramedics radioed through that the infant was in a very bad way and had bruises inconsistent with the alleged fall. They called us and took Martha to A&E, but she was DOA. The parents were brought in, examined by Scene of Crime Officers and their clothing removed and are still here but since the Chief decided that you had to take it on, it means the PACE clock has been ticking and they have not been interviewed.'

'Thank you, Inspector, that was a good and clear briefing. If we need you further we'll call.'

The Inspector knew when he was being dismissed.

'Thank you, ma'am.'

'We must interview as soon as possible. I'll do the man with Frankie; Jodie, and Darcey, the woman. Ahmed and Warren, find Amanda Stone, wherever she is and bring her in – no excuses, she comes in.

'Yes, boss.'

'Belinda, you are case manager. Ask Kelly to find anything she can on the parents, and then get her here. We may need to see anything that's on WhatsApp.'

'Yes, ma'am.'

'Then take first shift in the Audio Visual room with Belinda, to hear what the man says before you see the woman. Frankie and I will interview first.'

They went into the Interview Room and awaited the arrival of Delaney, wearing a white suit. He was tall and in his mid-30s with grey beginning to appear at his temple.

Frankie began, 'Present: PC Peter Delaney, his solicitor, Mr Edward Clarke, Detective Chief Superintendent Joanne Enright and Detective Inspector Francesca Wawszyczk.'

'Constable Delaney,' began Jo, 'as you will be aware, your daughter died on the way to hospital following what was described as an accident during a nappy change. As yet a post mortem has not been performed so we cannot know for certain the immediate cause of death.

'Can you please confirm that you were present in the house when she was taken away by ambulance?'

'Yes, ma'am.'

'And how long had you been in the house before whatever events that brought about the injuries to your daughter?'

'I completed my shift at 4:00 and came straight home, as Su was intending to go out for the evening, and I had to get Martha ready for bed, normally by 7:00.'

'Where was Susanne going?'

'A girls' night out she said.'

'And at what time were you expecting her back?'

'Not late. Ten o'clock was the normal time.'

'How regular was normal?'

'Twice a week.'

Frankie interrupted.

'Did you have sex on the nights when she had been out?'

'Not if I was on the early shift next day.'

'That wasn't what I asked. Did you have sex on the nights when she had been out?'

'I can't think that has anything to do with what has happened and I certainly did not keep a diary.'

'I think, Constable, that we are the judges of what did and did not happen. As far as you can remember, on the evenings on which your partner went out with the girls, did you or did you not have intercourse?'

'Sometimes she had been drinking and sometimes, as I mentioned, I was on an early.'

Jo, who trusted the thinking of Frankie, even when she had no idea what it was, spoke again.

'Last night she arrived home earlier than normal. What time would that have been?'

'About 8:00.'

'That was unusual. What reason did she give?'

'It's her house and she doesn't need a reason to come in.'

'But you were surprised?'

'I suppose so.'

'When she arrived, was she accompanied by anyone, perhaps some of the girls she had been out with?'

'She came in with a man.'

'Was this someone you recognised?'

'No.'

'And his name?'

'Ma'am, if I tell you his name, my life might as well be at an end.'

This told Jo and Frankie a great deal: they were dealing with someone who was almost certainly a criminal.

'Tell me what happened between the time of their arrival at 8:00 and when the ambulance arrived.'

'I had a friend with me. She was from the Social Services and had first come to see Martha after some busybody made a complaint. We got on well and would call in on the nights when Su was out.'

I assume you are talking about Amanda Stone.'

Delaney hesitated.

'Er, yes. When her dad died, Su inherited the house – it was one of the many less than impressive council houses sold off by Mrs Thatcher but it was hers. Sometimes she threatened me with eviction, mostly as a joke, but I assumed the baby implied my security. Then last night she came in and found Mandy and I in what might be called a compromising position on the sofa.

'"This is exactly what I've been hoping for", she said with obvious glee. "You can go home with your slut, and make sure you never come back, and I mean now. Pack your bags and bugger off".

'I said that we had a baby and that I knew the law.'

'That was when the man she was with appeared. He was big and rough looking with an Eastern European accent. "I'm not sure you heard the lady correctly. Now means now. Pack your bags or we might have a disagreement, and you won't be the first copper I've put into intensive care" and I think he meant it. Mandy indicated with her eyes that I should go upstairs. I threw some things into a bag but most important of all I picked up Martha and came downstairs with her.

'Su yelled out that I was not taking the baby. Once again the man said as before, "I'm not sure you heard the lady correctly – the baby stays with her mother as I'm sure your social worker would agree when you're not screwing the arse off her". I backed off into the kitchen, still holding Martha.

'Amanda told me to let her stay and then suddenly the man lunged forward and punched me on the side of my head causing me to lose hold of Martha. He grabbed her and I violently kicked his shin. Holding her he reached up and threw her down to the ground, causing him to drop her on her head. As I went down to pick her up I became aware that he had disappeared, as had Mandy. That ma'am, is exactly as it was.'

'Ok, we will leave it there for now. This must be extremely difficult for you but given your anxieties about the name of the man, I think it would be wise for you to remain here where you will be protected, but you are not under arrest and if you wish to be somewhere else, you can, provided you let us know where. The Recording is terminated.'

Jo smiled at him.

'Thank you ma'am. I need to think where the best place to be is, because I'm not sure even being in a cell downstairs here is in fact all that safe.'

'Mr Clarke, as the interview is now complete, there is no need for you to remain and you can see your client in a few moments. There is just something PC Delaney and I need to discuss briefly not related to the matter of Martha's death.'

The solicitor looked at his client, who nodded.

Once he had left the room, Jo asked: 'Perhaps you could tell me what you mean about not necessarily being safe here? This is not being recorded nor transcribed.'

'Conversations overheard in the canteen, no more than that, of certain officers being in league with big time villains and the claim that if you want a tom, they're readily available.'

'Any names?'

'It was in the canteen. Names would be stupid.'

'Yes. But thank you. I'll reunite you with your solicitor.'

5

Before they swapped over with Jodie and Darcey, the four detectives looked through the initial report from Socos which was largely unhelpful but provided an opportunity to talk over the interview just completed.

'Why did you ask about the absence of sex on nights when the partner was out with the girls, Frankie?' asked Darcey.

'Going out for two nights each week with the girls seems excessive and how many such girls are there working for Greggs with her, but not if she was actually out with a man. If she had just had sex with this other man, then she might be less willing to repeat the process on arrival home, though it seems he also had a night in with the girl.'

'Ahmed and Warren brought her in, boss,' said Darcey.

'Good. She'll keep. Ok, you two, get to it.'

'Boss,' said Kelly on her phone. 'This is a bit odd. I checked through Peter Delaney's work file as you saw it earlier. I've looked again online and there's something there that wasn't in the one we both saw earlier. There is now a reference to Delaney's temper, for which he had to be spoken to though not disciplined. It suggests it might have been doctored.'

'Who is the author?'

'It just says MH.'

'Thank you, Kelly.'

Jo and Frankie sat in the AV Room watching and listening as Darcey made the initial announcement for the benefit of the tape.

'Present: Susanne Day, her solicitor Maddy Groom, Detective Superintendent Jodie Lovelock, and Detective Chief Inspector Janice Bussell.'

'Superintendent,' began the solicitor, 'my client has just experienced the loss of her baby. I object to this interview taking place in the context where criminal investigations are held.'

'I fully understand, Ms Groom,' said Jodie, 'but until we can ascertain the events of last night, we cannot judge how best to take the investigation forwards which is why what we are doing here has to be recorded and witnessed externally. Your client is not under arrest nor under caution and I will make this as easy as possible but we are dealing with a child murder at which your client may have been present or in the house.

'Ms Day. At what time did you leave the house yesterday evening?'

'Peter gets in at about 6:00 and I left a little before then.'

'Leaving your baby alone?' asked Darcey. 'Are you aware that doing that is a criminal offence?'

'In her cot she has never come to any harm.'

'Where did you go last night when you left home?' continued Jodie, who was barely able to stop looking at the solicitor.

'I went out for a night with the girls.'

'That phrase,' said Darcey, 'is normally used to describe time spent away from work, with those you work with. How many such girls are there working part-time with you at Greggs?'

'It was also with some of the women I met at ante- and post natal gatherings.'

'Where did you go last night when you left home?' asked Jodie.

'I can't remember.'

'I shall require from you the names of the companions you call "the girls" as we need to speak to them.'

'No. That would be unfair to them, involving them in matters that have nothing to do with them.'

'Can I confirm that you are refusing to give the names of those you were with last night shortly before your baby died?'

'As I say, I don't want them involved. It has nothing to do with them.'

'Are you in regular contact with the girls to make arrangements or just to engage in chat?'

'Of course, at work and using WhatsApp.'

'Very sensible.'

'Last night you returned home at what time?'

'I had developed an awful headache, a reaction, I suspect, to the cocktails we started with. I should know better.'

'Yes, we've all been there. Your partner would have been surprised to see you back so early.'

'Oh, he was I can assure you, as I found him with a woman, and they were having it away on the sofa.'

'Did you know this woman.'

'Yes, she was Mandy Stone from the social services. She came following a complaint from an interfering neighbour that I was neglecting Martha. I could tell at once that she was taken by Pete, and she obviously came again.'

'Who brought you home last night?'

'What do you mean?'

'You were not too well, a little worse for wear, so I imagine that one of your girl friends must have brought you home in the car that was parked outside.'

'I was a little the worse for wear, as you said and though I was grateful for the lift, precisely which of my friends gave me the lift I can't actually say.'

'Can't or won't?'
'Can't.'
'Tell me what happened when you got into the house and came across Pete and Mandy *in flagrante delicto*?'

'I was shocked and told them I wanted them both out of my house – it is my house – and I wanted them to leave now and never return. I had to repeat this a number of times before Mandy indicated that Pete should go and get his stuff. I got really cross when he brought Martha down and insisted she was going with him. I told him she would be staying and I went to remove her from his arms. He said that if I wouldn't let him take her he would make sure neither of us would have her and that's when he deliberately dropped her onto the hard kitchen floor on her head. I screamed and picked her up and immediately rang for an ambulance. The social services bitch had buggered off. I kept hold of Martha until the ambulance came and they called the police. Pete had sat on the kitchen floor in tears.'

'There are parts of your account of what happened last night that need verifying without which neither we nor a jury would be convinced you have told the truth. We shall have to know the identities of the girls with whom go out at least twice a week, and then the identity of the person who brought you home last night and came into the house with you.'

'No one did.'

'And I have grounds for thinking someone did. Until you are able to provide us with the names we are asking for, I regret to say you will be placed under caution and have to remain in custody.'

Her solicitor was not happy.

'I repeat what I said earlier that my client is newly bereaved of her 6 month old child, and that a prison cell is an entirely inappropriate place for her to remain.'

'I am anxious to discover the truth about the death of baby Martha and whether any criminal activity has taken place, Ms Groom. I would have thought that your client was too, so perhaps you can convince her that in this way the truth might emerge fully. The recording is now terminated.'

As Su was taken back to the cells, Jodie spoke to the solicitor.

'How is it you are here Ms Groom, or put another way, who is it you are defending?'

'According to PACE every person being questioned is entitled to a solicitor.'

'When I'm arrested, I hope you might come and defend me.'

'Have you any particular crimes in mind?'

Jodie smiled.

'You never know.'

The team had drinks in the Canteen and commented on the recent interview and the issues to be developed in the next with Amanda Stone, and Jo decided to throw Ahmed and Warren in at the deep end, with Ahmed taking the lead.

'Present:', began Warren, 'Amanda Stone, duty solicitor Mr Foster,

Detective Sergeant Ahmed Hussain, and Detective Sergeant Warren Rolle.'

'What were the circumstances of your first contact with Mr Delaney and Ms Day?'

'We received a concern from an a neighbour that their baby was being neglected and I was sent to check this out.'

'And what did you find?'

'Nothing untoward and two caring parents.'

'But you found yourself caring for one of those parents more than the other. Isn't that so?'

'Yes. I think it was mutual attraction and we realised that a good time for us to be together was when Su was out, which was conveniently quite a lot.'

'This would hardly be approved of by the department for which you work, would it?'

She shrugged.

'It was not in work time, but my own, and I had already reported that everything was fine.'

'So were you there every time Su went out?'

'I suppose so.'

'Does than mean yes?'

'Yes, but, as I say, in my own free time.'

'Where was Su on these evenings?'

'I don't know, but apparently she went out for evenings "with the girls", whoever they were.'

'Normally what time did you leave?'

'About 9:30, as she was due back at 10:00.'

'Let's talk about last night, less than 24 hours ago. Please describe it.'

'I arrived at 6:00 as usual and the first thing we did was to get Martha ready for bed and she went down at about 6:45. We then sat together on the sofa canoodling.'

'Ms Stone, which century do live in? The Oxford English Dictionary has not recorded a use of the word since 1921. Perhaps I should make a note and pass it on to them. From what others have said, what you were doing was a little more than canoodling. Is that the case?'

'I suppose so.'

'You suppose so. You *were* there, weren't you?'

Those in the Interview Room could fortunately not hear the roars of laughter in the AV Room, nor the expression of amazement that Ahmed could quote a reference from the OED.

'Of course.'

'And were you interrupted, though not in the sexual meaning of the term?'

'I heard a shout or scream, and looking up saw that it was Su.'

'Was she alone?'

'No there was big, and I mean big, man with her, who told me to bugger off, which I did.'

'Did you hear a name for this man?'

'No. I'd never seen him before and haven't since.'
'Did he speak other than to tell you to leave?'
'Not whilst I was there.'
'Is that the extent of your knowledge?'
'My car was round the corner.'
'Did you see any other vehicle outside the house as you departed?'
'There was a big silver car, but I've no idea what sort it was.'

Ahmed turned to Warren, but he shook his head.

'The recording is terminated. We may wish to speak to you again Ms Stone, but you are free to leave but remain under investigation and I am sure your solicitor can explain what that means.'

Jo was swiftly out of her seat and in the corridor as Ahmed left the Interview Room.

'Very well done, Ahmed. That was excellent.'
'Thanks, boss.'

She led him and Warren into the AV Room, to find that Kelly and Belinda had joined them. Belinda spoke first.

'That was the first infant post mortem I have attended. It was not as noisy as that for an adult without the necessity of an electric saw. Dr Israel was really nice. Her report will say that Martha died as a result of a broken neck having fallen from at least 2.25 metres, but that indications of bruising from her body suggest she received thrust from whoever was holding her. Her report will say we are talking about a deliberate attempt to inflict injuries on her from which she died.'

'Thank you, Belinda. That cannot have been easy,' said Jo. 'We are therefore talking about murder, infanticide. Thoughts please on what we have heard today.'

'Boss, can I add something to the melée?' said Kelly.

'I came down via the Socos laboratory where they have been examining the phones of the parents but with little success but which, with the help of Colonel Kim and the Security Service, we are able to read and hear messages on WhatsApp fed back to us from the Coffee Shop. I will receive full transcripts tomorrow but whoever I was dealing with told me with the approval of the Colonel what they contained.

'Delaney's mostly consisted of soppy messages to a girlfriend called Mandy and arrangements for the next free evening together. Day's messages were quite different, however. They were mostly to a man she called Ivan, from whom she received instructions about visitors at a property in Hall St and some she had to call on in the nearby Travelodge. Now, I'm not a detective, but to me that suggests she was on the game.'

'Kelly, my dearest darling, you're one of the very best detectives I know,' said Jo. 'Any hope that you have a number for Ivan?'

'They can only find that with the phone in hand.'

'Of course. Bag it and we'll take it to Kim and Sharon's and stay the night if possible. My mum and dad are doing the children. So come on, people, let's

In The End, Love

have some thoughts, please.'

'It's clearly more than a domestic tragedy,' said Jodie. 'So should we bring in Vice? They ought to know what's going on under their noses if anyone does.'

'Yes indeed, but our concern is different to theirs. We are dealing with a murder and they with a pimp and we don't want crossed wires. Arrange to see them first thing, Jodie, and take Warren with you. Keep their eyes focussed on who Ivan might be: having an affair with Day and therefore in the house and finding her partner screwing on the sofa. You know the form.'

'Yes, Jo.'

The door opened and in came Darcey laden with hot [ies and sausage rolls.

'I just popped into Greggs, and innocently asked about how many women they employed. There are three, all-part-time, but apart from Su Day, the other two are teenagers.'

'Well done, Darcey,' said Jo, giving her a beaming smile. 'About the goodies from Greggs, I mean!'

Darcey stuck out her tongue.

'In the morning knock on doors. Someone must have not only seen that car but know what sort it is, and someone may have seen the driver. Be at your first front-door by 8:00am.

'I've got a Press Conference to do at the house now, and I need you Belinda alongside me as I do it. The rest of you can go home and thank you for today.'

Jo phoned Sharon and Kim, old and special friends and asked if she could stay with them overnight, which they were delighted about. Jo told them about Jude which they were shocked to hear. Having been one of the earliest couples to engage in that form of IVF with egg swap, Jo and Marie had followed suit, and Ollie was the wonderful result, they were nevertheless shocked at what had happened, and nearly happened, to Jude.'

Now she had to meet the Press which she was used to doing but hated all the same, even though the Press knew she wouldn't allow herself to be hassled by them.

'Good evening, everyone and please accept my apologies for keeping you waiting so long.

'At about 9:00 pm last night there occurred an incident in the kitchen of this house which tragically brought about the death of a six-month old baby, Martha Delaney-Day. We are seeking to ascertain how this happened, though investigations are at an early stage. It is possible that at the time of the incident there were three or four people in the house, one of whom departed before the ambulance arrived. Outside there was also a large silver coloured car which drove away before the ambulance arrived. We would like to trace the driver of that car, but if you saw this vehicle please come forward.

Understandably for all living hereabouts this is a distressing time but no less so for my officers. We want to complete our investigations as soon as possible for the sake of the baby's parents. This is a tragedy. Thank you.'

'Have you arrested anyone, Chief Superintendent?' shouted a voice as Jo turned towards her car. Jo stopped and turned. 'Who shouted that?' A hand went up. Jo glared at him dismissively and then continued towards her car, whilst behind her there was a lot of laughter, though she heard one person say to the miscreant, 'You're lucky she didn't give you lines. Nobody does that to Dame Joanne.'

These last words tickled her as having picked up Kelly, she drove towards London and made her report on the car phone to the Chief Constable.

'It was possibly an accident and I'm not ruling that out but at the moment I'm unconvinced that either parent was responsible though both are holding out on the name of the person who may well be. Making use of my contacts at MI5 we have discovered that the mother was on the game and that her pimp was called Ivan. He is our target tomorrow.'

'Jo, did you say MI5?'

'Oh, I wouldn't worry about it, Adam. No security issues are at stake.'

'I'm glad I'm on your side, Jo.'

'What on earth makes you think that, Adam? Don't forget I once sent a Police and Crime Commissioner to prison.'

'My colleagues and I wish you could do that to a few more.'

Jo laughed.

There was a danger that just about every man and certainly every woman fell in love with Sharon. She was highly intelligent, extraordinarily beautiful and very amusing. Kelly had come with Jo because she and Sharon were working on a book on women in prison. Kelly had first-hand experience but had used the experience to learn the inner workings of the internet and had one of the most enquiring minds Jo had ever come across. She had gone from prison to MI5 where she had learned even more things about the internet and they were hoping she would one day return. Kelly was was not gay and attached to Ed, a former member of the team now at medical school, in pursuit of his passion for dead bodies and the work of a pathologist, but Kelly adored the presence of gay women because they were as feminine as she was and loved talking about clothes and make up and other real things rather than football and criminals.

Sharon had been headteacher of a major girls public school before meeting Kim, who was now Deputy Director of MI5, a soldier and one of the finest technical brains anywhere. Jo handed over to her Susanne Day's phone. She had a small machine ready and plugged the phone it, pressed some keys and there on the machine was a list of numbers, which she copied down for Jo.

'The last one called has been called the most times. Let's see where it abides.'

She removed the phone from one machine and plugged it into another.

'Chelmsford and Barking – and both are in your area I believe. Good Press Conference by the way. And tell me, I'm very much hoping you brought Kelly to leave her with us for good!'

'Perhaps it will happen sooner than you think. What's happened to Jude has made me consider the future. I know I've done a good job on the whole, but I'm ready now to stop and change direction completely. When that happens, I suspect the team will be broken up. I'm trying to promote people so that they can get senior jobs when this happens, but Kelly can only come to one place, and that is you.'

'We wouldn't complain, but don't rush, Jo. For the police to lose you would be to lose a great deal and next time but one you would be a shoo-in for the Met.'

'And that, Kim, is another reason for leaving. I can do so proudly now, but jobs like that are impossible and cannot make use of my skills. I don't want to be a manager and held responsible for all the crime in London as Cressida was.'

'What does Jude think about this – doing a Wittgenstein and losing yourselves in the middle of nowhere?'

'Norway, did you say? Now, that's a great idea.'

'You know what I said. And what about duty?'

'You're a soldier and you're defending the realm. You're strong and extremely able, but you've not lost two loves, and almost three.'

'Yes, you're right, Jo, and forgive me when I sometimes overlook that because you still seem so strong.'

6

Jo and Kelly were back in Chelmsford by 7:30am and soon the whole team were busy at work doing their various appointed tasks. Jo herself visited the baby's parents in the cells.

'I would like to think you will be out of here today, able to go wherever you wish to go, but a great deal depends on what you are able to reveal to us when you are interviewed later about the identity and location of Ivan. That will be essential.'

Neither of them had replied but at least she was making them think and it was vital that one or the other broke their silence.

Jodie and Warren met with a couple of officers from Vice and asked about a man called Ivan.

'Any clues, ma'am?'

'Big and driving a silver car, possibly running toms here in Chelmsford and using the Travelodge for the same.'

'It sounds to me like the man we know as the Teddy Bear. 6'4" and shaven headed. Runs toms but keeps moving them from house to house and always seems to be one step ahead of us. When we raid, neither the girls nor the Teddy Bear are to be found. He's not limited to Chelmsford. We've tried various tricks to find out where he lives but he's always one step ahead.'

'Why is he known as the Teddy Bear, and do you not also know him as Ivan?'

'I'm not being evasive ma'am when I say I don't know the answer to either question..'

'Get up his file for me?'

'Are you entitled to see it, ma'am? Only someone of Superintendent level can ask to see our files.'

'Absolutely right, sergeant. What time is it, Warren.'

'8:20, ma'am.'

'Good.'

She reached into her pocket and produced her Superintendent warrant card which would expire in 40 minutes' time. She held it in front of the sergeant's face.'

'Sorry, ma'am, I thought you said Chief Inspector when you came in.'
'Actually you did, ma'am,' added Warren.
'I am rapidly becoming brain dead.'
'O God, is it catching, ma'am? I've been showing symptoms too, said the sergeant, laughing.'
Jodie and Warren laughed with him, achieving a less defensive officer before them. He turned towards a computer, as Jodie and Warren gave each other a knowing glance..
'Here you are,' the sergeant said.
Jodie and Warren approached the screen. There was no photograph and very little information.
'I can see you've had very little to go on. What about the girls? Haven't they come up with something more than this?'
'Most of this came from them.'
'Which means we are going to be as frustrated as you.'
'I wish I could offer you more, ma'am.'
'That's the nature of policing, I suppose. Anyway thank you.'
Warren and Jodie walked along the corridor and up the stairs without a word, and into an office where Jo, Kelly and the soon-to-be Superintendent Belinda were looking at mugshots on a computer. They turned.
'Anything?'
'We were given nothing at all, except a new name for Ivan: the Teddy Bear, but I think it quite likely Ivan has a friend in Vice it would be good to smoke out. He's always a step ahead of them. We were shown a file but it contained nothing.'
'But it did, Jodie.'
'I didn't see anything.'
'If Kelly had been with us she would have done, and I did. Kelly, what do you make of "FS 45100876514"?'
'It's the address of a secret file annexe, but even if I'd been there I couldn't have remembered it. Did you write it down?'
Warren turned to Jo with a grin.
'Ma'am, don't sit idly by when I am insulted in this way.'
'Let's see what we see first.'
Kelly asked for a repeat of the numbers and typed them in. Immediately a face appeared and a great deal more information about the man known as Ivan Aleksandrov.
As she read through the file Jo realised that this was an insurance document, drawn up and kept by officers protecting their backs. Jodie had been quite right. Someone or more than one of those in Vice was up to no good. Here was a document which would prove, if anything went wrong with this arrangement, that Vice had been on to him all along and were just waiting for their moment. It was, she knew the perennial temptation of all those who worked in Vice: money and women. But today they would have to come second. Their primary task was to arrest Aleksandrov.

'Before we do anything, I must phone the Security Service to find out what they know of him and anything we need to leave alone,' said Jo, leaving the room.

'Ok, Mr Memory Man, how did you do it?' asked Kelly.

'To be perfectly honest I have no idea. I just have an odd twist in my brain which enables me to remember at one glance all sorts of things, but it can come in useful I suppose.'

'Welcome to the team, Warren.'

'Thank you, Kelly.

Jo returned.

'Five are aware of him but as a criminal more than a security risk. They think he probably leans on police officers. Now there's a surprise, but they say that he is almost certainly dangerous and that great care should be taken if we seek to arrest him. Superintendent Gorham, call the the troops in.'

Everyone was in by 9:30 but with little to further assist their pursuit of Ivan, the Teddy Bear. Belinda took charge.

'We either storm his property, all guns blazing, or build a case by speaking again with the parents of the baby, and I think it should be the latter. Anyone disagree? Good. I suggest the same pairings of Jo and Frankie, and then Jodie and Darcey. I'm afraid you'll get it in the neck from their solicitors, but you're big girls now.'

Darcey was so impressed by her wife's authority as she spoke, but even more by Jo's appointment of her to this senior role, a position that seemed made for her.

'An impressive promotion,' said Frankie to Jo as they walked towards the Interview Room.

'Thank Kelly and Jodie for that, though you would hate it, Frankie, and be utterly wasted doing that job. You, my darling, are a quite brilliant detective and, if truth be known, next in line for my job. That very first day we met, when you tried to arrest me in the University Library, I knew at once how special you were. Call it intuition or over-active libido, but I was right.'

Frankie was stunned by this admissions they entered the Interview Room and it took the voice of Jo calling her name to do what she had to do, turning on the recording machine and naming those present. Once done, Jo began.

'Constable Delaney, as I intimated to you earlier, full co-operation on your part would be good news for us both. That means two things. The first is that you give me the name you withheld yesterday of the man who entered your house at about 8:00 with Susanne Day, in the hope that it will match a name already in our possession which will indicate to me whether or not you are telling the truth.

'The second, which follows on from that, is that you revise your account of what happened to cause Martha to lose her life.'

'It's easy for you to ask these questions, because you do not face repercussions for answering them as I am quite likely to. He's put coppers into intensive care, as he said, but he's also put people into the ground.'

'Has he said so to you?'
'No, but we all know he has.'
'Who is we?'
'Ask the twats in Vice who are scared stiff of him.'
'Name, please.'
'Ivan Aleksandrov, from Russia, and as nasty a piece of work as you can find.'
'Peter, answer this carefully. What happened in the kitchen?'
'He was threatening me. Susanne had told me to leave and indicated that Aleksandrov and she were intending to use the house as a knocking shop, but she said Martha had to stay with her, and he agreed. We tussled over her and then said "Neither of you will have her" and threw her down. He then left and Su called for an ambulance.'
Jo left a period of silence.
'Leaving here today, where will you go and can we provide protection if you wish to have it?'
'For a moment I was going to say that the cell downstairs would be the safest place, but I'm not sure it would be, if you take my meaning.'
Jo nodded as did Frankie. They both knew what he meant.
'There are no further questions and we shall not hold you any longer. Please accept our deepest commiserations for the death of your daughter and I can assure you, Peter, that we will move heaven and earth to ensure right will prevail in every aspect of this matter. Before you leave, Superintendent Gorham will come to visit you. Please tell her where you will going, and she alone will have access to that information, not even myself, her superior officer. She will also deal with important practicalities. Ok?
'Yes, ma'am, and thank you.
'We want you back working as soon as possible.'
Delaney and his solicitor left the room. In the AV Room Jodie was quickly filling Belinda in on what she had to do when she met Peter Delaney.
'Just remember, Belinda, he is a free man now, not under investigation and if he does not wish to play ball with you, there's nothing you can do about it.'
The Chief Constable entered the room and everyone stood.
'Is Jo about?'
'I believe she's having a think down the corridor and then to the left, sir'
'A drink or a think?'
'Definitely, the latter, sir,' said Belinda.
'Does she share her thinking?'
'Yes, always, when she's ready.'
'Dare I interrupt her?'
'Oo, er, gosh, dangerous,' various voices said as one, each accompanied by broad grins.
'I ought to put all of you on traffic duty.'
They laughed.
'Ok, I'll take my life in my hands. Meanwhile, thank you all.'

The CC walked down the corridor ands turned left. On a seat deep in thought was Jo. She shot out of her seat when she was aware of his presence.

'Jo, can you spare me some time, not long?'
'Of course, sir.'
'There's a café across the road I like.'
'Do they serve better coffee than the canteen here?'
'It's how I discovered the place.'
'Lead on, if you can. Just let me issue some instructions to the team?'
'Of course.'
Jo opened the door.
'Belinda.'
She came to the door.
'Yes, ma'am.'
'When you're ready, get on with the Day interview. I'm having coffee with the Chief. If he sacks me, Frankie can take over.'
'I'm not sacking her, Belinda,' said the Chief with a grin.
'Oh well, we'll just have to keep hoping,' replied Belinda.
'Sorry to disappoint!'

As they sat and waited for coffee, the Chief said, 'You have built up a splendid team, Jo, the only team I feel I can joke with and let them tease me. I suspect it's because women are in the majority. I am aware that it is sometimes called "Jo and the Lesbians" but Jesus, that is because everyone knows how good you are and have won a lot of affection because of it, even if also they feel indirectly threatened by your successes. But tell me what's happening here and now.'

Jo told the Chief everything they had discovered, that PC Peter Delaney had now been released though might need protection, and that even as they spoke, Susanna Day was being interviewed for a second time.

'We believe she knows more about the man we believe responsible for the death of the baby and also for running a drug and prostitution string here in Chelmsford, as well as elsewhere. She will need to cough up a great deal before she can be released, though she had no part in the death of her baby.

'The man we are concerned to interview is a Russian, Ivan Aleksandrov. The Security Service know his name but do not see him as a state security threat but said they believed he leans on police officers to make sure he is safe.'

'Here in Essex?' said the Chief.

'Adam,. said Jo, 'you are Chief Constable and if you order me to tell you what I know, you can rely on me to do so. At the moment not even all my team know about this and for the sake of security I want it to be so for the present.'

'Changing the subject,' said the Chief, 'I was so sorry to hear about your own very recent loss and that Jude has been quite poorly in hospital. For security's sake I cannot tell how this information came to me,' he added with a grin.

'Touché. Yes, well, I'm hoping she might be released tomorrow. Her life was saved, and this is odd indeed, by the surgeon once married to my own former wife, Marie.'

'The man whose release you brought about from Frankland Prison?'

'We were visiting him as he is the father of my daughter Josie, whose birth mother was Marie. He took one look at Jude, saw bad signs and whisked her off to hospital and into the operating theatre. He thought the baby had died inside her somewhat earlier.'

'Appreciative as I am of what you are doing here, Jo, shouldn't you be with her.'

'I speak to her regularly and because of a baby being at the heart of this case, we both feel I should stay.'

'Yes, but pull out when you need to.'

'Thank you, Adam.'

'Present: Susanne Day, her solicitor Maddy Groom, Detective Chief Inspector Jodie Lovelock, and Detective Chief Inspector Janice Bussell.'

'I believe, Chief Inspector,' began Maddy Groom, 'that yesterday you were a Superintendent. How come you are not so now and will you be a sergeant by the end of the week?'

'I was "acting Superintendent" until the appointment of a new permanent Super which has now been made. I was more than happy to stand down so as to engage in more direct policing.

'Now Ms Day, I understand that you had a brief visit to check on your wellbeing from our Chief Superintendent in which she expressed the hope that you might be released today.'

'Yeah.'

'That can certainly come nearer if you can confirm the information we already have about the name of the man who came home with you two nights ago.'

'If you already know, why are asking me?'

Jodie did not reply.

There was silence for about ten seconds before she turned to her solicitor and whispered something, and then replied.

'Ivan Aleksandrov.'

'And are you aware that this Aleksandrov man runs prostitution rings in the East of London and here in Chelmsford?'

She shrugged.

'For the benefit of the recording, Ms Day has just shrugged,' said Darcey.

'And were you one of those girls?'

'My client does not have to answer that question as it has no bearing on the matter of the death of her daughter,' said the solicitor.

'When you and Aleksandrov turned up at the house, do you recall his informing your partner that he had to leave as he had plans for the house?'

'No. When we got there we found him otherwise engaged. What Ivan might have said I certainly did not hear. I was attending to the other woman.'

The door to the room opened and Ahmed came in.

'Detective Sergeant Hussain has come into the room, and he and Chief Inspector Lovelock are leaving,' said Darcey.

'Shouldn't you suspend the interview?' said the solicitor.

Darcey ignored her.

'How often had you met Amanda Stone before that night?'

'Just once. Some busybody neighbour had been in touch with Social Services. Stone called in and was perfectly happy with what she found.'

'Were you informed of the identity of the complainant?'

'No. She said that was not the practice for fear of retribution.'

Not quite sure where to take the questioning further, Darcey was hugely relieved when the door opened and Jodie returned.

'Detective Chief Inspector Lovelock has returned,' she said.

'Ms Day, when you were brought into the police station two nights ago was it made clear to you that you were not under arrest?'

'Yes.'

'Were you provided with the facility to make a phone call.'

Yes. My phone had been taken off me at home but I was allowed to use the landline here.'

'And did you?'

'No.'

'You didn't call a solicitor for example?'

'No. I didn't need one, I assumed, as I wasn't under arrest.'

'You're quite right and we are bound to make one available in the absence of your own. Is that not right, Ms Groom?'

'You are here to ask questions of my client, not her counsel.'

'Correct. So, Ms Day are you aware that without having asked anyone for a solicitor, one suddenly appears that is on the payroll of Mr Aleksandrov, has defended some of his "goons", his heavies, some of whom you must have been aware, when in court for various offences including those of assault against some of those girls you know, and who is therefore ideally placed to report back to Mr Aleksandrov what you do and don't say here?'

'No, I did not know this.'

'Mr Aleksandrov exercises care for those with whom he works and that includes legal support, an example of which is that he asked me to come and take care of Su in the face of the terrible tragedy should just experienced,' said the solicitor. 'And surely you know I have nothing to report back, as you put it. You were aware of Mr Alexandrov's identity and asked my client to do no more than confirm it, and as to what happened in the kitchen when the baby died, she cannot know anything as she was not there. May I express a point of view on behalf of my client, that you are more obsessed with finding fault with Mr Aleksandrov for whatever reason, than finding out what happened to a baby.'

'Oddly, we think the two are one. Ms Day, we shall be taking out an injunction preventing Mr Aleksandrov or anyone employed by him, making contact with you. Failure on his part to observe the court order will result in his arrest. We do not believe you had any part in the death of your daughter and this we will inform the coroner.'

'And Pete?'

'He has been freed. And you are now free to leave.'

As she walked to the door, Jodie held the solicitor back.'

'When you began, did you have principles?' she asked with an edge of sarcasm.

'May I call you Jodie?'

'Of course.'

'And might we go and sit somewhere we can talk in private but outside this building?'

'I'm told the coffee shop across the road is very good.'

Walking across the road they met Jo and the Chief Constable coming the other way, the three police officers not even slightly acknowledging the others.'

Once in the shop, Maddy said to Jodie. 'You just passed the Chief Constable.'

'I know, but he might not want to have been recognised.'

'Even when walking with Dame Joanne, super cop?'

'Maybe it was she who didn't want to be recognised with the Chief Constable.'

Maddy smiled.

'She's an attractive lady.'

'Probably less attractive when she's just put cuffs on you.'

'*I* wouldn't complain at that – sorry, I shouldn't have said that. But look, Jodie, you asked me a question as we ended that is troubling me. In my experience people I've worked with are not out and out bad people from the start, but find themselves drifting into things, sometimes completely losing sight of earlier aspirations.

'At Uni I was very good at debating and wanted to be a barrister but I didn't have the money so I started as a solicitor feeling I must be second best and quite disgruntled, even though when dealing with the law I strove to do my best and I found myself doing criminal law most of the time, which is how I fell into the world of Ivan Aleksandrov.

'It was a silly police mistake in court, that anyone worth their salt would have picked up, but I was the one who noticed it and the client was released, but Aleksandrov was apparently pleased, and I was offered a retainer. That made me as stupid as the original police mistake that got me noticed, because the house rule is that once you are a member of the Aleksandrov domain, you don't leave.'

'Maddy, would you be willing to meet with my boss? You will know when and where it would be most safe to do so.'

'Could you also be there?'

'That would be for the boss to decide, but I would like to be as she doesn't know you and I do.'

'And might you want to get to know me more? Do you have a WhatsApp number?'

Jodie gave her one of the numbers she used.

'Perhaps you could let me leave before you,' said Maddy.

Jodie continued to drink her coffee and looking at Maddy as she crossed the road and made for the car park. It was then she noticed an officer she had seen earlier in Vice following and then catching up with Maddy and stopped her. They spoke for a short time before she continued on her way and he returned to the station.

7

Jo sat to watch the recording of Jodie's interview, and then invited the team to share thoughts about the way forward. It was Frankie who spoke first.

'Day was not present in the kitchen according to both Delaney and her own words and, as yet, we have no reason to doubt that, so was not involved in the tussle over the baby. Delaney may be telling the truth about how the baby died but as yet we have not had the chance to speak to the other person in the kitchen, and until we have done that we can be no further on.'

'Has anyone anything further to add?' asked Jo.

'I can see no alternative,' said Belinda, 'to inviting him to come in to give his account of what happened in the kitchen. After all he must know we know he was present and delaying an invitation will look increasingly suspicious.'

'Yes. Ok, Kelly do the business if you will.'

'Certainly, boss.'

'Tell him he will be seeing Detective Sergeant Hussain – let's not scare him with higher titles, and say he is welcome to bring a solicitor.'

Kelly returned.

'His PA, and I've never known a pimp with a PA before, has said he will come at 3:00 this afternoon.'

'That will give us all some time to get some lunch and I recommend the Indian down the street. Be back in time to be in the AV Room half an hour before he arrives. Warren, come for a curry with me, as there is something I want you to do.

By 2-30 all but Warren and Ahmed were in the AV Room. Warren, after a curry, was now in the window seat of the café across the road with a piece of chocolate cake on a plate before him, the very last thing he wanted to eat, but what he did have was a superb view of ingress and egress across the road. He saw Aleksandrov arrive together with two others, a man who was clearly a bodyguard and a woman whom he recognised from the earlier interview with Susannah Day, the lawyer Maddy Groom. Just before they entered, someone from inside came to speak to them briefly, and then preceded them inside.

Warren texted Kelly with this information before leaving the shop and the uneaten chocolate cake, and crossing to the car park, where he took photos of the car Aleksandrov had arrived in.

'Thank you Mr Aleksandrov for coming in and I apologise that it has taken so long to make contact. As I'm sure you can imagine the death of a baby is a matter of considerable pain to all those involved which is why it has been handed over to a special unit dealing with sensitive matters.

'We know that you and Ms Day arrived at the house at or around 8:00pm, and surprised Mr Delaney and a Social Worker engaged in sexual union on the sofa.'

'Surprise certainly, if not shock, when I discovered that the woman was meant to be keeping an eye on the welfare of the child.'

'And what was the reaction of Ms Day?'

'Hysterics and an absolute determination to throw the woman out, which she accomplished. She then told Mr Delaney that he had to leave too. The house belongs to her, apparently and, I presume, she had every right to throw him out. I encouraged him to do what she was asking and in the heat of the encounter, I probably threatened him, before he withdrew to put some clothes into a bag. When he returned he had the baby with him. I did not want to become involved in such a struggle, but intuitively I felt so young a baby should stay with the mother until the court could decide the matter.'

'That was wise of you.'

'It might have been had the father been willing to accept what I said but, whether through guilt at having been seriously compromised, he became angry and snatched the baby out of her basket and went into the kitchen. I followed him and tried to reason with him, and tried to take Martha from him to give her to her mother. I would be being less than honest if I said I knew exactly how the baby fell.'

'You left straight away, instead of waiting with the couple. Why would you do that if you didn't have something to hide.'

'Sergeant,' said Maddy Groom, 'my client had just seen a terrible thing happen and knew he was not responsible. In those moments you don't think straight. It was an awful shock.'

'Thank you Maddy, for your support, but I was at fault and I should have stayed and I apologise for not doing so. I have no excuses.'

'You will realise that you have not been placed under caution here this afternoon. You will nevertheless, being present at the time of the baby's death, be required to make the statement you have just made in the coroner's court and he will decide the verdict or ask us to look into the matter further. But I thank you for your candour and willingness to respond to our invitation so promptly. I am so sorry you had to be present for so ghastly an experience.'

'Thank you, sergeant.'

The three of them stood.

'And thank you, sir.'

They left the room and Ahmed showed them out before retreating to the AV Room.

'I think,' said Jo, 'that we shall not get much further with this way of handling it. Aleksandrov is a sharp operator,.'

'Does that mean we give up on the charge of murder?' asked Darcey.

'By no means. Instead we have to pay a visit to the mortuary and be guided by the pathologist with regard to the size of the bruises on the sides of the baby and the size of the hands that made them. I think I should call Dr Colville and see if she might meet us. She it was who proved without a shadow of doubt that a ten-year-old did not have hands of sufficient size to have caused the bruising on a baby thirty six years ago, and more recently to have shown that bruising on an arm was indicative of someone being pulled inwards and not pushed outwards, which otherwise would have been a miscarriage of justice. In the meantime you can all go home. To repeat: we are not giving up on this.'

As the team began to disperse, Jodie sidled up to Jo.

'Something has happened you need to know.'

'Belinda, hang on,' said Jo.

Although it was her first day in office, Belinda was part of the senior team, and Jo was determined she would not be left out of anything important.

With the door closed, Jodie outlined all that Maddy had said and her express wish that she and Jo, and also Jodie, could meet together well away from Chelmsford.'

'Oh, and I think she fancies you!' Jodie added.

Ignoring the final comment, Jo asked Jodie for an analysis of what was going on in these encounters with Maddy.

'She's clearly very able and good with words. Her mind operates swiftly and she was at first stimulated by defending members of the Aleksandrov gang, sometimes against considerable odds. It was then she cottoned on to the fact that he was not just a businessman but that his business consisted of brothels and betting shops and other less than delightful enterprises. She also learned that, against her will, she was permanently indentured. I think she wants to tell.'

'Where and when?'

'She's going to call.'

'Belinda?' asked Jo.

'A wire?'

'She's not stupid and I wouldn't want to lose what may be her trust,' said Jodie. 'I said to her that you would decide if it was one or both of us?'

'If she wants you there, then so be it.'

Jodie's phone sounded.

'This will be her.' She looked at the screen. 'Bull Inn, Long Melford @ 8-00. That's almost next to our office.'

'Is that a coincidence?' asked Belinda. 'My concern, boss, is that this may be a trap in which Aleksandrov may want to come and tell you to lay off him with accompanying threats.'

'Yes, that occurred to me too.'

'Do you want me to call everyone back?'

'What do you think, Jodie?'

'I think you should authorise an armed operation, with you, Belinda in the bar from at least 7:30 with Darcey. Frankie and the boys should arrive after she arrives when you text her, only to enter if called in by you.'

Belinda and Jodie looked to their boss.

'I always do as I'm told,' said Jo.

Jodie grinned.

From her car as she drove back to the office, Jo spoke first of all to Josie and Ollie, asking how school had been and promising to take them in the morning. She also called Jude who was beginning to feel very much better and was looking forward to coming home tomorrow.

'What time will you be allowed to escape?'

'The doctor says that I will need a final BP and urine test. Normally the results are back by 11-00. If they're ok I can dig a tunnel and be free.'

'I'll be there to rescue you.'

'Oh, thank you, my love.'

Jo was pleased that the pub was busy, and seeing Jodie ,at once joined her. The table nearest to the door was occupied by a lesbian couple who were all over each other, both of whom under their left arms wore a Glock 17 gun which both of them knew how to use to maximum effect. Jo watched them wishing it was her kissing Darcey. Why was it, she wondered, that although she now had Jude, and Darcey had Belinda, every time she looked at Darcey she had a profound longing for her, and knew it was mutual?

Just before 8:00 the door opened and in came Maddy Groom. Out of her official sober work clothes she looked very attractive to Belinda and Darcey as she passed them on her way to where Jo and Jodie were sitting.

'Let me get you a drink,' said Jodie.

'Sparkling water with ice and lemon, please. I am so pleased to meet you Dame Joanne. You have a formidable reputation in law and order circles.'

'Please, I'm Jo. The dame comes in handy sometimes but I don't make use of it unless it helps'

'It is said you were awarded it for courage beyond the call of duty in the face of an international plot.'

'O good, that's the story I like to hear. Impressive but completely false.'

Jodie returned.

'She won't tell you,' said Jodie, overhearing the end of their conversation, 'but on the subject of doing things well, I was impressed with you this morning, defending Susanne.'

'Thank you, but honestly you didn't have much to work on, as I think you knew, so it wasn't too demanding.'

'And you hardly spoke,' said Jo, 'when your boss came in.'

'He told me I had to be there "just in case". I can't help you in the matter of the death of the baby. Mr Aleksandrov is far too cagey to let anything slip about what did and did not happen. So I can't help you there, but there are others matters in which you might find me useful, and all to do with the Vice squad.'

'Go on.'

'I am well aware that my boss runs prostitutes, not just in Chelmsford but also in the East End where, of course he has competitors. He has a hold over them however, because the Vice Squad are encouraged to harass the opposition and to let him know when they are planning to raid a property in adequate time for him to move out.'

'When you say they are "encouraged", do you mean financial encouragement or payment in kind?'

'I would think both, wouldn't you?'

'Are you suggesting that everyone in Vice is involved?'

'No, but you must know the reputation of those who work in Vice anywhere. It tends to corrupt.'

Jo didn't reply.

'We've been suspecting something like this,' said Jodie, 'not least since I saw you being approached by one of their team after we met today.'

'I hoped you might see that. He's DS Bowlby, an absolute shit of a human being from South London.'

'Ronnie Bowlby?' asked Jo.

'Yes. Do you know him?'

'When I was with the Met in Lewisham, he was a PC.'

'He wanted to know what Jodie and I were discussing, and I told him you were considering leaving the Force and training to be a solicitor. He seems to have the brief of being the eyes and ears of Mr Aleksandrov in the station but the person who is in charge, if that is the right word, is DI Mark Hendry who makes frequent appearances at the Alexandrov home in Barking.'

'How do you know you have not been followed this evening?'

'I don't, but my car is in my drive at home. If someone is following me, he waits at the entrance to the cul-de-sac, so tonight, leaving by my back door I cross the field at the back of my house and my friend Val waits there for me, and here we are. Well, I'm here and Val is on the table next to your people by the door.'

'How on earth did ...?' asked Jodie.

'Because they look like plain clothes officers trying very hard not to look like like plain clothes policemen!'

Jo got up and approached the table.

'Guys, this lady on the next table is called Val. Please buy her a drink (non-alcoholic as she's driving). Val, please come and join this lot and help them to relax.'

'Of course and thank you, Dame Joanne.'

Jo returned to Jodie and Maddy.

'On television they never show the Chief Super having to nursemaid the team.'

Jo and Jodie laughed.

'Forgive me if I've got this wrong, but my instinct tells me that the best way for us to find a way of obtaining evidence against these two would be for you two to work on this without me present. I've often found that two is better than three. The thing is, Maddy, Jodie is by far and way the finest member of our team in every way, and that includes me. If honours should be given, it is to her above all. So I will leave you. I have two children to attend to and a partner coming home from hospital tomorrow, so don't expect to see me. Just get on with it, Jodie.'

'I sometimes think you got your DBE for flattery, boss.'

Maddy laughed and Jo leaned forward and kissed her cheek, before heading off.

'That's most odd,' said Jodie. 'I've never known her get up and go when a serious matter is being addressed,'

'When things were being handed out in the beginning,' said Maddy, 'you two received more than your fair share. Courage, intelligence, humour.'

'There's a negative side to that though. Jo had never had a boyfriend or girlfriend until she was nearly 30, and then met a black DI who looked like a supermodel but who died following a car crash. Then she met someone in the course of an investigation which won her the DBE. They married and had an IVF baby, and then the partner became a senior officer in the RAF.

'Unfortunately, she was also highly efficient in the art of adultery with men, and on a large scale, though Jo only discovered this after her death. She accepted an appointment with the American Air Force in California and committed suicide. Jo was besotted with Marie and it blinded her totally to all the terrible things she did, including murder and bringing into the country an extremely dangerous chemical agent smuggled out of Russia. Worst of all was Marie's decision to pretend she was a lesbian so she could be protected by living with and marrying Jo.'

'Jesus!'

'And just a few days ago Jo and her present partner (an ex-vicar believe it or not) lost their baby with pre-eclampsia, and Jo nearly lost her partner too.'

'What a story and you assume when you see a successful person that it must have been plain sailing. And you?'

'I love my job. I seem to do it well.'

'Married?'

'A year ago I might have thought that by this time I would be. But it wasn't right.'

'Does that mean there's hope for me?'

They looked at one another and Jodie left the question hanging.

'Let's give some thought to the matter in hand – for now,' said Jodie.

On her way back to Saxmundham, Jo spoke once again to Jude.

'I'm more than ever determined to resign when the case is resolved which is the most we can expect – I don't think there's a lot of chance of getting it solved.'

'That must be so frustrating. Never mind, tomorrow I'm coming home all being well. Are you still able to come?'

'You bet and I'm hoping to catch a word with Nathan too.'

'I have so missed you, Jo.'

'And you, my favourite ex-vicar.'

For Jude, the highlight of each night had come with the visit of Abby. Even when not on duty she had come in to spend time with Jude, a time of laughter and joy for them both. Jude wanted to go home but wondered how she could live without Abby, and knew that this was not good news.

Once at home, Jo crept into the bedroom of the children where Ollie was already asleep but Josie was reading.'

'What on earth are you doing, Josie? Shouldn't you be on your phone?'

Josie laughed.

'I like books. Can I ask you something?'

'Of course.'

'I'd like to begin calling you "mum". I know that was what we called Marie, but I shan't confuse you.'

'I would be very happy for that and you can offer it to Ollie as well.'

'Thank you, mum.'

'Sleep well, my darling. I'll take you to school in the morning.'

8

It was clearly going to take Ollie a little longer than Josie to use the maternal diminutive "mum" but with the example of Josie, Jo thought it wouldn't take that long. The complication was less that "mummy" was either childish or upper class, so much as in her suicide note Marie had asked Jo to tell the children their mum always loved them. Even from the grave Marie could wreak havoc!

Jo drove them both to school. She was not intending to say anything just yet to them about the possibility of moving, but she would do so to Jude this morning.

She called into the office and spoke to Belinda who had heard from Dr Colville, and had agreed to meet the Paediatric Pathologist who had conducted the post mortem on baby Martha, to consider the nature of the bruising on her arms and side.

Belinda wanted to know what should happen next in the matter of the two officers in Vice on the payroll of Aleksandrov.

'At the moment, we don't know what Maddy Groom was up to in meeting us last night. Was she telling the truth or was she spinning a line on behalf of her boss? We need more evidence one way or another before we hand it over to Professional Standards and greater insight into Ms Groom. Meet with the team and see if you can come up with a strategy.'

'Will you be in today?'

'I'm on my way to St Albans to bring Jude home from hospital, so I might not make it, but that doesn't matter. You're the senior officer, Belinda, and more than capable of doing anything and everything, and always remember the senior team of Jodie, Kelly and you, with whom you can't go wrong.'

Belinda was less convinced than Jo that she could manage, and she had failed to mention that Jodie was unusually quiet and detached this morning. She decided to call her into her office.

'You are an outstanding police officer, Jodie, courageous, intelligent and always capable of getting into the minds of villains, and I have barely any of your experience, but for better or worse, and I think you had a hand in it, I find myself as your superior officer. That means I cannot hold back when I see you as you are, because at any moment I may need you to be on top form.'

'And this is why we knew how totally equipped you are for your job, Belinda, because you are perhaps the only one, apart from the boss, who would address this directly because you would know it might interfere with operational matters. It's why every one of us respects you and looks up to you.'

'Thank you, but let's get back to you and what's going on inside.'

'People have probably noticed that I haven't mentioned Stuart recently. We remain friends but I think both of us knew it was not going anywhere. For some months, then, I've been living a celibate life. And then yesterday I met someone who made me tingle in a way I haven't known since I won the inter-police shooting competition in Derbyshire by a country mile.'

Belinda laughed.

'What utterly surprised me about this was that the person I met was a woman. You have had this experience but I most certainly have not, and the best or worst part of the experience is that it was obviously mutual. She said she had an experience of being with a woman when she was at university but not since, until she met me.'

'I take it you are talking about Maddy Groom, whom you met with Jo.'

'Yes.'

'Oh God, this is an awful question, Jodie, but did you spend the night together?'

'No, give me some credit. She was driven home by a friend called Val. I drove myself home and I spent the night alone and very confused.'

'I knew the answer before I asked the question, but the question had to be asked. But let's talk about the confusion.'

'The confusion is that I'm not gay and yet here I was powerfully drawn to a woman in a way I have always only associated with heterosexual feeling.'

'Even when you've seen it in colleagues?'

'But none of you make a song and dance about it, and to be honest I never gave it any thought, you were just a group of people I liked and, more importantly, trusted. Sexuality, male or female, never came into it, unlike it often does in a predominantly male police station. I got sick of that and was why I chose firearms and being a PPO, before coming to work with Jo.'

'Don't underestimate the Jo factor,' said Belinda. 'We would both acknowledge that she's not in the drop dead gorgeous category but is there anyone more attractive, physically and mentally? I wanted her the first time I met her, and Jo makes makes all things possible and quite without song and dance as you put it. I think we're all in love with her and it's catching. You know how ghastly it can be working with men and how they regard women as simply there for their own enjoyment and exploitation. Jo has shown me something different and perhaps you as well. I love being and working with women, and I find female sexuality wonderful, even glorious.'

'Belinda, I need to tell you officially that I have not overstepped the limits of relationship which would be a serious disciplinary matter if I had. I must also say that in coming on to me, I have to consider whether the info she supplied was deliberate misinformation. She gave me the names of the two officers she named in the Vice Squad who are bent: 'DS Ronnie Bowlby and DI Mark Hendry. It could of course be a deliberate deception, and I am alert to that possibility, but we have to start somewhere. I am willing to work with Kelly on that, if you're happy.'

'Yes, of course, and I thought I might send the others on a brothel hunt, to see if there are common patterns of ownership, and get Darcey to call on Susanne Day to see what, if anything, has come to mind since the death of her baby.'

'Good idea.'

'Thank you Jodie, for our conversation. If it helps, I've always thought you are quite lovely and desirable.'

'No Superintendent has ever said anything like that to me before,' she said, laughing.

'You need to get out more.'

They laughed.

'Thank you ma'am,' said Jodie as she left the office.

9

'Did you get to see Nathan?' asked Jude, as they drove out of the car park.'
'Yes, but it wasn't about you but about the baby who died in Chelmsford.'
'And was he any help?'
'He told me that the bones in the neck of a baby are very soft which is why a baby's head has to be supported. He's not a paediatrician of course but he thought it unlikely that a baby that fell from someone's hands accidentally, at waist level, would have that degree of injury. The paediatric pathologist's report is full of detail, and that was her job, but I've asked Sheila Coalville to do a second post mortem, which I am entitled to do, under the guidance of the first pathologist, focussing not on the neck but on the bruising on the baby's sides about which she has previously done work in the Nottingham case which freed Alice.'
'Jo, has the loss of our baby affected your approach to the death of this baby?'
'I would have thought inevitably so, though to what extent I cannot say. I have totally withdrawn from the case today. They're a good team, now being led by Belinda Gorham.'
'Belinda? I thought Jodie was your deputy.'
She wanted to return to more direct action, so she's back to being a DCI and director of operations, but Belinda is extremely able and was recommended to me by Kelly and Jodie together. We've also got two new men, Ahmed and Warren, who are also outstanding, not to mention Darcey and Frankie. I still need another couple to ensure continuity after I'm gone.'
'I know you've mentioned leaving before, but this time it sounds like you're drawing up plans. I would have liked to have known about them before now.'
'Well, so would I. The fact is that it's only since you nearly died that I've given more serious thought to it all and this is the first chance we've had to talk about them.'
'Well, come on then, talk about them.'
'Because we have the aeroplane, distances are much smaller.'
'Jesus, how far are you thinking we should move?'
'Far enough away so that no one knows or cares about who I am. It was fun

being called Dame at first but I'm ready to shed it.'

'To renounce it, you mean, send it back to the Queen?'

'No, that would hurt those who are most proud of it – the children, your mum, my parents, and you, most of all.'

Jude smiled.

'Of course I am and so should you be. You earned this the hard way. You excelled in the face of something terrible and people should know that.'

'I also got utterly hoodwinked by someone.'

'Yes, well that serves to remind you you're not quite as perfect a detective as you might otherwise think.'

Jo laughed.

'You'd make quite a good vicar, you know. Have you ever thought of that?'

Jude laughed.

'Ok, Dame Joanne. Out with it. Tell me what you have in mind. I know you well enough to know that you only speak when you are clear inside yourself.'

'What a terrible thing to say to your partner,' said Jo with a grin.

'You're quite right, I apologise, but now tell me.'

'I want us to go to live in a remote part of Scotland, to acquire a croft and spend our days engaged in farming a smallholding – subsistence farming.'

'Oh thank God for that, I thought you were going to suggest we do something we know nothing about in a place we don't know, knowing no one and with no income.'

'There is a croft available at the present time near Oban.'

'Oban? That's near Iona. But Jo, a croft is not like an allotment. From what I have read, it's a 24/7 undertaking, and what knowledge have either of us of animals.'

'You forget that I was brought up in a kennels, with horses and hounds and terriers.'

'I'm not sure fox hunting is allowed even in the West of Scotland.'

'Sentimental nonsense. Any fox coming anywhere near our sheep will get short shrift from me. Don't forget I'm a crackshot.'

'No you're not. At your last training day on the range, you told me the instructor said those behind you were more at risk that the targets ahead.'

'What did he know? He is only a firearms instructor and I'm a Dame'

'That will be a great comfort to the fox. Anyway, what sheep do you have in mind?'

'Tough and hardy. Swaledale from the Pennines or Herdwick, from where you mum lives in the Lake District. Or we might have some Scottish Blackface or North Country Cheviots.'

'And where would the children fit into this, and Katia who has the flat in our house, and our house for that matter. Have you thought all these through?'

Jo had no time to reply as there came through a message from Kelly.

'Jo, Maddy Groom has been found unconscious at home this morning and is now in Colchester General Hospital. Jodie is with her. I know you're taking Jude home, but the you're needed. I'm sorry, boss, and I'm sorry Jude. Where

In The End, Love

are you?'

'On the A12 near Witham.'

'Go straight to the hospital and I'll come and take Jude home to Saxmundham.'

Jo looked across to Jude, who nodded.

'She'll be in the hospital café.'

'Hasn't she suffered enough?'

Jo switched on the blue lights and siren.

'This is why I want to get away,' said Jo.

'Don't you think Scotland's a bit too near?' said Jude. 'There's always Iceland. They can't easily call you back from there!'

With Jude deposited in the café, Jo made her way to A&E to find that Maddy had been taken to a single room on a ward where the maxillofacial consultant would be coming to see her.

Jo made her way to the ward where an officious staff nurse blocked her way.

'There's already one visitor and we don't allow two.'

'Are you the staff nurse in charge?'

'Yes.'

'I'm Detective Chief Superintendent Jo Enright and I am going in there. She is the victim of a serious crime.'

So saying, she literally pushed the nurse aside and went into the room.

She looked terrible with appalling bruising around her eyes and what seemed to Jo to be a depressed cheekbone. Holding her hand was Jodie. Jo asked nothing, knowing that it was better that any conversation should take place outside the room when the consultant came. They didn't have to wait long.

A young woman came in, wearing a lovely multi-coloured jumper and skirt of such a length as to make her legs noticeable wherever she was in her place of work.

'Hello,' said the young woman. 'I'm Miss Dawson, the maxillofacial consultant. Please stay if you wish, but I'll come and talk to you outside when I'm done if you prefer to leave, though please don't be rude again to the staff nurse in charge.

'Maddy has been x-rayed and I gather this was an unpleasant person or persons unknown who are responsible for this and you two are going to arrest them.'

'Miss Dawson, you watch too much television.'

Leaving the room, Jo sought out the staff nurse.

'Truly I'm sorry for my rudeness when I know how important a job you do. Sometimes when you are in a position of authority you tend to abuse it. I ask your forgiveness.'

'Even staff nurses do the same sometimes. Thank you, and you are forgiven, and just ask if I can help.'

Jo and Jodie walked a little along the corridor.

'What do you know?'

Anna's friend, Val, whom you met, dropped her off at her home at about 10 o'clock. She says there was nothing untoward, no cars or people, and she drove home. It was one of her neighbours, leaving very early for work, who noticed her front door was open and went to investigate. He found her unconscious in the hall and called an ambulance and us, but look at my phone. I took the photo as soon as they let me see her. Behind her right eye she was clearly punched by a signet ring of some sort or other and it has left a mark and you can see the outline of a horse.'

'That has to stay known only to you and me. By the looks of her, Maddy is going to be in a lot of pain, but you and I, Jodie, have an important task ahead of us and it needs us both.'

'What are you going to do?'

'At the moment I have no idea, so I'm hoping for inspiration, but we might pay a visit to Vice to have a conversation with DS Bowlby about the chat he had with Maddy following her lunch with you. I gather from Belinda that Darcey is visiting Susanne Day to see if she is interested in opening up further about Aleksandrov. Belinda herself has gone to meet the two pathologists to see if the baby's marks suggested she was being tightly held prior to be being violently thrown. I asked Nathan Vickery this morning about this and he said he thought that this was the only way the neck of the baby could be broken. Frankie and her boys I've pulled off the brothel hunt and I'm sending them to visit Aleksandrov to inform him that his tame solicitor has been violently attacked and that they want to examine the hands of all his goons.'

'They'll be lucky.'

'Of course, but it might put the wind up them and that often causes unexpected fruit to fall.'

At that moment Miss Dawson appeared.

'She's come round and she's asking for you, she said to Jodie.

She returned to the room.

'She's taken one hell of a walloping, by one person I think. Her left eye socket is fractured and her left cheek bone has Zygomaticomaxillary fractures – what a wonderful word, which means it will hurt for for some time to come and we have to hope she doesn't get a cold because blowing her nose really won't help her recovery and would cause intense pain. But, the good news is that by the time I've finished with her in theatre, whether once or twice, she will soon be as lovely as she was before.

'Now, Chief Superintendent, what you need to know is that there was just one assailant, and that he is right-handed. Generously he has left you tiny amounts of flesh under her nails and I have therefore bagged her hands until your boffins can get to work.'

'Miss Dawson, you are a wonder.'

'I know, even if not yet a Dame.'

'You have just spoiled everything.'

They laughed.

Jo immediately called for Forensics to come to the hospital, as the observations of the surgeon could be a real breakthrough. She also called Frankie to let her know about that possible development. She would know how to respond in terms of holding back when interviewing the goons.

Jodie once again held Anna's hand.
'I can't smile because it hurts,' said Maddy.
'I'll smile for you. Did you see who it was?'
'Is it wise of me to say so? After all, on the next occasion Broznik might come and finish me off.'
'You're right. Best not to give me his name.'
Jodie leant forward and kissed Maddy on the lips.
'Did that hurt?'
'I might survive another.'

Jodie left and found Jo waiting for her.
'The man in question is called Broznik. Until we get the skin fragments removed from Anna's nails I would like protection for her.'
'Do you want to stay yourself?'
'It's not the best use of a DCI. No, but I'll wait until we can get someone here.'
'It so happens I've already sent for someone: PC Tommy Carter from Colchester. He's a big lad I like and trust a great deal, and he reminds me of Ed Secker, and between you and me I'm hoping to recruit him to the team.'
'Trust you to be one step ahead of me, but you're right, I miss Ed a great deal. I'm so pleased he and Kelly are still together, unlikely though it might once have seemed with him a bobby and she an ex-con, both a tribute to your ability to recruit.'
'And here is the man himself. Good morning Tommy.'
A huge man, at least 6'5", came towards them, grinning from ear to ear.'
'Good morning, ma'am.
'This is DCI Lovelock.'
Good morning to you as well, ma'am.'
'Oh Tommy, stop it, you make me feel old. We know each other well enough to dispense with titles.'
'How do you know each other?' asked Jodie.
'A little moonlighting Tommy and I did in my time off. Tommy had worked out that there was a smuggling operation using Aldeburgh fishing boats and he knew where I lived so he called on me and we set a little sting together, well actually quite a big sting, and we caught all sorts of goodies in our nets with the help of the coastguard. I did nothing really – it was Tommy's op from first to last.'
'Which would never have happened without your guile, Jo. What a fabulous criminal you might have have made in a parallel universe.'
'Flatterer. Jodie will brief you on your charge. Someone from Socos will

come to remove skin from her nails which is why they've been bagged. Otherwise doctors and nurses only.'

'Of course, Jo. Ok, lead on, ma'am.'

'In the circumstances, you'd better call me Jodie.'

'Are you *that* Jodie, the one who saved Jo's life with an extremely well-placed kick in the balls?'

'I have that distinction.'

'In which case, may I walk behind you, please?'

Jodie walked on, struggling to hold in her laughter.

Darcey pulled up outside the house and could see Susanne at the kitchen window, and Susanne could see Darcey as she emerged from her car and assumed she was either from social services or the police. Darcey rang the doorbell and had her warrant card to hand. She didn't need to speak.

'Come in,' said Susanne, and Darcey followed her into the lounge, where she was invited to sit.

'I'm Detective Chief Inspector Janice Bussell, but I'm usually called Darcey.'

'You do have a lot of women in your setup,' said Susanne, 'not that I mind. A couple of the men coppers I've met are absolute shits.'

'However did you come across them because I can assure you they were not from our unit?'

'I'm sure by now you know that I have been operating as a sex worker. We worked in a particular location, and then would have to move to somewhere else, and keep going round the houses. Those two called in to see us, not least in the hope of trying it on.'

'And did they succeed?'

'It was that or rape.'

'How many sex workers were there?'

'I never saw most of the girls, but I would guess there were about a dozen including a couple under age for those who like that sort of thing. I think they got paid in drugs which they could either use or sell on.'

'Do you know the names of these two men?'

'You're kidding me, aren't you? I'm not the prettiest face in the world but I would be a lot worse after they had finished with me, as they had with Dorn.'

'Did you visit the Travel Lodge?'

'I think we all did.'

'And did someone there know what was going on?'

'Unless they were blind and stupid, they must have done, so I imagine they were paid to keep their eyes firmly shut.'

'Presumably this provision was for businessmen.'

'Well, not for families, that's for certain.'

'Susanne, these two police officers you've spoken of and not wished to name, and I fully understand that, are working for who, do you think?'

'Isn't that for you to work out?'

'You have been used and abused and possibly raped by so-called police officers. Do those who control you arrange for regular medical checks? What percentage of the money you earn is yours? What was the controller doing here with you on the night Martha died? How often has he or one one of his men been round to find out how you are or to bring you some money to help with the funeral?

'I want to get these men and put a stop to what they have been doing, though you're right to worry about what they might do to you if you give us help. Late last night your solicitor when you were being questioned, Maddy Groom, had a drink with one of my female colleagues, and on returning home was viciously attacked in her home and is now in hospital requiring surgery on her face. It doesn't take much imagination to work out who was behind this.'

'Will she be alright? And she has such a pretty face.'

'We have to hope she will again, but how are we going to prevent a repeat, and a repeat of a baby's death when a man gets angry. We are having a second post-mortem today.'

'Yes, I had a call informing me from someone called Kelly Jones.'

'She is our administrator and by law you had to be told. I can't pre-empt what will emerge, but there is a reason why we asked for this on what was the advice of a consultant obstetrician and gynaecologist who told us that the chance of a baby of Martha's age breaking her neck by being dropped accidentally less than a metre, was more or less nil. We shall know much later today, but Su, you can make a great of difference by confirming what I have spoken to you about.'

'And how will that help me if instead of your car parking outside, it is Ivan's or one of his men. He is a big man and a bully. You do what he tells you because you dare not and any of the girls that dares to stand up to him soon regrets it. They either get a violent slap across the face from him or a visit at home from one of his men who threatens to give the good news to her family and neighbours what it is she does in her spare time.'

'And is that why he was here then, to tell Pete what you did?'

'He had decided that because I own this house, it would be ideal for one of his houses, provided he could get Pete out, and that's why he came round, to tell Pete his time was up.'

'Have you had any contact with Pete?'

'He came round last night to see me. We have practical matters to discuss with regard to the funeral, and to be honest and I suppose I'm a bit ashamed about this, if we could get rid of Aleksandrov, Pete and I agreed that we would like to make a fresh start. '

'If it's any help, you have not told me anything I didn't already know, but did Pete tell you anything you did not know? After all, he was present when Martha met her death.'

She hesitated.

'He said Aleksandrov took hold of Martha, lifted her up and then with considerable force, threw her to the kitchen floor.'

'The evil bastard!' said Darcey. 'I shall leave now, but just tell me who Dorn is and where I can find her.'

Darcey received the information. Her sat nav showed she was not far away and she set off for the address. Dorn had probably been a pretty woman until recently, but her face showed the ill effects of crossing Mr Aleksandrov – more or less the same sort of injuries for which Maddy would be being treated in hospital but had not been attended to.

'I'm Detective Chief Inspector Bussell and I'm investigating the killing of the daughter of Susanne Day and Peter Delaney, and, by the looks of you, the assault you received.'

'Come in.'

'Who did it, Dorn, and why?'

'I told Ivan I was leaving and he said something like "O Dorn, I don't think so". He said I was a good earner and that perhaps I needed a few days off, but there was no question of leaving. I told him I was, and he sort of shrugged before leaving.

'About an hour later there was a knock on the door. I recognised who he was. He was a policeman who had raped me before, but on this occasion he was nice as can be and even accepted a cup of coffee. He then said he gathered I was quitting the business and he would like one last sample of the merchandise. I assumed I had no option, so I led him upstairs, and it was when he was presumably satisfied, that he turned very nasty and began punching me with considerable force, and the result is as you can see.'

'Can you describe him?'

'I can do better than that. He went to the toilet to wipe off some blood and as he came out I took his photo with my phone.'

'Tap my phone with yours,' said Darcey.

10

Frankie and her two male colleagues had parked in the drive in such as way as to prevent anyone getting out. There were a number of vehicles parked around the house.

In response to their knock on the door, and unexpectedly, a smartly dressed early middle aged woman opened the door. The trio showed their warrant cards and were admitted into an ante-room. After three or four minutes the door opened and in came Ivan Alexandrov.

'Good morning sir. I'm sorry to disturb you but we have a matter of mutual concern to deal with.'

'It must be important for you to send three officers to see me.'

'Oh don't worry about Ahmed and me, sir,' said Warren. 'We are trainees and are here as observers of Inspector Wawszyczk.'

'Wawszyczk sounds to me like a Polish name. You are from Warsaw or Gdansk possibly?'

'Nottingham. Where do you think the name Broznik hails from?'

'Why do you ask?'

'I ask the questions, sir, not you.'

'It could be Polish too, or from the Ukraine, somewhere like that. I could look it up.'

'Of course but it would much easier simply to call Broznik and ask him to his face.'

'He's almost certainly not here.'

'Late to bed was he?'

'He's not on duty until noon, and although my people are loyal and well rewarded, if they have an evening off, I don't ask what they were doing or with whom.'

'Were you aware that the solicitor you use in business, Ms Maddy Groom, was attacked last night in her own house and badly beaten by person or persons unknown, such as has required urgent surgery this morning.'

'That's terrible news. I must get to see her.'

'That's not possible, I'm afraid. She's under a 24 hour police guard and we are waiting for her to regain consciousness so we can see if she can remember anything, though I'm told that may not happen, as who ever attacked her brought about serious head injuries.'

'That saddens me greatly but I'm not sure where Mr Boznik comes into it.'

'Oh, it was not from her. Anyway we shan't trouble you further.'

Jodie and Jo arrived at the police station at much the same time.

'Any chance of getting Tommy transferred soon?' asked Jodie. 'He seems to me more than slightly able.'

'He is and a definite replacement for Ed. The Chief will owe me one once we get this sorted and I am determined that I shall get Tommy.'

'Oh God, if the villains get to know you're "determined", they'd flee, let alone the Chief Constable.'

'We shall make a start in here with the gentlemen of Vice, but don't forget we can't do the work of Professional Standards.'

'You mean be nice to them and utterly detached?'

'How did you guess?'

Jo walked into the office of the Vice team and everyone stood.

'As you were,' she said. 'Where is DI Hendry?'

'In the office at the back, ma'am,' said one of the officers.

She went to the office and knocked and entered. From the sound emerging from his computer before he had time to mute it, Jo knew he had been playing a game. He stood up.

'Are you winning. Inspector?'

'Just a short break from serious work, ma'am.'

'Do sit down. I would like an informal conversation with you later, but I'm just letting you know I also need to have a chat with Ronnie Bowlby, and I'll borrow him from you for a short while. Actually I knew him some time ago when he was a new PC in Lewisham, though we won't be discussing old times.'

'Of course. I'll tell him.'

'No need,' said Jo in a way that members of her own team recognised as not worth arguing with. She smiled, the sort of smile the team would also recognise as determined.

She returned to the main office and approached Bowlby.

'Ronnie, it's some time since we were together in South London. How's Chris and the kids?'

'We're still married which must be some sort of record for coppers.'

Jo laughed.

'You're not wrong. Anyway, there's something I need to chat with you about, not officially. Hendry says you can.'

'You could overrule him anyway.'

'I wouldn't do that. He's your guvnor and I respect that.'

She led Bowlby out of the room and down the corridor into an empty office where Jodie was sitting, reading the paper.'

'Ronnie, this is Jodie, my DCI.'

In The End, Love

'Hi.'

Once seated and trying to be as relaxed possible, Jo let Jodie do the leading.

'As you know we are concerned with the death of a baby which your Chief Constable wanted us to investigate because of the involvement of a police officer which makes some sense, I suppose. Do you know Peter Delaney, the father of the baby?'

'I've seen him about the station and occasionally chatted with him in the canteen.'

'And your thoughts about him?'

'You will know more about his record, I'm sure, but as a bloke I think he's ok.'

'A temper?'

'I've never seen evidence of it

'He was involved in a tussle with someone over his baby daughter. Perhaps you've heard about it. The tussle was with someone you know well, Ivan Aleksandrov.'

'I've come across him in the course of work, but there's no way I could say I know him well.'

'Good,' said Jo. 'We're discovering that those who get on the wrong side of him tend to come out of it not at all well. That happened during last night. Someone you made a point of speaking with when she ended her lunch with DCI Lovelock here.'

'I can't recall that.'

'I believe DCI Lovelock filmed the encounter. Would you like to refresh Ronnie's memory, Jodie?'

She took out her phone and turned on the video.

'There is Maddy leaving the café and there you are intercepting her. Do you remember now?' said Jodie

'Of course. She is a brief often used here and I just wanted to find out how she was.'

'And you can see through walls, can you? From your office it's not possible to see the café, which suggests you were waiting for her, and her account differs from yours; not so taken up with social niceties.'

'People remember things differently.'

'That's certainly true as every copper knows,' said Jo, 'and to be honest one of the difficulties in our case is to know who is telling the truth between PC Peter Delaney and Ivan Aleksandrov. Who would you think is the more reliable witness?'

'I have no idea. It's not my case, ma'am and my opinion is not evidence, as well you know.'

He stood up.

'I think I'll go back to some real police work now, not doing what they call on television news programmes *vox pop,* a survey of opinions.'

He left the room.

'I'm impressed he knew some Latin,' said Jodie.

'I shouldn't be surprised if, by the time we've finished he doesn't know another: *incarceration*.'

'Oh Jo, it's only based on Latin. Surely you knew that? Do you want me to fetch Hendry?' asked Jodie.

'No, I'll go. I shall be interested to see if Bowlby is in with him and I'll do my Latin homework later..'

She entered the room and went straight to Hendry's office where she found Bowlby talking to him.

'Mark, you'll have plenty of time to compare notes later. Can you please come with me now.'

'We're discussing something important, Chief Superintendent. As it is only an informal conversation you are wanting, please supply the questions in writing and I will answer within ten days.'

'Sergeant, leave the room and ask DCI Lovelock to join me here.'

He did so and Jo smiled at DI Hendry.

'Where are most of your operations carried out?' asked Jo.

'In the East End, often working with City Force and the Met.'

'On?'

'The normal stuff of Vice everywhere: drugs, toms, illegal gambling and the like.'

'That's hardly what I would expect in Chelmsford.'

'You're right but until our base is moved, this is where we function.'

Jodie entered the room.

'DI Hendry, this is DCI Lovelock, who is the Director of Operations in our team. I have a simple question for you, DCI Hendry and it is this: why are you so often to be found in the house of Mr Ivan Lewinsky?'

'He has proved most helpful in the past couple of years in dealing with the things that we are concerned about. I know that he sounds like a typical Russian gangster, but in fact he is a businessman who is very concerned about the ways in which corrupt practice makes it difficult for legitimate business to function and I feel it's important to support him and also to learn from him what is going on that we don't know.'

'And what about his own enterprises and businesses. Do you look closely at them or is there a quid pro quo deal between you that in return for the support and help he gives, you will not look too closely at what he does?'

'As you should know, Chief Superintendent, the concerns of Vice are not yours and I don't have to answer you.'

'We have been brought in to deal with the tragic death of a baby, the daughter of one of the officers based at this station, but it is slightly complicated because Mr Alexandrov was present at the time, and we are trying to clarify any part that he might have taken in what happened, especially as he was in the company of a prostitute, the mother of the baby, who maintains Alexandrov was running a string of girls. I have already questioned DS Bowlby and ascertained his view of the Russian, and so I ask the same question of you.

'I don't know what Ronnie said to you, but I certainly think that Mr Aleksandrov is a man with the welfare of families at the heart of what he does and the very thought that he has been involved in this must be a source of great distress to him. It's a terrible thing to happen and Mr Aleksandrov feels these sorts of things deeply. I haven't actually seen him since it happened but you asked me my opinion and that is it, but we have investigated claims about a string of toms, and found nothing. It sounds to me as if she's a loner looking to heap blame on Mr Aleksandrov. We have found no evidence.'

'It's certainly helpful to have the opinion of a senior police officer who knows him well. I am very much hoping that we shall be able to conclude matters soon, as we are having a second post-mortem done today. That will, I think, take us further forward and get us out of your hair quite quickly. You've all been most helpful here in Chelmsford and I am sure you're as keen to get rid of us as we are to return to our station to get on with other matters. So thank you for your time.

'But tell me, DI Hendry, what sort of future do you see for yourself? Are you intending to stay in the force?'

'I would imagine so. I've been in a long time but not being a woman I have not advanced with the speed you two have.'

'I suspect quite a lot of men think in that way but we didn't make the rules. Just one other thing, and you will find this out when you reach the dizzy heights of being a superintendent or above, and that is officers at your level do not threaten those at my level, so do not refuse to provide the information that is now being asked for. You can ask me questions and I can make *you* wait 10 days for an answer, but you can't do that to me. Just worth remembering next time you come up against one of those wretched women who have stolen your jobs.'

Without another word and without a backward glance Jo and Jodie left the office.

'Let's try the café across the road shall we,' said Jo.'

'Before you sent for me, I had a message from Belinda at the post-mortem. She said Dr Israel and Dr Colville had been able to agree on the cause of death of Martha and that if you can give them a call, they will let you know what is now going to be in the final report. They wouldn't tell me because I'm not SIO on this case.'

Once inside the café Jodie went to collect the tea and a cake, whilst Jo remained outside to telephone Sheila Colville.

'Please apologise to Jodie for me,' said Sheila, but I was with Dr Israel and I think she is something of a stickler for protocol. You are the SIO and she insisted that only you could be told in advance of the official report.

'To break the neck of a six month old baby is extremely difficult and would require considerable force, and that is what we have decided must have happened. Examining the sides of the baby, even through the rest of that she was wearing there is clear evidence of strong hands squeezing before the baby was thrown. That means the baby would've been in pain at the point of being thrown down and we think it must've been from a height greater than the waist or chest where a baby might have been held and we have concluded that this was murder. This baby was deliberately thrown down with the intent of causing maximum injuries. All this will be in the report, together with photographs. The hand marks were big and I would suggest that if you have a suspect then the size of the hand should be also photographed holding something comparable to the size of a baby.'

'By the way we had an unexpected visitor with us at the PM today. Someone must have tipped him off what we were doing and I do see him from time to time as you know, but I adore Ed and you will be greatly encouraged to know he managed to get a bacon sandwich. Please give my thanks to Kelly.'

'As always Sheila, I am hugely grateful to you and so is the whole body of those concerned with bringing criminals to justice. When will the official report be with us?'

'That will depend wholly on Dr Israel but I suspect it will be with you either tomorrow or definitely on the following day. In the meantime, how is Jude?'

'She's home, thanks. I think she's traumatised by what happened.'

'I'm not surprised. She needs time to talk and to talk with you, don't forget. You've put together an outstanding team, and you don't have to do their work for them. Even you are not indispensable Jo.'

'Well?' asked Jodie when Jo had joined her over a cup of tea.

'I should have rung Dr Israel. She wouldn't have told me off as Sheila did, for not being with Jude at home.'

'She has a point.'

'Be quiet, Chief Inspector.'

Jo now passed on Sheila's verbal report.

'I shall go home, but first I must be in touch with Belinda and share my thoughts as to what she should do next.'

'We need to talk again to Peter Delaney,' said Jodie.

'And she should send someone, perhaps Darcey and Frankie together to go the Travelodge and bring in the manager. And she needs to ensure a watch is kept on Susanne Day and Delaney. I'll ask Kelly to get us some background on Bowlby and Hardy.'

'You have their records already, surely.'

'Oh, I'm sorry, Jodie, I was meaning the sort of background that only Kelly and her friends in London can find, and I'm not referring to Scotland Yard.'

'Oh, that sort of background.'

'In the meantime have you heard anything from the hospital?'

'Yes, Tommy called to say she's back from theatre. Nobody has tried to get in to see her.'

'Then here's your chance.'

'I'm not sure what you mean, boss.'

'To see if the experience can prompt her memory, not just of last night but her previous work with Aleksandrov. What else did you think I meant?'

'Nothing.'

At that moment two men in their mid-20s who had come in whilst they were talking, came over to their table.

'Can we buy you lovely ladies a cup of tea?' said the taller of the two.

'A gin and tonic in a bar might have been a better chat up line, but tea would be more than acceptable,' said Jo.

The young man went and ordered two more teas and then joined his mate as they sat next to Jo and Jodie.

'So, are you from Chelmsford?' one asked.

'Bury St Edmunds,' replied Jodie.

'We should come up and meet you and get you that gin and tonic.'

'Can I take it you are both policemen, plain clothes policemen?' asked Jodie. 'I saw you leaving your car in the police station car park.'

'That's right,' said the one who bought the tea. 'We're CID.'

'What, all of it?'

'We've been doing a special job today so before we head back into the station, we decided to have a cup of tea, and just look at what we found.'

'It must be exciting doing your work. Is it like on tele?' said Jodie.

'Almost exactly like it is on *Line of Duty*.'

'And do you have *Anti-Corruption* like they do?'

'Oh yes and what about you two ladies?'

'I'm a Detective Chief Superintendent and this is a Detective Chief Inspector, as you can see from our warrant cards, and you two are a pair of wankers we could arrest for impersonating police officers, but you did it so badly I'll let you off. You are however nice lads, a bit young for us but you've lightened our day. Just be grateful our officer called Frankie isn't here or you'd be up shit creek by now. But thanks for the tea, and off you go, and don't forget to move your car, but I'll look out for you as you now owe me a gin and tonic.'

Sheepishly but with emerging smiles, the two of them stood.

'If I ever have to be arrested,' one of them said, ' I hope it's by one of you and do you do a strip search?'

'Scarper,' said Jo.

The two women burst into laughter as did the lads.

11

Having parked the car in her drive, Jo was surprised to see her dad come out meet her.

'Darling, you should know before you come in that Jude is not in a good way.'

'Do I need to call the community midwife?'

'I don't think it's a physical thing, though it may be. It's more a psychological thing I think. But she's not good. Keeps crying and asking for you.'

'Well, I'm here. When did this start?'

'Kelly said she was like it all the way from when she picked her up at the hospital.'

'Oh shit! I'll go and be with her. I have the phone number of her consultant and if need be I can call her.'

Jo went on into the house, greeted the children who were clearly anxious about Jude, and then went straight into their bedroom. As she approached her it was almost as if was a different Jude from the one she had collected earlier in the day. Her face looked anguished, her hair was a total mess but her colour was most odd. She was unusually pale and her eyes were almost exophthalmic.

Jo came to her and took her in her arms and held her, but there was surprisingly little response, almost as if she wasn't aware of Jo's presence. Jo stayed like this for a while and tried to engage in even a little conversation, but quite without response. Jo was now anxious and tried to think what should do because she knew something was very wrong and something had to be done.

Jo left the room and called Julia McAndrew in St Albans, and described what had happened.

'I saw her before she left this morning and wouldn't have let her leave if she'd been as you describe. It could be what's called cerebral oedema, a swelling of the brain, a delayed symptom of eclampsia. It's vital you get her into hospital as soon as possible and here is too far. Dial 999 and and ask for an emergency ambulance. She'll be going in to Ipswich and I'll call ahead so that she can get into ITU as soon as possible after arrival.'

'Julia, I have blue lights and a siren which will halve the time at least.'

'I'm sure you have, but Jo, it needs to be an ambulance in which Jude can lie down and be safely held down. They will receive instructions where to take her. How far is it?'

'30 minutes.'

'That's over an hour for an ambulance there and back. Ok, Jo, you do it but have someone else with you. I have your phone number and I presume you can take calls in the car, so I'll get the hospital to be in touch and direct you on arrival.'

Katia helped Jo move Jude to the car, and could see that Jo was shaking.

'Do you want me to drive, Jo.'

'I'm travelling with lights and siren, Katia, which means you can't drive, but I'll be ok once we're under way. You get in the back with Jude and hold her nice and tight, and we'll be off.'

The journey took no more than 15 minutes and yet Katia felt completely safe. They had a call to take Jude to the ambulance bay of A&E.

A team transferred her to a trolley and she was whisked away, Jo was directed to Reception and gave in Jude's details. She and Katia then sat in the waiting hall for two hours.

'Might it not help if you were to tell them who you really are?' asked Katia who was getting restless.

'I'm certain it wouldn't help Jude and that's my primary concern.'

'I can't believe how unlucky you are, Jo. Ellie, Marie and now Jude.'

'Jude is going to recover, Katia!'

Eventually, a nurse came towards them and invited them to follow her through swing doors, down a corridor and into a room where they were disappointed not to see Jude. There was however a man in a suit sitting and the edge of a desk and talking to another man in blue scrubs.

'Hi there,' said the man sitting on the desk, 'I'm Tim Berners, A&E Consultant, and this is Alwyn Berners, who doubles up sometimes as my brother, though I have no idea what he does – he hangs about the place and gets in everybody's way, though this evening he has taken responsibility for Jude. So I'll take the risk of letting him talk to you.'

'Thank you for those kind words, Tim. In fact I'm the Psychiatric Reg. We received a message from St Alban's that Jude might be suffering from cerebral oedema following eclampsia. It's not very common and odd that it should just come on at this stage. However, we've done a brain scan and a lumbar puncture, and we can say with certainty that she is not suffering from cerebral oedema.'

'So what is it?' asked Jo.

'PTSD: Post Traumatic Stress Disorder. She has just come through a massive trauma, which no doubt for very good reasons, you were not able to go through with her. In addition to eclampsia Jude also had the death of a baby to contend with.'

'It was my baby too as she was carrying my fertilised egg. You have heard of lesbian IVF, I suppose? And I assume you both know what it is to be on call and away from those you love.'

'She said you were called away. Could not other police officers have dealt with it and allowed you to stay with her?'

Jo smiled wearily.

'Even in extremis, Jude would be loyal and discrete, and so, would no doubt not have mentioned that I received a call from Chief Constable to take charge of the investigation of a child murder because I am a Detective Chief Superintendent, obviously not as important as a patronising doctor, but then, you don't run the risks I do.'

'And she's a Dame of the British Empire, awarded for immense and extraordinary courage in the face of terrorists,' added Katia.

The doctors looked as if they had just been slapped across their faces with a kipper and said nothing.

Eventually, Alwyn spoke:

'Jude said nothing of this; the only thing she said was that she experienced something that happened on the way back from St Albans but can remember little more. But please, accept my apologies.'

'How is the hunt for the murderer?' asked Dr Berners from A&E.

'I know who he is but there are reasons why I'm not ready to arrest him yet, but I shall.'

'That's an awesome responsibility.'

'You do that all the time. What now with Jude?'

'She can go home and might benefit from a specialist PTSD counsellor.

'Thank you, gentlemen.'

Katia and Jo left the room.

Behind them, the two doctors looked at one another.

'Quite a woman,' said one.

'Yeah, not a bit like the dames I saw in the pantomime with the kids last winter.'

'However did a woman like that get to be a lesbian?'

'Perhaps by being wiser than you and me, and especially you. In future, if I were you, I should leave the preaching to the chaplain.'

The journey home was quiet, and the only conversations between Jude and Katia. Jo could sense a measure of deliberate non-communication and desperately hoped that her radio would not burst into life demanding her presence. Fortunately, either Kelly, Belinda or probably Jodie, had the nous not to be in touch which in any case was exactly as it should be.

Jude was welcomed by Marian and Sidney and offered food, but said she wanted to go to bed. Jo let her do so whilst having supper with her mum and dad and Katia.

'Thank you for standing up for me, Katia, in the face of those two doctors who were treating me as if I was a village yokel. I've often noticed how utterly arrogant some medics can be.'

'The psychiatrist was especially so and I was sorely tempted to tell him before we left that he should consult a psychiatrist.'

Jo smiled.

'And yet he was the one who gave us the results which we were overjoyed to receive, and now I think is the time for me to go and be with Jude. No calls of any kind even if the Chief Constable has been shot by one of the team.'

Quietly Jo opened the bedroom door. The bedside light was off but she could see the outline of Jude under the duvet and she reached out her arm and touched her.

'Oh, Jo, ignore me, leave me be, I have so failed you in every way. There is no way I am worthy of your love.'

By now she was pouring tears and Jo had her in her arms.

'Don't ever think that my work matters more than you, because it doesn't. To be happy with you, I would resign in the morning and have no regrets. That's why I want a new life for us both to share together. I can't become a vicar and you can't do what I do, so let's do what we can together.'

Jude was crying again and held on tightly to Jo's hand.

The team gathered at their office in Stowmarket for Belinda to allocate tasks for the day ahead, or at least for her to allocate the tasks Jo had decided on the previous day.

'Will Jo be with us today?' asked Frankie.

'I don't know,' replied Belinda. 'Jude was rushed into hospital last night, but what happened thereafter I don't know.'

'It's so very unfair,' said Darcey. 'First she lost Ellie, the love of her life whom Jo's parents still think of as their second daughter and have a large photo of the two together looking so happy. Then of course Marie and her suicide, and now she's lost a baby and may lose Jude. Why should such things happen to someone so wonderful and committed to the service of society as Jo?'

The were murmurs of agreement.

Only Kelly had been facing the door and seen Jo quietly enter, and Kelly could keep a straight face in almost any circumstance.

'It's true,' said Jo, as every face swung round. 'My mum and dad did lose a daughter when Ellie died. My mum still cries for her, as do I, and they still have that large photo in a prominent position in their lounge. It's such a wonderful photo of a wonderful person who just happened also to be stunning. Sadly she didn't have time to teach me about clothes, which you now understand accounts for what I wear and my almost total inability to put on make up, but she taught me how to use my intuition as a detective and that has been her greatest legacy to me and, I hope, to you.

'One other thing before we get this case finished is the news that Jude is feeling much better this morning. She came home last night and is still suffering from PTSD but she will make a full and total recovery. My mum and dad are with her.

'Have you let everyone know what they are doing?' Jo said to Belinda.

'Yes, Boss.'

'We have a new member of the team, temporary in the short time but will become permanent. He's DC Tommy Carter, about 8 feet tall and most like Ed, whom we all miss, except Kelly, who I'm sure sees as much of him as possible. Going to visit and arrest Aleksandrov, which I want to do today will require the combined efforts of Warren and Tommy. You've met Tommy, Jodie.'

'Yes, he is huge but don't ever let the word get around that he's a big softie.'

The team laughed.

'How is Maddy Groom this morning, Jodie,' asked Jo.

'Still very bruised, black and blue, but that surgeon has put back into place the needful and I could see her real face taking shape again.'

'Is there any chance that we might get Dorn, the former sex worker, who was appallingly disfigured by DS Bowlby after he had just screwed her, to see the surgeon?' said Darcey.

'Could you take her to see her GP and get a referral,' said Belinda'

'It's more urgent than that.'

'Then, after you've finished your work this morning, pick her up and take her in to see Miss Dawson.'

'Yes, she seemed frighteningly able. I've arranged for a PC from Colchester to stay with her. Frankie and Darcey, off you go to the Travelodge. If need be, bring him here not to Chelmsford.'

'Ahmed's not here, boss,' said Frankie.

'Sorry Frankie, I should have told you but he's been observing Aleksandrov since 6:00. I need to know where he is, so I woke him at 4:30. Kelly will coordinate, but we need to get going. Tommy will be with Ahmed now.

Frankie and Darcey parked the car in the space reserved for kitchen staff which immediately prompted a man in a suit to come out to remonstrate.

'I'm sorry, but you can't park there.'

'Why are you sorry?' asked Frankie.

Darcey almost burst out laughing, knowing that when working with Frankie anything was possible. On their first meeting Frankie had wanted to arrest Jo, and after Marie's funeral had arrested the vicar for hate crimes. Darcey also knew Frankie was an outstanding police officer.

'What I mean is that you can't park there.'

'I'm Detective Inspector Francesca Wawszyczk and this is Detective Chief Inspector Janice Bussell. We're here to speak to the manager, James Barnes. Can you take us to him, please?'

'I am Mr Barnes, the manager. How can I help you?'

'You can invite us inside first of all,' said Frankie.

He led them to his office which overlooked the car park, and they sat down, James behind his protective desk.

'So how can I help you?'

In The End, Love

'By telling us the truth about those women who come here as prostitutes for the benefit of some of your guests and arranged by you, and for which you receive payment.'

He laughed nervously.

'I haven't the first idea what you're talking about. I can assure you there is no prostitution allowed in this hotel and if someone claims there has been, it can only be as a result of their own initiative. Any guest inviting someone to their room is wholly within their rights, and has nothing to do with the management.'

'So a guest, in this case one travelling in business, came to the manager and asked he where might find some female company for the evening,' said Darcey, 'is told that this can be arranged and that a young lady would call on him for a certain amount. Do you recognise what I am saying, Mr James?'

'I do occasionally arrange escorts for guests.'

Darcey paused and breathed in deeply.

'Mr James, you are a blatant liar and you leave us no choice but to arrest you. Before you are locked up, be sure to tell your wife and daughters that the charge will be keeping a house of ill repute and providing sex workers, and I am pretty sure you can say farewell to your job. My colleague told you that if you told the truth none of this would be necessary. So please stand and turn round so you can be cuffed.'

'Hang on, hang on,' said James. 'You are arresting the wrong guy completely.'

'Oh,' said Darcey, 'tell us more and tell us the truth this time.'

'I had a visit from a Russian, a Mr Aleksandrov, who said he would provide me with money if I was willing to allow the young women in his escort agency to come spend time with any of my guests interested in having company. I suspected that they might be prostitutes and asked the Vice Squad in Cheltenham to come and see me. Two came, an Inspector Hendry and a Sergeant Bowlby who listened to my story and assured me that Mr Aleksandrov was a bone fide businessman who ran a clean operation, including the provision of escorts. So I agreed. And the odd thing, and this came from one of Mr Alexandrov's team who called to check, is that we began to get more guests, unaccompanied men in the main which he said was a result of advertising they were responsible for. I couldn't argue with that.'

'How long did these guests stay?'

'Just one night.'

'And they all asked for an escort?'

'Most.'

'They are not committing any offence and we shall not be disturbing them, but it would help us a great deal if you can get from them where they came across the adverts for here.'

'Does that mean I'm not under arrest?

'We are not here to concern ourselves with you,' said Frankie, 'and all we needed to hear from you was the truth, though you will be asked to make a statement, repeating what you have told us. However at some stage other officers from those you named from the Vice Squad may call to see you.'

He looked at them, mouth agape.

They stood.

'Good morning sir,' said the two officers in unison as they left the office and returned to the car.

'I'll call Belinda and let her know how we've got on, and she can tell us where to go.'

'That must be really odd. At home you're totally one as a married couple, but at work she's your boss.'

'It's not a problem. Belinda's a natural Officer-Leader. She thinks methodically in a way I don't. I can't do her job but she couldn't do mine. It works and I'm pretty sure Jo, Jodie and Kelly knew it would when she was appointed.'

A message came through from Jodie. They were to gather at the police station in ten minutes time. On arrival they could see Jo, Jodie, Ahmed and a huge man they discovered was Tommy Carter who had been brought in from sitting with Warren outside Alexandrov's house.

As Director of Operations, Jodie gave the briefing. Jo had already cleared the op with the Chief Constable so no one could stop them at any time, and she would lead them into the offices of the Vice Squad followed by Tommy, and then the rest of the team. Hendry and Bowlby would be arrested and taken in separate vans to the station in Ipswich. There they would be charged by Ahmed. The rest of them would then move to Alexandrov's house.

Jo led the way down the corridor and stopped just before reaching the door. She looked round, and then proceeded to open the door. Those who saw her stood at once, and the others slowly made their way to their feet.

Jodie passed her and went into the office of Inspector Hendry and told him to come into the main office.

'Inspector Hendry and Sergeant Bowlby,' said Jodie, you are both under arrest. This is by order of the Chief Constable. You will be taken from here and held elsewhere before you are transferred to the jurisdiction of Professional Standards. Please come forward leaving your desks exactly as they are.'

They did so and were handcuffed by Tommy, who led them out of the office.

'The same condition exists for all the rest of you. Leave your desks and computers exactly as they are and return home until the day after tomorrow. Sergeant Galbraith.'

'Ma'am.'

'You are now acting Inspector in charge. Can I remind you that you are forbidden to communicate with each other and anyone else about any aspect of this. You can now go.'

They did so.

'Tape the door,' said Jo. 'Kelly is coming after lunch with techies from

In The End, Love

Professional Standards.'

12

'Warren, block the drive and when we arrive, pull right in.'

'Yes, ma'am.'

It was an unmarked car and he was not in uniform, so was greeted gruffly by a man coming from the house.

'I don't know what you're doing here, blackie, but you have five seconds to get out or you will be forcibly moved.'

Warren opened the window.

'I'm sorry. Perhaps I have the wrong address. I was looking for the home of Ivan Aleksandrov. Is this not it?'

'Why would Mr Aleksandrov want any sort of business with the likes of you?'

'You must ask him,' replied Warren, hoping to hear other cars arriving soon.

'He's mentioned nothing to me.'

'He did say that his men were none of them very bright, so that may be the reason.'

Finally, to Warren's relief, the posse arrived and he moved his car as far forward as he could. Everyone was out of the cars in seconds and were wearing their knife proof jackets.

Jo and Jodie led the way to the front door and rang the bell. It was answered by Aleksandrov himself.

'Good morning sir,' said Jo. We are looking for one of your employees, a Mr Broznik who we think can help us with our enquiries into a serious assault.'

They could almost hear Alexander's's sigh of relief.

'He is the man over there,' he said, pointing at the man who had been arguing with Warren earlier.

'Ask him to come here.'

He did so.

'Alexei Broznik you are under arrest on suspicion of the assault of Madeleine Groom. You do not have to say anything. But, it may harm your defence if you do not mention when questioned something which you later rely on in court. Anything you do say may be given in evidence.'

Jodie handed him over to Darcey who led him away.

'That is bad. I assume you have the evidence you need.'

Jodie did not reply.

'Now there was one other matter though it has rather slipped my mind,' said Jo putting her hand to her head. 'Oh, now I remember, Ivan Aleksandrov, you are under arrest on suspicion of the murder of Martha Delaney-Day, and other charges which you will hear in detail later, relating to prostitution in Chelmsford and blackmail. You do not have to say anything. But, it may harm your defence if you do not mention when questioned something which you later rely on in court. Anything you do say may be given in evidence.'

'You really are getting desperate. It will be my word against that of a man with temper on his record.'

'And how were you made aware of that?'

'I can't quite remember.'

'Even though it was you who asked that it be added to his record, but you see my technical wizard had already copied his record prior to your wish to have it tampered with, and there is no mention of temper at all. Hendry and Bowlby are both already in custody and now you are going to join them. Constable, please take Mr Aleksandrov out of my sight, said Jo to Tommy.'

Vans took Boznik and Aleksandrov away. The former to Chelmsford but the latter to Cambridge. Meanwhile the team entered the house and eventually took away paperwork and two computers.

'A satisfactory morning,' said Jo to Jodie.

Jodie did not reply and had to get to Ipswich to interview the two Vice officers with someone from Professional Standards, though en route she was calling in on Maddy in Chelmsford Hospital, where there was a possibility she might be discharged.

Jo and Frankie would meet up in Cambridge to interview the Russian, whilst Belinda and Darcey would give their attention to Broznik. Jo called them altogether before they set off.

'Excellent work, you lot. What a team! However I'm looking to recruit at least two more members in addition to Tommy, whose promotion to DS I am announcing here and now.'

Everyone turned and applauded.

'You all know what has to be done to conclude the day, so, lovely friends, go and do it.'

Before heading to Cambridge, Jo went back to the Chelmsford station and into the Vice office where Kelly and some others from Professional Standards were at work on computers.

'Anything, Kelly?'

'Loads. Why are some coppers unbelievably stupid? If only they bothered to do a course on computers they would know how impossible it is to remove material from a network even if the hard drive can be wiped by various means such as removing it and attaching it to a stick of dynamite.'

'Can you download dynamite from the App store?'
'No, only from Amazon.'
'So tell me.'
'He was up to all sorts of scams, I'm afraid to say, betting shops and the like. I think he thought that earning a combination of small amounts was more likely to be less noticeable, but of course they added up. He liked to think of himself as a friend of prostitutes but he was the sort of friend we could all do without.'
'What about Hendry?'
'He was much more circumspect with his computer than Bowlby had been and clearly thought that his phone, and WhatsApp in particular, was completely safe to pass on communication. Last night I passed on the phone to MI5 who can occasionally help in providing access to WhatsApp communications. They revealed a close link between Hendry and Aleksandrov, in which he was at the behest of the Russian. One of the more important recent calls concerned the murder of a baby in which Aleksandrov asked for the names of the police officers who would be investigating and, details of their records. He wanted dirt. That included you, Boss.'

At the hospital Jodie found Maddy sitting on a chair in her room reading. She was still bruised but improving.
'The surgeon was in this morning and said that I could go home today provided there was someone there to take care of me.'
'And what did you say?'
'I think I said that I thought there just might be, or at least I hoped so, someone who is as surprised as me at how life is turning out.'
'Surprise? More like a bombshell, Maddy. And it happened just like that. Up to that moment I'd just assumed ... you know.'
'Oh yes, I know too.'
'And suddenly there it was, there you were, and I thought to myself, O God, I love this woman. And since then, during a demanding investigation, the strength of that bombshell has only strengthened, and although the bomb has only just gone off, I feel it all more than ever. I love this woman, and you are this woman. And although most of my team are lesbians, and I could never hitherto even slightly understand that, I now find myself in love with you.'
'And me with a bashed-in black and blue face.'
'Your face is simply beautiful, but look, I've got to go to Ipswich and question and then handover to Professional Standards two police officers. I will come straight back and take you home.'
'Sounds like I'm missing out on earnings.'
'Their loss and my gain. You were rather good.'
Jodie came to her and kissed her gently but with passion.
'Is it true you have a medal for bravery?'
'It was nothing really.'
'A likely story.'

'I'll tell you one day.'
They kissed again before Jodie left.

Professional Standards had sent a DI to work with Jodie and they shared info before they began. They saw DI Hendry first. After the initial naming of those present, Jodie began.

'This is not a formal interview, but one in which DI Allen from Professional Standards will assess the evidence and decide the next step.'

'My client is entitled to be questioned only by someone of one rank senior to his own,' said the solicitor.

'Of course', said Jodie. 'DI Hendry, how often are you in communication with Ivan Aleksandrov, not including your visits to his house.'

'Not often. There is no reason why I should be.'

'And have you had reason to think that he might be engaged in business that would take him into the realm of your concerns in Vice?'

'Only incidentally.'

'Go on.'

'For a while one of my own team has been skating on thine ice in terms of our work, and getting far too close to Mr Aleksandrov and his business activities. Before I could put a stop to this, I had to confirm from Mr Aleksandrov that this was the case. So I went to see him a few times and our conversations confirmed what I suspected.'

'What sort of things are you talking about?'

'Mostly petty, to do with toms at a hotel. In a way this officer was exercising a caring brief for the girls.'

'And you were not involved in this, even though you were tolerating one of your team being involved?'

'I was gathering evidence.'

'According to the manager of the hotel, after the deal to use prostitutes, which he called escorts, made with Aleksandrov, he was visited by two police officers which he named, one of whom was you.'

'We were not aware of anything illegal and he wanted reassuring about the probity of Mr Aleksandrov.'

'It never occurred to you that the work of Vice is putting an end to illegal activity rather than endorsing an enterprise which you must have known was corrupt?

'On his computer, DS Bowlby failed to hide from our technical department, some illegal involvements and payments. There are also entries containing the initials MH where he was describing joint enterprise and payments.'

'Martin Hill, Michael Henderson, Murray Haig – there must be hundreds if not thousands of MH in the world.'

'But you are the only working on the matters in hand to which he refers and it may be that a search of your financial affairs will help us appreciate what MH was earning.'

He said nothing.

'How often would you estimate you were on the telephone to Aleksandrov?'

'Never. You have my phone and I imagine you have checked and can see for yourself.'

'You're quite right, for your EE account. However you made your calls and received them on WhatsApp.'

'You can't possibly know that.'

'Why?'

'Because all calls are encrypted.'

'Any attempt to de-encrypt them would be regarded as an illegal search,' said the solicitor.

'That is yet to be decided in the courts and if the police deem it necessary they can always try to do so, and of course we cannot, but we know someone who can and in the course of the investigation of a murder offers appropriate help.'

'So, how often have you in, say, the last two weeks, been on the phone to Aleksandrov? Before you answer you should recall that you have received a caution and that as a police officer you are obliged to tell the truth to a superior officer.'

Hendry was obviously uncomfortable.

'I think you are bluffing, sir. I don't believe you can have access to encrypted phone calls or we would all have it.'

'So, how often in the last two weeks, have you been on the phone to Aleksandrov?'

'None at all.'

Jodie produced a piece of paper from the file she had brought in from Kelly and showed it to Hendry and his solicitor.

'This is a list of the 12 calls made from your phone to or received from Aleksandrov on your phone using WhatsApp in the last 14 days. As you look at them, do you wish to confirm the dates and times?'

Hendry looked at his solicitor, who merely raised his eyebrows in resignation.

'The majority of these calls do not concern me, but will be taken further by Inspector Allen. One stands out however, as I am part of a team investigating the tragic death of a 6 month old child. It was made by Aleksandrov to you, and both voices are recognisable, in which, just 2 days after the child's death, he asks you to provide him with certain information about the police officers investigating the death. He wanted from your access to computers their records and any dirt on them you could come up with. Do you recall the conversation?'

'No comment.'

'A team of officers are going through the papers we have found at Alexandrov's house, since his arrest on suspicion of murder. Do you think we will find papers fulfilling his request?'

'No comment.'

'He faces numerous other charges involving matters you should have been dealing with. I suspect he will not be landing most of these charges at the door of DS Bowlby as you began by wishing to do, but at your own door which those continuing to peruse your phone records are discovering.'

'Inspector Allen.'

'Thank you ma'am.

'DI Mark Hendry, you will now be removed to the care of Professional Standards and questioned on a range of offences of which you are a suspect. Please stand.'

He nodded to the uniformed officer, who came and placed handcuffs on Hendry and led him down to the cells.

'Thank you, ma'am,' he said to Jodie.

'I can hardly say "My pleasure". Now you have to decide whether it's worth while bothering with DS Bowlby. The evidence is considerable. I can't question him because he's not involved in our investigation though I will stay if you wish to go ahead.'

'No need, ma'am. As you say the evidence is already compelling.'

'Well, good luck with them.'

'Thank you.'

Jodie left the building and set off for the hospital in Chelmsford, to which Darcey had brought Dorn, after some persuasion and introduced her to the surgeon who said she had to be admitted at once.

Jo had not been in the Interview Rooms in Cambridge for a while but she was always welcomed by the station custody staff. Frankie always enjoyed working alongside Jo and was more than happy to operate the equipment.

'Present:,' she began, 'Ivan Aleksandrov, also known as Zinoviy Aleksandrov and Lev Baranov, the names he used when in prison in Russia, his legal representative Elizabeth Andrews, Detective Chief Superintendent Joanne Enright and Detective Inspector Francesca Wawszyczk. If you prefer we can use one of your aliases, otherwise we shall use the name under which you have been arrested.'

Aleksandrov shrugged and Jo sat silently for a little while.

'Ms Andrews, I have not had the opportunity to work with you before. Your client usually depended on Ms Madeleine Groom as his legal counsel and very good she was too, but unfortunately was badly beaten up in her home a few days ago and had to undergo surgery. Isn't that correct, Mr Aleksandrov?'

'I have no idea.'

'You mean Mr Boznik was lying earlier this afternoon when he maintained you had instructed him to make sure she had no contact with the police?'

'No comment.'

'I'm very interested to know from you what information about my police record and dirt you received from DI Mark Hendry in reply to your recorded request made on the telephone.'

'I made no such request.'

'On the second day after the murder of the baby, you asked Hendry for the records and any dirt he could find on the officers investigating. Deny it until you are blue in the face but we have the transcripts.'

'May I see them?' said his solicitor.

Jo passed them over.

'These are inadmissible; they have no police identifiers. They could be fictions with fabricated identifiers.'

'Indeed they could, so would you welcome a short break to check with more experienced colleagues the identifiers used by the Security Service?'

She looked up, startled.

'In which case may I ask you how you obtained these?'

'I'm a detective. It's what I do. Now Mr Aleksandrov, now that that we know what you asked for from DI Hendry, what did you learn about police records and the dirt you asked for, with which I assumed you were hoping to find material with which to blackmail myself and others?'

'No comment.'

'In a short while I am expecting to hear from a Forensic Team taking your house apart, of impressions they have made of your hands from the prints you have left behind. They will be comparing them to the handprints left in the form of bruising on the body of baby Martha and recorded by two pathologists who have performed two post mortem. They are consonant with someone squeezing the baby tightly before throwing it down to the ground head first from a height level with the head. Have you anything to say?'

'Until that evidence is available it is pure speculation, Chief Superintendent,' said the solicitor.

'I agree,' said Jo, 'but it fits with the account of Police Constable Peter Delaney, the father of the baby, who had the confrontation with your client in the kitchen where the baby died. His hands are far too small to have left the bruising.'

'He is a policeman,' said Aleksandrov, 'so his evidence is worth nothing as you will defend him completely. He killed the baby not me.'

'Even though at the time you maintained that the baby fell between you,' said Frankie.

'I was confused by the shock of what had happened.'

'Why were you in the house in the first place?'

'I was giving a lift to Susanne Day, a friend.'

'From where?'

'I can't recall.'

'Ms Day maintains you collected her from the Travelodge where you made girls serve as prostitutes by arrangement with the manager Mr Barnes, as you did elsewhere in the town.'

'That's just nonsense. Day is an absolute slag but that has nothing to do with me.'

'Even though another woman we have spoken to was beaten up on your orders for refusing to continue to work as one of your girls.'

'That's simply ridiculous.'

'And you ordered DI Hendry to insert a sentence to PC Delaney's record to the effect that he has a temper about which he he had been warned at work. And you brought Ms Day home because you knew she owned her house and wanted it for one of your mobile brothels.'

'You are talking nonsense, and might I suggest that what you are saying is simply a manifestation of uncontrolled lesbianism that you have forced upon your police unit and led you into a relationship from which her only escape from you was by suicide.'

'May I congratulate you, Mr Aleksandrov,' said Frankie, 'on your amazing psychological analysis of Detective Chief Superintendent Enright's succession of total failures, not least her arrest of yourself, which have led to to her present position of leadership within the police force. What a pity you didn't look more closely at yourself. You might have been able to avoid repeating your previous times in prison, the use you have made of your own prostitutes, and the possibility, if not likelihood, that you will spend considerable time in prison here before being deported.'

Jo expected the solicitor to register a complaint at this point but it did not come. What did come was a message from the Forensic Team for which Jo had to leave the room temporarily. Once she returned, she looked straight into the eyes and gave him one of her "death by smile" stares.

'Forensic evidence is now 99% certain that the intense bruising on the side of the baby was made as a result of you squeezing her as you lifted her up and thrust her down, neck first – your act of murder.'

He did not reply.

'There will be other charges to follow in relation to criminal activities, but I am now contacting the Crown Prosecution Service, presenting them with evidence and seeking their agreement to charge you with murder. You will then appear before magistrates who will decide your future. Recording terminated.

'Constable, please unlock Mr Aleksandrov from the desk, ensure he is then handcuffed on two wrists and accompany him to the custody suite, together with DI Wawszyczk.'

'Yes, ma'am.'

After her call to the CPS, Jo rang home to speak to Jude, who had enjoyed a peaceful day, a walk with Marian on the beach at Aldeburgh, and a nice call from one of the nurses in St Albans.

'That sounds good. I won't be too long. I'm waiting to hear from the CPS about a prisoner and then I'll have a debrief with Frankie, and then ... I'm coming home.'

The call from the CPS took longer than usual, and Jo and Frankie were enjoying tea and cake in the canteen when it did come.

'Chief Superintendent Enright?'

'Yes. I'm Charles Sudgeon, Assistant Deputy Director of the CPS. You cannot charge Ivan Aleksandrov and should release him at once into the care of his solicitor.'

Jo paused before replying.

'What? Why?'

'I'm not allowed to say, Chief Superintendent. However, changing the subject completely, on my way in to work today, I noticed the new title of the Foreign, Commonwealth and Development Office.'

'That's most interesting, Charles. Thank you.'

Jo put her phone down.

'The Foreign Office have prevented charges and we have to release him.'

'That's terrible,' said Frankie.

'It's also how the system works sometimes.'

'Isn't there something we can do?

'Inspector, I'm profoundly shocked that you should suggest I use links to newspapers and other outlets to make known the man who murdered a baby and who whose release was ordered by the government.'

'I'm profoundly shocked too, Jo.'

They smiled at one another.

13

'You never usually talk about your work,' said Sidney, Jo's dad.

'It's true that I would never speak about a case that was ongoing, even to Jude, but this one is apparently finished in that I received instruction that I was to release a man who had murdered a baby and ran a chain of prostitutes and ordered women to be beaten up. He is not under arrest so I am perfectly happy to speak about him.'

'Who gave the instruction?' asked Marian.

'That question I cannot answer as it is an Official Secret.'

'But you know?'

'Yes.'

'Is there anything you can do?'

'I shall be seeing the Chief Constable in the morning. He asked me to investigate and I will report to him in full. I shall also inform him of my intention to resign to all four Chiefs.'

There was silence.

'O come on, you all knew this was what I had in mind. I've given of my very best in this job and a great deal has been asked of me. I want now to fly more often and care for animals rather than a team who need to freed from me so they can show their own great talents. Tommy has joined the team and Willie will be back soon, and I've secured a very able Geordie lass to replace Kelly, because when I go, Kelly will back to MI5, and a woman from North Wales called Gwyneth who feels she's stuck and from her record she shouldn't be. So the future is secure.'

'But who would take your place?' asked Jude.

'They may appoint from outside but I hope they will appoint Jodie as Chief Super.

'And what will you be?' asked Jude with a laugh that was covering an anxiety.

'Well, you and I must talk about that together.'

'Are you going to be leaving Saxmundham? asked an equally anxious Katia.'

'Whatever we decide together, and I mean all of us five and the children too, there is no way you are going to be abandoned, Katia, and that for two reasons. The first is that we all adore you, and the second is that you and your mum remind me of the most important and very best thing I was able to do as a police officer. Forget Norfolk and my DBE, it was in Nottingham that I knew all I had done was worthwhile.'

'Thank you, Jo, and you will never be forgotten by my mum and I.'

As they lay in bed, Jude said, 'Clever old you. You didn't answer your dad's question about what you were intending to do about this Russian being released other than make your report.'

'Surely you're not suggesting I might telephone Sharon and ask for the name of someone who is interested in that sort of story, of which of course I could not tell her?'

'It had occurred to me.'

'Well, I'm definitely not intending to do that. And my main reason is that I've already done so on my way home in the car.'

'You are so very good with words, that I have to keep my wits about me. I should really call you Rebekah, who tricked her husband Isaac into giving a blessing to Jacob instead of Esau. But Jo, I don't want to be tricked by you. I think you already have something in mind, and in fact you told me about Oban, so please I think I am entitled to know first.

'If I remember the story of Rebekah from my schooldays aright, she was doing more than tricking Isaac, she was arranging to cheat and wholly redirect the whole of subsequent Jewish history.'

'I'm impressed.'

'Yeah, well don't test me on anything else. My point is that I am not proposing any form of cheating or even trickery of you. In case you'd forgotten, it is just a few days since we lost our baby, and you were extremely unwell, and I had to come to terms with the dreadful possibility that you might die. I know you have suffered from PTSD and that has been terrible for you. My feelings about it all have had to go on the back burner even as I investigated the murder of another baby, but please don't think I have no feelings. I too want to cry and be held and if I find myself wanting to change life in a fundamental way, together with you, I can only hope you can help me and be with me as I explore another existence.'

'Oh Jo, I'm sorry for being so self-involved that I've thought you could handle it all. Shouldn't you be stopping work?'

'If you remember, I've just returned after a three month break, but you're right. The Chief Constable is going to love me.'

'I do, so why can't he?'

The message from Belinda was that the Chief Constable invited Jo and Belinda for coffee at 10:00 and a Press Conference at 10:45. It would have been Jodie until a week ago before she chose demotion, but since last evening her mind was less on police operations and more on Maddy Groom, and the astonishing new reality of her life about which she barely knew how to think, let alone communicate to another, even Jo. By the end of the night however, a night in which they had discovered, each for the first time in life, what love and commitment meant, she could hardly care less what anyone else, anyone else, might think, so joyful she felt. But then she smiled to herself and knew that Jo would smile too at her new life.

Jo collected Belinda and drove her down to Chelmsford. Both wore their best uniforms and laughed at the other. It was the first time Belinda had worn the uniform of Superintendent, but Darcey saw them both just before they left and said she was proud to see them showing all that they were.

The Chief Constable had not yet heard of the turnabout with regard to Aleksandrov and was still a happy man. Over coffee, Jo spelled out all that had happened.

'The thing is, sir, we have unassailable evidence that Aleksandrov deliberately murdered that baby to make the point that he would not be stopped by PC Peter Delaney from taking over the house to use as one of his mobile brothels – for no other reason. This morning he should be at the magistrates and instead the Foreign Office ordered his release wholly without explanation. This a man who had ordered that the faces of two women of whom he no longer approved should be damaged beyond recognition. One may never be able to recover and the other to have emergency surgery, and the latter was his solicitor. If I may say so, sir, he was an absolute bastard of the first order.'

'I didn't know we could classify them, Jo, though if you have decided that, I will recommend it to others.'

'I shall address the Press directly, sir. It has to be done wholly with your agreement, sir, but I will take the responsibility for it, and no one will ever know that you knew. Belinda is the soul of discretion. Is that not true?'

'I have early dementia, ma'am. I can't remember anything.'

'That's a great gift, Belinda,' said the Chief, 'cherish it. So tell me what you have in mind, Jo.'

'It's my feeling, sir, that the people of Chelmsford will be outraged that for unspecified reasons a government department has demanded the release of the murderer of a child, who did so wholly because he could not get his own way for extending his empire of prostitution.

'Yes, you're right, but what can you do about it?'

'I was appointed to investigate the brutal murder of a child, in the course of which as we gathered irrefutable evidence and became aware of other serious offences. We made an arrest and communicated this to the Crime Prosecution Service, but they were prevented by the government from allowing me to charge him and send him to the courts. And I will say this, and then that already this morning, my team has re-arrested him, and regardless of government interference, he will be in court later today. Fait accompli.'

'Ok. It is an important matter of principle.'

'It is, but please don't say so, sir. In fact after introducing me, it would be better if you said nothing and allowed me to answer the questions. You're too important to be dropped in hot water.'

Jo led them out and as she did so, the Chief whispered to Belinda: 'She's taking a big risk.'

'That's because she's a woman, sir!'

He smiled at Belinda.

The room appointed for the Press Conference was packed with tv cameras and other cameras.'

'Good morning,' said the Chief Constable. 'A few days ago I was made aware of the tragic death of a child here in Chelmsford, and I immediately turned to the Sensitive Crime Unit, led by Detective Chief Superintendent, Dame Joanne Enright to investigate. I will now hand over to her to give an account of her investigation.'

'Oh dear,' began Jo, 'when my superior officer makes use of my full rank and title, I feel uneasy.'

Everyone laughed.

'Thank you sir. The SCU team responded at once to the request that we, rather than the local team, should investigate this death, as one of those present at the time was a police officer here in Chelmsford. The investigation has led to further criminal involvement in Chelmsford, unfortunately necessitating the arrest of two police officers. Our investigations together with forensic reports led me to arrest yesterday morning a foreign national who has been operating a prostitution ring in the city, and one of whose staff maintains that this man ordered the beating up of two women, one of whom may be permanently disfigured by it, and another who has undergone extensive maxillofacial surgery. This latter lady was in fact the solicitor employed by the foreign national and had been seen having a cup of coffee with a member of my team by one of the the police officers now charged with corruption. The man responsible for her assault was wearing a ring with a particular motif which left an impression on the face of his victim, which was photographed before it faded. He was wearing a ring with that same motif when arrested. That man has been charged but has provided us with information of further criminal activities by the foreign national.

After his arrest he was interviewed by myself and another officer. We had already learned that after the baby's death he had requested police records of the investigating officers, together with any 'dirt' that could be found about us. The evidence that we would present to the courts, which obviously I cannot share with you, led me to make representation to the CPS that we charge him murder and numerous other offences.

'They took an unusually long time to get back to me and when they did I was informed that they rejected my application on the order of a government department and that I was to release the man immediately.'

A journalist spoke out.

'When you received the DBE, the citation spoke of courage and integrity in the face of terrorism. Is this the same and do you fear that the government will take away your award?'

'I have been a police officer for a long time and still feel that the police force has an important job maintaining law and order, and removing from society miscreants, whoever they may be. If foreign nationals live in this country they are bound to keep our laws. If the Foreign Secretary wishes to do so, let him try debating this in parliament with the other representatives of the British people.

'As for the DBE, it was the award of the Queen, not the Foreign Office. I serve wholly at Her Majesty's Pleasure and always have. I earned my award in the service of my country and am proud to have done so. Any officials who wish to take it away are welcome to come and arm wrestle me. Any other questions will be dealt with by Superintendent Gorham. Thank you.'

'Chief Superintendent,' said a voice from the middle of the room, 'just before you leave I have a question that calls into question your own integrity,'

Silence fell as Jo turned to look at the man whom she now recognised as the reporter with whom she had crossed swords at her last Press Conference.

'Please continue,' she said.

'As you mentioned you were awarded the DBE for your part in the Norfolk troubles. What you haven't mentioned is that you also received £50,000 to prevent you arresting the ringleader, the sum paid directly into your bank account which perhaps accounts for the fact that you are able to run a private aeroplane.'

'Thank you for mentioning this though I ought to begin by saying that for that crime I would regard £50,000 a paltry sum and would have wanted at least a million. Second, the name of the benefactor was of someone who didn't exist as I found out by tracing back the payment to a Swiss bank account, and seems to have been an attempt to blackmail me, even though I could not have spent the money as it didn't exist. Finally, on the morning I learned about this having appeared in my account I sought an immediate interview with the Head of CID and then with the Chief Constable of Norfolk and reported what had happened, and if you had seen my next statement, you would have seen that the money had gone. It is my belief that two people were responsible for this. One is in prison and the other has died and both used the same alias to confuse us. And you are right about one things – I do own an aeroplane and am a qualified pilot, but you are totally wrong about its provenance. It was a gift from the RAF where she was a pilot, to my wife, Marie, and when she committed suicide in the United States working for the USAF, was passed to me. It's wonderfully generous of you to bring such matters up now.'

As she turned to leave the room, she noticed the Chief Constable laughing and that she was leaving to applause. She had a reputation for being warm and attentive to individual journalists but not this one.

'That was Martin Fellowes, ace reporter on the Essex Chronicle and are you good at arm wrestling, Jo?' asked the Chief.

'I've never tried it. But, Adam, before Belinda comes back, I have to tell you that I have realised this week with the death of our baby, and the near death of Jude with her, that I have decided to resign from the Force. I lost my first love following a car crash. Marie committed suicide in Los Angeles, and Jude was nearly the third. We shall not go through the IVF process again, but I want and need a change of life completely. Too many deaths, too much grief and too many horrible people including journalists.'

'And what of the SCU? It is so important.'

'It never has been about me only. I am making appointments and recommendations including Jodie as my direct replacement as Chief Super. She is a superb detective and unbelievably courageous, but best of all she is a fine leader and they all look up to her, and to tell the truth, Adam, so do I. She was once a PPO to my friend the former Chief Constable of Manchester, Dani Thomas. I have also been building up the unit with others. The unit will be in good heart.'

'Jodie is the officer who saved your life with a kick. I sometimes look in the Law Reports to see what the judge said when the victim complained of pain in his balls seven moths on and wanted compensation: "You had an assault weapon in your possession with which you were about to commit murder. The officer also was armed and could justifiably shot you, so I think painful testicles was a small price to pay for surviving."

'The thought of losing you, Jo, is awful but I can understand what you are saying, I've seen enough of Jodie at work to echo your words, but she will never be you.'

Belinda came into the room.

'Oh! I thought what I heard out there was incredible, but what I've just heard as I came into the room was devastating. Jo, you can't leave us. We owe everything to you, all of us. Please refuse her, sir.'

'Oh, these are words I never thought I would ever have to utter to a serving officer: "Please don't cry, Superintendent".'

Now both Belinda and Jo started to laugh.

'What might you do, Jo?' asked the Chief.

'A life of crime, sir?'

As they drove towards Cambridge, Jo said to Belinda, 'I need to find out how that scumbag of a journalist found out his information about what was on my bank statement. I cannot believe anyone at Norfolk Police HQ leaked it.'

'I'm not sure you should be looking into this, Jo. Without hesitation I would say it is a job for Frankie.'

Yes, thank you, it should be Frankie.

Belinda said, 'There's another matter, Jo, to do with your resignation, and we both know this. This will finish Darcey off. She's totally devoted to you, more than she is to me."

'Don't be daft, Belinda, you're married to her.'

'Yes, and we love one another, but I warn you now that wherever you go, Darcey will follow and want to be near you, not me. You should be married to her, not me, and I think you know that, because Darcey does.'

'Tell me what happened when you were at the Press Conference,' said Jo, rapidly changing the subject.

'I was dreading it but in the end it went well. I studiously avoided giving them any intimation of the evidence we have gathered despite their every attempt, and I did talk about what it felt like as a police officer attending the unexplained death of a child together with my admiration of the work of of a paediatric pathologist. By this time they had quietened down, and just before the end someone asked what I thought might happen to you as a result of taking on the government. I replied that you had spoken earlier on this subject and I knew that every member of our team would endorse your words.'

'Thank you and well done. You will have more of those in the months and years to come.'

'So you want Jodie to lead the team on a permanent basis?'

'Don't you?'

'Yes. There's no one else, really. What's happening about her and her boyfriend Stuart? She doesn't seem to mention him any more.'

'She may have someone else, but I guess she'll tell us when she's ready.

At that same time: 12:30 pm, having watched Jo at the Press Conference on tv, Jodie had got up, made some breakfast and two cups of coffee and returned back to bed where she first kissed her companion and then handed over cereal and toast.

'Did you know you made breakfast and were walking about with no clothes on?' said Maddy.

'Just trying to tempt you!' said Jodie.

'You don't need to try. But what did you think of Jo?'

'You're the lawyer. What did you think?'

'I thought she was compelling and if the government are wise they will now leave well alone but she's flying near the sun, and I only hope her wings don't melt. There will be quite a few people in government and in the police who won't mind seeing her fall into the sea and drowning.'

14

Belinda thought Jo was going an unusual route to get to Cambridge.

'That's because we're not going to Cambridge though the journalists behind us think we are. Soon we shall head off back to our office and get a sandwich for lunch in the tea shop.'

'But what about Aleksandrov?'

'He appeared before magistrates this morning in Chelmsford and was remanded in custody. He was picked up by Tommy and Warren and we were represented by Frankie, I guess that at the moment he will be on his way to prison. In fact it was all over before the Press Conference began.'

'Did the Chief known that?'

'Sometimes it's best to say nothing that will in anyway compromise them, and the suggestion for doing it in this way came mostly from Dani Thomas herself who knows a thing or two about the Press from her time as Chief Constable of Greater Manchester.'

'That's where Paul and Esther have gone. Had that appointment anything to do with you?'

'I don't make that sort of appointment, Belinda.'

'In which case I'll make a Jo Enright response. Yes, but had that appointment anything to do with you?'

'The Home Secretary was taking soundings and I gave her a name or two.'

'Did she want you to do it?'

'Yes, but there was no chance. Now we need to turn here and see how many vehicles follow us.'

Belinda turned.

'Three.'

'Ok, I'll stop and save them a fruitless journey.

They all stopped behind her and she passed on the news that an appearance before magistrates had already taken place and the suspect would by now be in prison.

'What might happen to you, Jo?' asked one of them. 'We've just had word that the Foreign Secretary is going to speak in the House.'

'I've done all I can. If he is released again, I cannot stop the process now he in the hands of the courts, and that includes the court of public opinion. But to release a man who has been charged with such serious offences will be to set a dangerous precedent. Now, I have a partner recovering from a serious illness and surgery, and we too have lost a baby this week, so I'll love you and leave you.'

As they continued their drive, Belinda asked, 'Jo, what are you going to do and where?'

'I have a couple of ideas in my mind but I have to talk them through with my family first. Whatever else I do, I want to spend more time in the air. I haven't flown for a wee while and I need to do so.'

'Can I tell Darcey?'

'I think it should come from me, don't you?'

'Do any of the other members of the team know?'

'Just you, Superintendent, which is proving to be a good appointment.'

'But it's your capacity to recognise potential in people that we shall most most miss. You transformed my life, Jo, and you saw in Kelly things that nobody else would have recognised in someone who had served time.'

'I admit to feeling very proud of you and Kelly, though everyone in the team knows your qualities and looks up to you.'

'What does Jude say?'

'Hey, she's just come through one hell of a week, and to be honest that's the same for me; it was my baby as much as hers, and perhaps more so. Since this lot came up we've hardly had ten minutes together though she knows I'm ready to stop.'

They were now back in Stowmarket and Jo asked Kelly to come out for a walk with her.

'You were on the lunchtime News, boss. In fact you *were* the lunchtime News. Your support was considerable, though there was a total wanker of a government spokesman who said that the government was elected and you were not and you shouldn't be allowed to overrule the elected representatives. The interviewer asked him if he was elected, and of course he was not, but as I can imagine you realise, this is going to run and run.'

'I have no regrets.'

Jo then disclosed to Kelly that she had informed the Chief Constable of her decision to resign from the Police Force.

'The team won't be pleased Jo, but you're right to do so. I thought this was likely to happen soon. You've been doing this job long enough and Ed and I are happy to re-focus our life together in London when he qualifies.'

'I've really missed him, Kelly. I don't need to tell you, but he's such a wonderful man. With the exception of my dad, I don't usually relate to men very well. But Ed is simply wonderful and I wish you both much joy together.'

'I haven't told him but he would make a great doctor, and that he'd be wasted as a pathologist.'

'Don't you dare.'

'What are you going to do, Jo?'

'I've had no chance to talk it over yet with the family given the last week.'

'Of course, though the Press might be taking more interest in you in the next few days. And then there's Darcey.'

'Darcey?'

'Jo, don't be stupid or pretend you don't know. She may have just got married to Belinda, and I'm sure she loves her, but you are everything to her, so for heaven's sake be extremely gentle with her.'

Jo arrived home shortly after 6:00, and was greeted by Ollie announcing that he'd just seen her on the television which he thought was most exciting. Others were getting excited too. Some, perhaps most, were right behind her but a government spokesman had said she was interfering in affairs bigger than she was and had brought about a major setback in international affairs for which she should be stripped of her DBE, and put back on the streets conducting traffic.

'Are you going to reply to any of these idiots?' asked her dad.

'No way. I've done what I think is right and no further comment is needed.'

Jude had been washing har hair and came out to Jo with her head in a towel.

'I think you were wonderful at the Press Conference. I was so very proud of you,' she said.

'I am sure the government knows it has lost this case, but neither of should underestimate the vindictiveness that might be unleashed in the next few days, looking for dirt with which to smear me.'

'What sort of dirt?'

'That I am a lesbian, though they will have to take care with that not to commit a hate crime. I am sure my relationship with Ellie will be mentioned and that I was awarded a gong for what I did in Norfolk even though one of the principal criminals was married to me, and fled to America where she committed suicide, despite heroics in Saudi and Egypt. That sort of thing. My best hope is that Sharon will endeavour to use her contacts to shut them up, but civil servants believe they are sacrosanct and no one should be allowed to get in their way.'

By the time of the 10:00 News things had changed, and it featured a smiling Foreign Secretary endorsing the actions of SCU in dealing with the murder of a small child. Earlier spokesmen from the Foreign Office had not been made properly aware of what the Police had uncovered. Chief Superintendent Enright enjoyed the full confidence of the government and it had nothing to do with a ministerial fear of arm wrestling her!

'I would say you have won,' said Jude.

'In the case of the death of a child, no one wins,' replied Jo, 'but at least we now have a chance to lock him up for a long time.'

As they lay in bed, Jude said, 'Are you any further on in your thinking about resigning?'

'I've completed my thinking. I informed the Chief Constable this morning after the Press Conference that I had come to the end of the road. Losing our

In The End, Love

baby has set everything in perspective for me, and I have had more than enough of dealing with people such as Aleksandrov and his henchmen who beat up the faces of women to teach them not to disobey him, not to mention politicians who metaphorically act in the same way and seek to abuse me in public.'

'What did he say?'

'He didn't try to dissuade me.'

'And did he ask what you are now intending doing with your life, and with your partner and children, not to mention Katia and your mum and dad? Did you say you were intending to move us all to a croft near Oban? Did you mention schools, housing and my work with Diane, who lives 50 yards away, on a book we are jointly writing, or do you only respect a partner if she has a military honour to match your own?'

'I'm glad it's too dark to see your face because I could not bear seeing your beautiful face exuding hatred for me.'

Jude was now sobbing.

'Oh Jo, I could never hate you. You are everything to me, and I am so sorry for what I've just said. I can't believe how horrible I was. Please forgive me.'

'Hey, it's ok. Better out than in, and you're quite right about it all. I think I've just got desperate enough to think of the almost ridiculous. I've only been back a week but it's enough.'

'Won't this mean the end of the SCU?'

'I don't think so, as I've set in motion a restructuring, but it only came into being because of me in the first place.'

'So what are you wanting to do?'

'I want to fly more. I really miss it and I'd like to do an Instructor's Course and I want a smallholding where we can have alpacas.'

'Alpacas?'

'Yes, they're quite wonderful and I shall take them to shows and win the occasional rosette, and be totally happy with no horrible people in my life, no Interview Rooms or Courts or prisons.'

'How will the team respond to this?'

'Jodie will be brilliant in the job and especially with the added support of her partner.'

'Stuart?'

'No. She's found a solicitor to keep her on the straight and narrow. No one will believe me, but Jodie and Frankie are by far and away the best two police officers on the team, far better than me even if I'm the best detective but together they're outstanding. Kelly will go to MI5 and she and Ed will get married. She wants him to be a doctor, but he will be an outstanding pathologist, provided the country doesn't run out of bacon sandwiches.'

'And what about me?'

'This will still be our home, allowing you and Diane to continue working together, and if by any chance you want to learn to fly or help alpacas mate, then we do that together which is more than we have managed working together so far.'

'Could we afford for me to do a Research Degree?'

'Of course, though a lot of research on alpacas has already been done!'

There were a number of matters for Jo to attend to on the following morning. The most urgent was to summon Frankie into her room and ask her to investigate how the information about the £50,000 had come into the hands of Martin Fellowes, the journalist from the Essex Chronicle.

'I know it didn't make it it onto the News, but somehow or other he obtained information that he shouldn't have had access to, and we need to find out how he came by it. You will be working alone and there are no limitations and whatever the results, please Frankie tell me exactly what you discover – the whole truth.'

'I will do exactly as you ask, Jo, and you know I can be relied on not to conceal anything from you. But reading between the lines, I wonder whether you already have suspicions.'

'Evidence, not suspicion, is what we deal with. In our team you know this best of all. Later I shall tell the rest of the team that I am leaving, and that will mean changes. You will be being promoted though details have to wait. I am endeavouring to to ensure the SCU can continue, and to show that it can do so without me.'

'That will be difficult, Jo, not least because all of us have come to work here because it means working with you, and you have uncanny ability to select people who are really good but might be the first choice of others. That's why I'm here.'

'Actually Frankie, you're here to make sure you don't arrest me as once you threatened me to.'

Frankie smiled.

'O God, Jo, we shall really miss you, I shall really miss you.'

'You, my lovely Frankie, together with Jodie are the key to the future of the SCU. Provided you continue to get results, no one can close you down. You are a brilliant detective, which is why I want you to do this other matter.'

'Jo, forgive me please for what I'm about to say, but my real concern is for one person above all, one person who in all honesty may fall apart when she hears that you're leaving, and I mean Darcey. To her, you're not just a superb boss and colleague, you are everything. I swear she only married Belinda to fill in time before she could come to be with you. Honestly, Jo, she adores you.'

'Thank you for your frankness, Frankie. I would like you now to get on with the investigation.'

'Of course, ma'am'

In the outer office the team were discussing the television news of the previous night and the morning papers, all of which were behind Jo, though one described the team as "the lesbian cops" which amused Ahmed and

Warren.

The only negative report was under a heading "Who does she think she is?" under which was a photo of Jo in her uniform. The paper, predictably, argued that if the police can ignore the strictures of government, why should any of us take notice of them? The police, it said, are not above the elected representatives of the people, though this particular police officer had already taken great pride in imprisoning a Police and Crime Commissioner who continues to protest his innocence from prison claiming he was set up by female police officers, mostly lesbian. The article made Jo's blood boil but she knew that the best defence was silence.

Jodie came into Jo's office.

'First of all,' said Jo, 'how is Maddy?'

'The swelling has begun to recede and I can see what a marvellous job the surgeon did.'

'And how has she reacted to yesterday's events?'

'She approved and thought you handled it all very well, especially as you gave no details of evidence. It struck me that we might well use a solicitor to guide us in what we do – part-time of course.'

'Of course, and you're right. But if you're willing and it will go no further than me, I would be happy to hear about the relationship between Maddy and the police officer I rate most highly.'

'Are you a detective by any chance?'

They both smiled.

'Go on.'

'Well, as you know, I've only ever sought to relate to men and I regarded the rest of you in the team as odd, including you, even whilst I thought the team and especially it's leader quite wonderful in so many ways. Stuart was the last throw of the dice. I thought he and I started well but I couldn't get to grips with sex, you know, what went where. My attempts with men never worked and I had begun to think I should probably have to manage on my own.'

'Then I had to interview Susanne Day, and Maddy was her counsel. She was superb and for someone who had once without hesitation tackled a man with a gun, I found myself shaking. When you and I met her for a drink this got worse. I suddenly realised that I found a woman so very attractive that I wanted to kiss her. It was a dreadful shock. When you left early, I was alone with her, and when I told her of my failings with men, she asked if that meant there was hope for her. If only I had taken her home and stayed the night I could have prevented what that bastard Boznik did to her. When I brought her out of hospital I told her I would always be there for her because I had discovered I loved her. She said, and I quote: "About bloody time too" and for the first time in my life I discovered the wonders of love between two women.'

'Yeah, well you can spare me the details, Jodie, as I've been there and I agree. Where is Maddy now?'

'At home, with her mum who has come from Southend.'

'Southend! Poor lady! Jodie, I have something to tell you. I am resigning with immediate effect and I have written to all four Chief Constables recommending your promotion as Chief Super, to lead the team. You are perhaps the best police officer I have ever come across, with the possible exception of Dani Thomas, and the members of the team respect and love you greatly. Bringing Maddy into the team is a superb idea, and I think you will lead the team onto greater things.'

'But what are you going to do?'

'I want to teach flying and raise alpacas.'

'If you're still around, can I consult you?'

'Of course, if you can afford me.'

'There is one thing, however.'

'Oh?'

'Have you told Darcey?'

15

The team crossed the road for the morning coffee break. Through the window as they ate and drank they saw a tv vehicle with a huge ariel on top, stop outside the station and ten minutes later, when no one could be roused, drive away. Only then did Jo send all but Darcey back to work. Darcey loved it when she had Jo to herself.

They refilled their coffee cups.

'Darcey, my dearest darling, I am leaving and I have already resigned to the our four Chief Constables.'

'That's a great relief. Increasingly the work of SCU will become more and more politicised and unkindly focussed on you and you neither deserve nor want that. You have been a terrific public servant.'

Jo was, as they say, gobsmacked. That was not the response she had expected.

'What are you going to do?'

'I am going to learn how to teach others how to fly, and I have one or two fantasies such as getting a smallholding and keeping and breeding alpacas.'

'Alpacas! Wow. They are simply glorious though they do spit, though probably not as much as football crowds did at coppers, when I was on duty at Carrow Rd. How many will you get?'

This encounter was not going as Jo had anticipated.

'Enough to make it all worthwhile to enable me to breed and show them.'

'And shear them. Their wool is very important and they're not like sheep in that you don't eat them.'

'I'm relieved about that.'

'And what about here?'

'Jodie will become Chief Super and head of the team with Frankie replacing Belinda, who will hear about her new job in the next day or so. I haven't told her yet but she made a great impression at her interview so, providing she accepts will be moving to the Yard. I think Kelly will be going off to MI5 and I have someone coming to replace her plus a couple of new team members, in addition which Steph will be back next week and Willie very soon.'

'Gosh, it's all going to look very different but it's been an exciting team to be part of.'

'Let's go for a walk up the road, Darcey.'

They left the shop and headed up the road.

'When you appointed me head of the Armed Response Unit in Norfolk I discovered that I had a gift for logistics. I never shot a gun even once on any shout, and I was far from convinced that functioning on adrenalin bursts was how I wanted to function. I wanted a different kind of policing and besides I was missing you badly, so I came to join you here.

'I'm not a super detective like you, Jodie and Frankie, and no one was more delighted than me when you promoted Belinda over my head to the job of Super and, as you recognised when we first met her, she is the one of us here, including you, who might rise to the very top as Commissioner of the Met. But those qualities we all recognise of order and logic in her work, are driving me mad. Cups, bowls, books, in fact everything in order. Absolute hell!'

Jo laughed.

'Without any bitterness between us, we both know I won't be going to London with her. And there's something else she and I both know, and that is all about you. I felt that you would be retiring about now and the events of the past week have strengthened that. I've known you longest, Jo, and although I know everyone laughs about it behind my back and maybe yours, I have been in love with you longest and I know you well enough to know that those feelings are reciprocated. Well, aren't they?'

'You were there in Norfolk with me; you and Ed know what happened there. You didn't know Ellie of course but you knew best of all what her death meant to me. I also remember your face when I told people I was going to live with Marie and you were the only one who saw through her from the very beginning and you tried to warn me, and yet despite my stupidity you followed me from Norfolk to the SCU. I can't tell you how overjoyed I was that you came because you're the one person whose judgement I've always been able to trust, even when stupidly I didn't act on it.

'Although I came to discover that Marie was to prove the great betrayer, the adulteress and liar, not just to me but to the Air Force as well, I remember well a number of occasions when it was all I could do to stop myself coming to you and wanting to make love with the person I most loved.

'Then you met Belinda and I assumed my hopes were over. My crass stupidity, my total folly, had lost me the most precious person in the world. It wasn't your lack of ability that made me shield you in terms of work, it was, is, my love for you. I needed to protect you from risk.

'After Marie left, I recall you telling me to be very careful with Jude, that I was trying to reach back in time to Ellie and that Jude could never be her and that she was on the rebound from being a priest. At the time I thought you were saying something quite bizarre. Only now do I know the truth, that you were right, as you were after Marie's funeral when you came up to me as we walked back to the house and warned me against getting married again "because it will just make matters worse" – your exact words.'

Jo stopped, turned to Darcey, and took her hand.

'So my darling, tell me now what we are going to do and how we set about it. Our day, at long last, has come.'

Abby Clarke had called Jude at least twice a day since she had left hospital, and they spoke for ages. At one level Abby, as a maternity nurse, could answer any medical questions troubling Jude, though there were few of them and merely consisted of what would happen at the removal of the plastic wound cover and staples that Jude would experience in a couple of day's time.

A second level was concerned with the wonderful liberation Jude had brought for Abby following their night time conversations on the ward, enabling Abby for the first time in her life to feel that what she was, could and should be, allowed out into the outer world.

Within a week there would be a third and quite astonishing level in her friendship and mentoring of Abby with which Jude would have to come to terms.

The other three Chief Constables – Norfolk, Cambridge and Suffolk, were also having to come to terms with Jo's decision to resign and spoke with each other on a conference call on Zoom.

'The things is,' said Chris Biddle, the Chief of Cambridgeshire who knew Jo best of all and with whom she had been speaking about this for some time, 'we all of us know how much we owe to her and the SCU, and her plans are not to take the SCU away as she is putting excellent people in place, so it would seem churlish at best not to accept her resignation.'

'I would hate, however,' said Norfolk, 'if it looked in any way as if we were forcing her to resign over this recent business about the Russian. And, I don't know about you two, I would resist any pressure put on us by government to ask us to do so..'

'Jo turned down an appointment as a Chief Constable, made in person by the Home Secretary herself' said Chris. The *Telegraph* may hate lesbians in the police, and women in high office generally, but that piece of information should be enough to shut them up.'

'Jo has asked Jodie Lovelock to take over,' said Norfolk. You may recall she saved Jo's life with an excellent aim of her boot, such that Eddie Jones will have considered her for the England First XV. Jo says she's a better detective than anyone she has known. What do you think about a meal, say in Bury St Edmunds, plain clothes, for the four of us, Jo and Jodie to say thank you and welcome?'

'It's a great idea,' said Chris, 'provided I can sit with Jo. I love that woman and it pains me to think I shan't be working with her again, but let's compare diaries and hopefully get out of a meeting with our Commissioners, and I'll call Adam and let him know. One other person I think should attend, and you may not like this, is Dani Thomas, who has played such an important part in Jo's life and work.'

'Dani? That would be terrific. I've long since fancied her and now she's divorced there may be hope for me,' said the Chief Constable of Suffolk, Mark Palmer.'

The others laughed, though Suffolk was much more in earnest than they realised.

It was Chris who rang Jo at home to say they had agreed to her resignation and wanted to meet with her and Jodie, and Dani, for a meal, an arrangement with which Jo was thrilled. The continuation of the SCU was so very important to her.

Ever since their conversation up the road, Jo and Darcey had not spoken to one another, except the necessary words at team meetings and these were kept to a minimum. The new members of the team were now present and learning something of how the team functioned. Jo completely withdrew from participation and allowed the new Chief Superintendent Lovelock to take over even before she was due to leave at the end of the week. Kelly would be staying on another week to work closely with Sally, the new administrator. Steph was also back, hiding by day from the Church of England though still loving going to bed with one of its priests every night, one who had already developed a healthy ambivalence for his new employer ("they really *couldn't* organise a piss up at the proverbial brewery" was his favourite description of the Church of England, delivered in his broad Irish brogue), but at least it allowed him a wife with whom he was besotted and a wonderful child, which for a former Catholic priest was a real experience of grace.

Jo had felt obliged to let Jodie and Kelly know that she had asked Frankie to do a special work of investigation with regard to the leak of her banking information from the Norfolk days, and neither saw a problem in this.

'I have some friends in London who might be willing to help out if Frankie gets nowhere.'

'"If Frankie gets nowhere"?' said Jo. 'That is tantamount to heresy, Kelly. You'll be telling me next you have a group of heavies who can be brought in.'

'I do actually and they've all played for England at rugby?'

'Men?'

'Don't be silly, Jo!'

'Oh, Kelly, my love, it thrills my heart to think of you and Ed sharing life together.'

'And mine. Apart from you, whoever would have thought when I was just out of prison that I would marry a copper, work for the police and end up with MI5?'

This morning Frankie had an appointment in the café near the Police Station in Chelmsford with Martin Fellowes. She had not identified herself but indicated that she had information he might well find beneficial.

He turned up on time.

'I imagine Martin, you may be smarting somewhat after the Press

In The End, Love

Conference.'

'It was the journalist's nightmare of only receiving some of the story when Dame Clever Clogs had it all.'

Frankie feigned laughter.

'I suppose over the years that I've always double checked a story. But look here's the dead. I have information about our mutual friend Dame Clever Clogs which you can have in return for something I want from you.'

'Oh? By the way, who do you work for?'

'I work for a firm that does not like the government being forced into a major retraction.'

'Goodness. Do you mean ...'

'I can say no more about it.'

'And what is it you wish to know?'

'We wish to know whether the information you received is a security leak that has to be attended to by those with whom I work, ultimately a leak from Switzerland or worse still, the Netherlands, from where, if you recall, the deadly agent Ricin was brought into the country. If it is then we may be on to something so very important, of which I cannot speak to you. It would be of national importance.'

'Blimey. Well, when I was given the statement it didn't feel that this was a matter of such importance but perhaps it was, someone working under cover, as it were.

'I telephoned Saxmundham, where Enright lives and spoke to her partner who had just has a miscarriage and feeling her partner should be attending to her instead of the world of crime. She invited me for coffee and whilst I was there, amazed me by showing me a bank statement she had found a little while ago in a drawer in a desk in the loft, which I photographed and returned to her.'

'Very well done, Martin. Did you pay her?'

'I gave her £100 in cash.'

'A shrewd investment.'

'And what is your information?'

'That the Dame is this morning resigning, indeed has probably already done so, and that the Chief Constables who oversee the SCU are to meet to discuss the Unit being wound up.'

'How accurate is this? I've just had my fingers burned, remember?'

'Martin, think who I work for. The Foreign Office are furious and have leant on the Home Office.

'Of course, though you haven't exactly named who it is you work for.'

'Would you really expect me to?'

'I suppose not.'

Frankie gave him another false smile

'I must go. Thank you so much for time, Martin and good luck with your career ahead.'

'I need this story for that. The Editor gave me a final warning this week about going solo. But what you have said will show him.'

'I think it will!'

Frankie now drove out to Saxmundham and Jo's house. Ever since Jo had asked her to do this, she had known this is where it would end, and she thought Jo had known that too.

Katia was waiting outside, giving no more than the impression of gardening.

'I had a text from Jo to say she thought you would be coming. I do need to tell you that about an hour ago I left the flat to go to the kitchen in the house, passing the spare room, The door was closed but I knew what I could hear from inside, if you know what I mean. I shocked them by knocking and asking if they wanted a cup of tea.'

'Thank you, Katia, and did they?'

'They might have preferred hemlock!'

Frankie smiled and moved to the door and rang the bell.

Jude opened the door looking dishevelled and in the sitting room she saw why. On the sofa where two had been sitting there was a young woman, introduced as Abby, also looking somewhat dishevelled.

'It's great see you, Frankie. Presumably you know Jo is at work.'

'Announcing her resignation, I believe, and looking to move to an isolated part of the West of Scotland. How do you feel about that?'

'I don't think she's made her final decision yet.'

'And have you made yours, Jude?'

'What do you mean?'

'I was just wondering if you'd managed yet to spend your £100, and incidentally, you were shortchanged. The bank statement was worth ten times that to a real newspaper, though as an ex-vicar you can correct me, but wasn't Christ himself betrayed for the paltry sum of 30 silver pieces?

'Betrayal may be a moral matter but it is not a crime, nor for that matter is adultery though as you are not married we are talking more about being unfaithful.'

'If we are talking about being unfaithful, Frankie, I had just lost a baby and almost my life, and I was abandoned for clearly more important matters. That happened twice in just a couple of days. On the second occasion I was dumped in a hospital café whilst my partner did more important things and Kelly had to come and get me.

'In all of this there was one person who stood by me, who cared and comforted and made me laugh again, who loved me. Abby has come all the way from St Albans even though she did night duty last night because we love one another.'

'You must have realised that handing that statement to Fellowes you were potentially destroying Jo. Is that what you wanted?'

'I was never in Jo's league. What I want is the simplicity of life that Abby and I can have together.'

'But it was unkind doing what you did, surely.'
'But Frankie, what happens is that things get out of proportion. You are dealing with people for whom that's true every day of the week.'
'You're right and that's just the members of the team.'
They all smiled, happily breaking the tension.
'Look, Jude, I've been here all this time and I would love a cup of coffee.'
Abby got up to make it, and Frankie raised her eyebrows in appreciation and smiled at Jude.
'You have very good taste, Jude. She's really lovely – hair, tits and all.'
Abby returned with coffee.
'Jude, would it be best if I left you alone now?' asked Abby.
'Are you happy for Abby to remain, Frankie?'
'Yes, please do so, Abby.'
'Thank you, but, you should know I have done little for Jude whereas she has transformed my life.'
'You know she will insist on compulsory hymn singing every morning when you wake up?'
'I may have discovered a way to stop that happening.'
'Say no more, or I shall be embarrassed. But look, Jo is not interested in any sort of confrontation and truly wants only the best for you Jude. She knew that you were the source of the information because it could have been no one else, and I know she hasn't ceased to want only the best for you. Ye Gods, I'm turning into an agony aunt!'
Jude and Abby laughed.
'But I think it might be best if you move out today, and therefore we've some logistical matters to consider. As a police officer I cannot allow you, Abby, to drive back to St Albans with no sleep behind you. Are you due to be working tonight?'
'No.'
'And, staff nurse, what is your opinion on Jude being able to drive?'
'I cannot recommend it. She still has staples in and a plastic covering.'
'So, lets book you in at the Brudenell Hotel in Aldeburgh. Can you drive that far safely, Abby?'
'Yes.'
'If I take your car, Jude, perhaps Abby can drive me back. Tomorrow, collect as much of your stuff as you can before driving ultra slowly to St Albans. How does that sound?'
'Frankie, why are you doing this?'
'Because I want to spare you and Jo unnecessary pain, and who knows, one day it might happen to me. The truth is that it is about neither crime nor morality but what happens to us human beings as we go through life. We make mistakes. So what?'
'The best aspect of it all for Jo, is that at last she and Darcey can be together. I've known, and I think everyone knows, that their marriage should have happened a long time ago.'

'As Francis Urquhart memorably said: "You might very well think that, I could not possibly comment".'

Back in the office, Frankie and Jo talked this over.

'You knew, didn't you, who it was who had revealed the bank statement?'

'I didn't think a burglar would have entered the loft and the house is hardly ever empty, so the only suspect was Jude, but she must have been sitting on it for a while as there is no way post-operatively she could get up there, and that bit hurts because it means she was keeping it in reserve, and indicates things had been in a mess for longer than I realised. I know she was profoundly hurt that I twice abandoned her for reasons of work, and in my life I will never do that again.'

'The last things she said to me was that she was so happy that at last you and Darcey will be together.'

'It might all have been different if I had been most true to my feelings and been with Darcey from the beginning, instead of my carnal instincts which chose Marie.'

'Jo, it wasn't like that; Marie chose you and knew why she did so.'

16

On the Thursday the team was called into action when two teenage girls went missing in Thetford Forest and suspicion fell on one of a team of workmen helping to rebuild a house. It turned out he had previous for a similar abduction four years earlier. A dog section worked with the unit though it was Frankie who made the breakthrough when she found a small piece of fabric from one of the girls' dresses close to a barn. Entering the barn she found the man and the girls who had been tied with tape and rope. He rushed at her with a knife but Frankie used her truncheon with incredible force on the wrist holding the knife causing him to drop the knife and scream with pain. This drew the attention of one of the dog teams and he rushed into the barn, his dog exercising control over the man whilst Frankie released the girls and dealt with their tears of relief. The knife was bagged and the piece of cloth.

'I know it was like Hansel and Gretel,' one of the girls said, 'but I thought it was worth a go.'

'It was simply brilliant,' said Frankie, 'and worked.'

Later Frankie and the two girls appeared on *Look East* and as she watched at home, Jo gave a smile of satisfaction. Any team that had Frankie had someone of quality. Less enamoured of her tv appearance was Jeremy Fellowes of the *Essex Chronicle* who now discovered that the woman to whom he disclosed his source, was not from MI5 but simply a copper. This might well be the last straw for the editor.

The team debrief on the following morning was going well until Darcey announced that this was her last day with the Unit. 'You kept that quiet,' said Jodie.

'Well, all the emphasis has been, and quite rightly so, on Jo's departure and I wanted nothing to detract from that. Jo has been the founder and leader of all that we are; I'm just a foot soldier. I've loved the team, but with Jo going I can't see the point of staying myself. The team, as we saw yesterday now has a fabulous leadership in place, but all I have wanted to do is to work with Jo. She recruited me and I shared in what happened in Norfolk before she asked me to come here. With Jo gone I shall do other things.'

'What sort of things?'

'Please don't interrogate Darcey as if she were a criminal,' said Belinda. 'This is her free choice and not, I think, entirely unexpected. Perhaps, however she can tell us how the questioning went last evening of our abduction suspect.'

'We all knew Arthur Billings had form. He maintained he would not have harmed the girls, despite the presence of a kitchen knife with which he attacked DI Wawszyczk. He said his intention was simply to tie the girls up and then release them, something I didn't buy. I took abduction and assault, plus attempted murder to the CPS and I charged him. Warren has accompanied him to the magistrates and he texted me to say he is on remand.'

'Well done, Darcey,' said Jo. 'You will be sorely missed here, I can tell you, and thank you for all you have done.'

The team applauded.

'No. It's Frankie who ought to get the applause,' said Darcey. 'She was brilliant and courageous and, I gather, is to be put forward for a bravery award. I have learned so much from her and I know you all will continue to do so. At our first meeting in Nottingham she threatened to arrest Jo and me and we both took to her as a person, but Jo did more than that and could see that was considerably more than meets the eye, and so she came here. Most of us still can't spell her name but Detective Inspector Wawszyczk is still en route to the top.'

Cheers and applause followed.

'I'm sorry to break up the celebrations,' said Kelly from her desk but work has come in. Unexplained death of a woman prisoner in Peterborough Jail.'

'Ok, Frankie, over to you, said Jodie. 'No more than two cars and we're still in Sheila's territory so only let the body be moved when and to where she says.'

'Yes, ma'am. So get going everybody.'

Jo, Jodie, Belinda and Darcey remained seated, watching the others move into action.

'It's called getting older,' said Jo. 'The four most experienced members of the team stay behind as the Young Turks take to the field.'

'Don't you wish you were with them?' asked Kelly.

'I found one gem freshly released from a woman's prison; I can't expect to find any more.'

'No one makes me feel better about myself than you, boss. Even Ed has a lot of catching up to do.'

Belinda received a call.

'That's very good news. The West Midlands Police and Crime Commissioner whom you put away has just been told he cannot make a second appeal.'

'His difficulty was that he was up against overwhelming evidence of rape.'

'I'm going to clear out my locker,' said Darcey. 'Leaving the Force after all this time is pretty tough.'

They watched her walk out of the room and only then did Belinda rise to follow her.

'Coffee across the road for the last time?' asked Jo. 'I can't imagine that they will be at the prison yet so we probably won't hear anything but you will have the phone, Kelly, and you Sally, need to learn how we function primarily from the coffee shop.'

'Yes, Boss.'

They all stood up to leave and were joined by Darcey and Belinda. Kelly held back as an email was coming in and she saw that it was from the Home Office. Reading it through she quickly printed it out and pushed it into her handbag, before going down the stairs and joining the others, who customarily were indulging themselves.

'I shall miss coming here,' said Jo.

'Me too,' echoed Darcey.

'I do hope, Jodie, that you continue to provide our hosts with business.'

'So do I!' said a voice from the kitchen, causing merriment.

'Who's in charge now?' asked Kelly.

'Jodie, of course,' said Jo.

'Not until 6:00pm,' said Jodie. 'Until then it's the Dame. Why do you ask?'

'Oh, nothing really, though when I say nothing, I really mean quite a lot.'

'In which case you'd better tell me what it is,' said Jo.

Kelly reached into her bag and withdrew the piece of paper which she handed over.

Jo read the email and handed it to Belinda, whose eyes widened, before handing it back.

'Shall I read it aloud, Belinda?'

'The email is yours, Jo.'

Jo hesitated.

'Ok. It's an email from the Home Secretary. It says that the Home Secretary is announcing today that Detective Superintendent Belinda Gorham of the Sensitive Crime Unit is appointed as Head of the Commission on the relations between Male Police Officers and Women. What the email doesn't say is that this position will be made at the level of Commander which Belinda will take up based at Scotland Yard but nationwide in its concern. She will have a team of senior officers, and will answer directly to the Commissioner of the Met. Congratulations Belinda. You know about this issue from the inside, having one experienced a sexual assault by an officer with whom you were working, and it's my conviction that you have the determination and skills to do this important job so very well.'

'Thanks Jo. If it hadn't been for you, that experience would have meant I was stacking supermarket shelves now, but this gives me the opportunity to make a difference, even though I know the resistance will be considerable. You also brought Darcey and I together and though even if such things don't, or more realistically, can't work out, and I think we all know why, there is no bitterness, just thankfulness, in our parting.'

Darcey put her arms around Belinda and kissed her cheek.

'And you Jodie, I'm sorry to say, need a new Super,' said Jo.

The team members in the prison were struggling because of the "never talk to cops" ethos. They interviewed those on the same landing as the dead woman and tried to find out as much as they could manage. In the end Frankie thought it might have come down to drugs, as many disputes in prison life did. It was late in the afternoon when Ahmed picked up something from one of the inmates about the nature of the dead woman's relationship with one of the male prison officers which made him wonder whether there was a link of a sexual nature in return for contraband, especially coke. It would, however, not be until the Saturday morning when the forensic pathologist, Sheila would let Frankie know what was in the blood and the sexual organs.

Ahmed shared his concerns with Frankie who at once engaged in much more formal conversations with some of the women again on the landing about male screws and how they felt about them. One name was mentioned a number of times: Prison Officer Dexter, but Frankie decided to leave matters for the day and to return and pick up these bits and pieces in the morning, not least when she had spoken with Sheila.

On the way back she laughed at the mistake made by Jodie when she said it was a message for Superintendent Wawszyczk. There seemed no content to the message but replied that there was as yet not a great deal to report but that she and the team would be back in Peterborough first thing on the following day. She thought nothing more but assumed it was obviously just a slip of the tongue given all the changes of this week..

Jodie and Maddy were going out for a meal, but en route they intended calling in to see Dorn who had just had her maxillofacial surgery on the same ward as Maddy, and Jodie had used all her influence with Miss Dawson to accept Dorn as another emergency victim of violence without the need for a GP referral.

Jodie transformed herself from senior police offer into a glamorous woman in next to no time, and Maddy couldn't get over how lovely she looked, and indeed even Jodie was amazed. She wanted to look lovely for Maddy; her world had been turned upside down and she loved every moment of it, and on top of that she was at the top in terms of her work.

Dorn was sitting by a bed in a four-bedded ward and was taken aback by the appearance of two attractive women coming to see her, though she could tell that one of them must recently have undone a similar sort of surgery to herself.

'Hello Dorn,' said Jodie, 'I'm Detective Chief Superintendent Jodie Lovelock, and this is my partner Maddy Groom, who recently underwent more or less the same operation you did, and we thought we'd like to come and see how you're getting on.'

'Good heavens. That is so kind of you. Nobody else has been in to see me, and all this is a result of that lovely person Darcey, who came to see me at home. I don't know what to say. I always thought the police were just as bad as Aleksandrov, as it was a copper who did this to me, but you're not the same sort at all.'

'I certainly hope not,' said Jodie.

'And I've never seen a copper dressed like you with proper makeup, not to mention the cleavage on show.'

'I thought you weren't going to mention the cleavage!'

The three of them laughed.

'But how has it been, Dorn?' said Maddy. 'The bruising will go down, you know. You can trust Miss Dawson to have done a great job. It's just going to take a few days.'

'I'll never be as beautiful as you though, will I, no matter how many operations I have?'

'Do you know, Dorn' said Jodie, 'I came to acknowledge my love for Maddy when she had recently come back from theatre, because I know the beauty that she has on the inside, and I don't adore her any more now looking as she does than I did then.'

'O God,' said Dorn, 'now you're going to make me cry and I shall look even worse. But isn't it a bit odd, I mean, being in love with another woman?'

'Not a bit odd,' said Maddy, 'because neither of us had the first idea that might happen to us until we met. Both of us knew we weren't wildly inclined towards men but didn't contemplate another possibility.'

'And I've been working for some years now with gay women,' added Jodie,' but never had even slightest sense that I was just waiting for this wonderful lady to come along.'

'I've had some pretty horrible experiences of men, I can tell you, utterly sickening and disgusting.'

'But you've also been courageous in getting out of what you were doing as a sex worker.'

'Until one of your colleagues came round to give me my redundancy package, the results of which you can see.'

'Dorn, I'm a solicitor. I would like to support you to get compensation from the police for your rape and battering. Would you like to work with me on that? I'm pretty confident we could get you a significant amount.'

'Good heavens. Yes.'

'Let's get you out of here first and then we can proceed. I'll call round and see you. No win, no fee.'

As they left, they held hands in a public place for the first time.

'That was such a generous offer you made in there, my lovely.'

'You don't mind my making it against your employer?'

'Not in the slightest. I just wish I could get access to Bowlby's scrotum with my trusty right boot!'

17

Jo left early on Saturday morning to fly to Tibbenham by 8:00 for routine maintenance which would take most of the day, and therefore she arranged to be collected by Dani Thomas, her old boss and closest of friends. In the afternoon they would fly together back to Crowfield where Jo's (and formerly Marie's) Pipestrel was hangared.

She had not flown for over a month and Jo wondered even if she would start, but there was no hold up and once she had done the full round of checks, she took off and set off on a North-East heading. Being a Saturday there was little or no military traffic and her flight was straightforward, but she was so thrilled to be in the air again and had already applied for the course to teach flying. Marie had loved this aeroplane and she could understand why. She was also looking forward to being with Dani again, both now *former* police officers, and to the dinner with the four Chief Constables on the following Monday.

Alice had said she was more than happy to look after the children until late morning when Katia was taking them swimming followed by lunch in Macdonalds in Ipswich. The morning newspapers had turned their attention from Jo to the new appointment of Commander Belinda Gorham to lead the Commission on Male Police Officers and their relating to Women. Inevitably, their least favourite paper had the headline "It's a lesbian once again", but Belinda would have to get used to that as well as the considerable opposition she would meet from many men in the Force. She began her descent and kept a sharp lookout for gliders.

'Hello, Dame Joanne,' said Dani as they hugged one another.

'Oh Dani, whenever I see you, I can't think of however I can live without you.'

'Well then, move back to Norwich and come each day to Waterstones and consult the manager.'

'Will I get free books?'

'Certainly not. Just because you've got a posh title. You have to pay like everyone else. No more freebies as when you were a police officer.'

'Hey, I never got any then, and in any case I would have had to declare them.'

'And have you anything else to declare?'

'I need to get some breakfast.'

'Ok, then, let's do so.'

Dani stopped at the sort of greasy food transport café beloved of Jo and both indulged themselves in the least healthiest of ways.

'Oh that was wonderful,' said Jo. 'Better than sex.'

'You would never have said that when you were married to Marie. For all her huge faults, you were never in doubt about that.'

'Ah well, it's all change. Jude has left. She's met one of the nurses who looked after her in St Albans.'

Jo told her about the leaked bank statement – an act of betrayal, which somehow felt familiar.

'I sent Frankie to investigate, despite knowing where the leak can only have come from. Before Frankie had arrived, Katia had come into the main part of the house from her flat and heard the grunting and groaning of two people having sex coming from the spare room. She knew who it was and knocked on the door saying that they should let her know when they they done so she could get them a cup of tea!

'She said that when they emerged rather coyly, the other woman was amazing to look at to the extent that Katia said she fancied her with an amazing half-shaven haircut and lovely body. So poor them being interrupted before Frankie was due to arrive. Clearly our sexual problem was me.

Dani laughed and laughed.

'Every evening when I get in', said Dani, 'I see that large photo of you and Ellie your mum and dad have. Unlike everyone else, I knew Ellie, and I can tell you having met Jude, she was not like Ellie one little bit. And if ever you meet someone else, you must take them on their own terms, not comparing them with Ellie, otherwise they will always fail and you will be bitterly disappointed. But, my darling Jo, I have to tell you this because your mum and dad won't or can't, you and Ellie were together for just a short time and it may be that things might have changed, as they often do. Do you think it even possible that you make a graven image of her, an impossibility that never was?'

'Tell me, Dani, do you sell lots of self-help books in your shop?'

'It's funny you should say that because in fact we do. It's big business.'

'We both know the answer but it's become part of my mystique, the story told by the team.'

'But you've got to stop believing it yourself, my darling.'

'It's only very recently that I have stopped crying for Ellie.'

'I have cried a lot for Ellie too. The day she died, was the day for me, God died. "The monkey trick of a spiteful imbecile".

'Who said that?'

'It was C S Lewis, the religious writer, about Beethoven going deaf. I read it when I was young and it has often seemed appropriate to me when confronted with deaths of various kinds.'

'I've just been dealing with the murder of a 6-month baby.'

'It's time to stop, Jo.'

'I know.'

Before the team returned to Peterborough jail, Frankie took a call from Dr Sheila Coalville, the Forensic Pathologist.

'There is considerable evidence that your prison officer had sexual intercourse with the prisoner and that he did so with considerable force judging from the extent of internal and external bruising. You will have seen for yourself the extent of the bruising round her neck which I am sure brought about her death. The evidence is clear that that this was rape, followed by murder caused by his attempts to stop her screaming. She clawed at his body and I found skin underneath her nails with a 99.5% certainty of matching his DNA. And both had blood containing heroin. So I imagine you can all have a Get Out Of Jail Free card today. I will send my full report today and the CPS will have no difficulty with my oral report.

'Thank you Dr Colville.'

'I think that when you get to the dizzy heights of being a Superintendent, I am happy to be "Sheila", and you "Frankie". Don't you agree? I hope you know that Jo thought you were superb, so I look forward to working with you.'

Frankie put down her phone and wondered what was going on. There was a lot to do in the prison today, taking statements from screws and inmates alike, and interviewing the senior staff and so on, but in essence the case was solved and she would need to devote time to interviewing the arrested man, making contact with the CPS and getting him to the magistrates in Peterborough before they went home which would necessitate a Saturday sitting.

There was another matter to be sorted first however. She rose from her chair and went to Kelly's desk.

'Kelly, who am I?'

'Detective Superintendent Wawszyczk.'

'Oh!'

'And do you need to know *where* you are or can you manage that?'

Frankie spoke to Sally, Kelly's replacement to be.'

'Please, please, Sally, be nicer to us when you take over next week.'

Sally laughed.

'I suspect you can all give as good as you get.'

'I'm going to prison now for a touch of sanity.'

Jo and Dani had flown back on the Sunday evening and with the big meal in the evening, Jodie had telephoned Jo at lunchtime.

'Jo, understandably Maddy is still pretty nervous at the prospect of being in alone whilst we are at the meal this evening. Is there any chance she could come spend the evening with the children and Katia.'

In The End, Love

'Katia will be fine but I cannot guarantee her safety in the presence of my children but if she's willing to take the risk that sounds like a great idea. Even better would be for you both to stay the night. Katia or I can drive her home after you've gone to work in the morning.'

'Thank you.'

'How is the situation in the prison going?'

'I'm sorry, but that has nothing to do with you – it's police business only I'm afraid.'

Jo laughed.

'Quite right, Chief Superintendent. I'll see you later.'

Jo and Dani went to the beach in Aldeburgh in the afternoon.

'You've told me a great deal about you and Jude, about your work, even about Nathan and David, both of whom you managed to get out of prison and had their convictions overturned in the Appeal Court – all typically brilliant Enright pieces of work and you know I don't mean that sarcastically. So there is just one thing you have not mentioned.

'I take it you are referring to getting my car serviced. Yes, it is such a worry.'

Dani paused.

'What's the temperature of the sea at this time of the year?' asked Dani.

'The sea? I've no idea.'

'Never mind, you can tell me after I've thrown you in.'

She put her arms round Jo as if to pull her.

'You're still strong, Dani, despite what you've endured.'

'Yet I was never strong enough to win your heart, Jo.'

'I was newly bereaved and you had just fixed me up with a job that would take every ounce of my being.'

'And yet you were seduced by Marie.'

'And it turned out I was not the only one. I think of her very much along the lines of Mata Hari, who probably was not the German spy the French executed her for, whereas Marie really was a traitor to her country, to me, to her children and in the end, to herself, and all because she couldn't live without excitement. It's terrible to say this of my former wife, but her suicide was the right thing, the only thing. I was stunned but I have never cried for her though I might have done for me and the children who'll grow up learning the truth about her.'

'And all you have to do now is to tell me the other thing, the one you haven't mentioned.'

'Before you became an ACC or a Chief Constable, you had a pretty impressive reputation as a detective, so work it out for yourself.'

'I'm still considering throwing you into the sea.'

'That's cheating, though if you came to my rescue you might have to to remove all my clothes and hug me close.'

'Don't tempt me. Alright, I'll try. There has long been one name on your lips more than any other, even that of Marie, even when it should not have been emerging from the mouth of a senior officer referring to a very junior officer who was promoted rapidly and even headed Armed Response. Am I getting warm?'

'Go on.'

'This name reappeared when you moved to Suffolk though I was totally confused when I learned that she had married, and after Marie's death you took up with the former vicar. It was wholly unexpected and always felt inappropriate.'

'I was as devastated by Darcey's relationship with Belinda, as she was mine with Jude and then there came the turning point when she told me two things whilst we were doing an obs together on a suspect in Braintree.

'The first was that Jude and I were both on the rebound, she from the Church and me from Marie, and it had no future. The second was that she had decided to split up from Belinda or she might go mad. What has made Belinda so able as a Super – her obsession with fastidious policing, her ordered mind and thinking, and why she will do the new job so well, but Darcey couldn't cope with this at home. Apparently she even had their sexual relationship worked out on a chart to fit in with their work shifts and schedules. Darcey, and I'm exactly the same, is perfectly happy with chaos and spontaneity.

'So, unbeknown to everyone, in that vehicle, on that shift, in Braintree of all places, just a short time ago, we each committed ourself to the other, we married, if you like. But, Dani, that marriage has not yet been consummated. Our love is common knowledge it seems but I have continued to observe the proprieties of my office, and whilst we were still working together and living with others, we did not have sexual contact, though, God knows, we both longed for it. Tomorrow night, after I fly you home, Darcey and I will begin to live together – at long last.'

Jo looked at Dani and saw tears on her cheeks.

'Jo my darling, no one deserves the very best in this life than you. You hold together a first-class detective mind with an unusual compassion even for those who have done terrible things and it wouldn't surprise me to learn that you still visit that awful woman murderer in prison. I wanted to be the person who shared your life but if it can't be me, then what a wonderful choice you have made and so has she.

Jodie and Maddy arrived in good time, so as to allow Maddy to meet the children (though Josie was growing up quickly and hardly counted as a child any more but still chose to share a room with her brother, and neither seemed to have inhibitions in the presence of the other). Maddy also instinctively took to Katia and they chatted all evening, Katia intrigued to hear about the work of a solicitor, and Maddy to hear all about the terrible existence Katia's mother and herself had lived for more than 35 years until Jo had found the real killer of the two babies in Nottingham. Katia also said that she was intending to write up the story now that Jo had left the Police Force.

'You will have to be careful because there will be all sorts of legal eggshells to be avoided. Can I be your advisor – totally free of course?'

'Yes and no,' replied Katia. 'Yes, that would be brilliant. No, only if I can pay you.'

'Can you afford me?'

'Can you afford not to be paid?'

They laughed.

'Mind you, you're not entirely wrong. I've become associated, through my own fault, with undesirables who will soon be spending time in prison. That has not done my reputation any good, and if I am to resume my practice it's going to require a move, either physically to a new location or to a different sort of work. Jodie wants me to work part time with her team and that appeals even if it's a bit like poacher turning gamekeeper.'

'I think that will make you even more useful to them. But when did you come out, Maddy?'

'It sounds ridiculous I know, but it was when I met Jodie. I sat on the opposite side of a table in the Interview Room from her and I found it difficult to concentrate and I couldn't work out why until she looked at me with her amazing eyes and I realised I wanted to be with this woman and no other, forever. Up to that moment I had never had boyfriends or girlfriends, even at school or Uni, and I'd never thought anything was lacking. Jodie has shown me that there was a real emptiness inside which only she could fill.'

'From the way in which they were chatting after you arrived, she obviously knows Dani well.'

'She was her Personal Protection Officer in Manchester and they worked closely together. She told me that Dani had a large framed photo of Jo in her office. Do you think she and Dani are getting together? Or is what Jodie says true, that Jo is now getting together permanently with the woman she has allegedly loved for a long time, and vice versa: Darcey?'

Katia smiled.

'It's not unlike a film, in which the actors keep getting things wrong and then in the final scene everything comes right, and no one deserves it more than Jo. The irony is that although both have been with others – Marie, Belinda, Jude – ridiculously, we have all known they are made for each other and always have been.'

'I shall cry in a minute. And what about you, Katia? When did you come out?'

'I never have.'

'Oh, I'm sorry, I thought ...'

Katia laughed.

'The thing is, Maddy, I never needed to come out, because I'm like Jo. I've never been anything but a lesbian, never had a heterosexual thought in my life, and to be honest have never thought twice about it. Living with Jo has helped me a great deal because we are alike in this and her mum and dad have been as wonderful with me as they were with her.'

'And your mum?'

'She lives across the road so I see her and Henry every day. She is happily married and I am so happy for her. She says it doesn't trouble her at all that I'm gay and I believe her, because after years together struggling to avoid journalists and corrupt police officers, she can see that I'm flourishing. She's keen for me to write the book.

'And what about girlfriends?'

'The deal with my landlady is that I can bring into my flat anyone I choose but no drugs and no smoking. I use neither so it's not a problem, and I don't have to sneak anyone in or out.'

'Jodie and I are learning about lesbian sex very slowly, perhaps too slowly.'

'Look on the Internet. There's plenty there. On the other hand I reckon there's much to be said for making it a voyage of discovery together.'

'Katie, I reckon you must be 50 years old at least. You know so much.'

'The terrible things that happened to mum, and then to me with her, have taught both of us a great deal in a short time. You must meet mum soon. She's most unusual – so much unspeakable treatment and not a trace of bitterness. And all of this because of Jo, and also Darcey, who worked on it with her.'

'Are you in love with Jo, Katia?'

'I suspect everyone who knows her loves her, but there is no possibility of my being in love with her. Like you, she's much too old!'

Maddy laughed.

Katia, you've just ruined a very lovely evening.'

18

The hotel in Bury St Edmunds was well known to Jo, as sometimes she had held Press Conferences there, being the most suitable place. As Dani, Jodie and herself entered the dining room she breathed a sigh of relief that all four of the Chief Constables had come in civvies. Both Dani and Jo knew them well and were on first-name terms, but Jodie found herself inevitably addressing them as "sir" and wondered what she was doing there. However Chris Biddle from Cambridge could see her awkwardness and was determined to help.

'Jodie, I've heard so much about you and I'm thrilled that you are taking over the SCU from Jo. Rumour has it that you are as tough as you are beautiful, that you crept up on a potential assassin and kicked his ass in!'

Everyone laughed and Jodie blushed.

'I think it was a little more painful for him than that.'

'Jodie was my PPO in Manchester until stolen by Jo, but she was utterly fearless and even without showing the firearm she was carrying, single-handedly broke up a crowd of rough and rowdy men.'

'Well for me, it's enough of a recommendation that Jo knows you are the natural leader of your team,' said Norfolk.

'Thank you, sir.'

'Have you a husband and family,' asked Suffolk.

'No sir. I'm afraid the reputation of my right boot has chased all the men away, but I do have a partner, as is the modern idiom.'

'I'm not allowed to ask whether the partner is male or female.'

'No you're not, sir, but I'll drop you a hint and say my partner's called Madeline and is a solicitor.'

'It's not much of a hint, Jodie,' he replied to general laughter.

'It's great to see you again, Dani, said Adam, the Essex Chief Super. 'We have missed you greatly at Chief's meetings, that ability you had to cut through the crap and show us how silly we were, like a teacher might.'

'I haven't missed them but it took me some time to adjust once I left. Moving to Norwich helped and now I'm manager of a bookshop which I enjoy, not that people read books as once they did. It's all social media and

Netflix, which is a great shame, especially among the young. If you were to ask me whether drugs or social media had the more detrimental effect on the young, I could not easily answer.'

'Are you on social media?' asked Cambridge.

'Chris, I still struggle with texting, and I hope that answers your question.'

Jo had a puzzled look on her face.'

'Jo, you're looking uneasy,' said Suffolk.

'It's just that there is a spare setting at the table and the manager here is usually so meticulous.'

'I see what you mean,' said Chris from Cambridge. 'I know, I'll just pop into the bar and see if I can find a volunteer to join us, perhaps not mentioning what the four of us do.'

'Good idea, Chris,' said Adam.

Jo sensed a con in progress, as she watched Chris go through into the bar and return just a few moments later with a vision in blue: it was Alice Watts.

The three Chiefs stood as Chris brought her to the table.

'Jo,' said Chris, 'we wanted to share this farewell evening with your greatest triumph as a police officer: liberating this brave and lovely lady from a hell even Dante never thought of.'

Tears were pouring down Jo's face.

'Alice, my darling, thank you so much for being here at the suggestion of these wicked gentlemen,' she said through her tears.

'How could I not? I know I see you across the road every day but a formal opportunity to thank you in this way was just too good to miss.'

'Well, come and sit down. And does Katia know where you are?'

'Of course.'

'Considering the appalling way you were dealt with by the police in Nottingham back then, sitting in a hotel with four Chief Constables, shows extraordinary strength on your part.'

'It's over and done with. I'm happily married, I have a happy daughter and I live over the road from you. As they say, what's not to like?'

The food came and conversations became limited to those on either side. Jo thought back to her own days in the past when her own superior behaved appallingly badly towards her and she spent almost ten years patrolling the streets of Boston as a constable. He had died a long time ago, but he would surely have been stunned if he could see her now. Now, she knew, it was quite likely that this would be the last time she would see three of the Chiefs, because Chris Biddle was a friend she would continue to be in touch with.

'Alice', said Norfolk, 'your story is remarkable and even if it doesn't necessarily reflect well on the police in Nottingham all those years ago, does it occur to you to want to turn it into a book or even a television programme? There have been books written about Mary Bell, and she *had* done what you haven't.'

'With encouragement from Jo, my daughter Katia has begun to write the story though she will need some legal advice, I suppose.'

'Does she live nearby?'

'Oh yes, she lives across the road with Jo, in a self-contained flat within Jo's house, and she works primarily as Jo's childminder.'

'I don't think she will have any difficulty getting a publisher.'

'Are there constraints on former police officers publishing their memoirs.'

'Yes, and rightly so, though most of our work is dull and routine, not unlike a jigsaw, little by little putting together evidence piece by piece. I know that on tv that is rarely how things are shown but it's the daily reality for detectives. On the whole that would make boring reading.'

At the conclusion of the dinner, Adam, the Chief Constable of Essex, stood and made a short peroration, thanking Jo for her service and handing her an envelope which expressed the four Chiefs' gratitude. Jo did however notice a long and very quiet conversation between her friend Chris Biddle and Dani, but on the way home, Dani would say nothing other than it was two old colleagues catching up, which instinctively Jo knew was a lie.

Once back in Saxmundham, Maddy reported that she had enjoyed a wonderful conversation with Katia, and hoped she might get the chance in the morning for her to meet her mother Alice.

'Here I am,' said Alice. 'I was the unexpected guest, present to help finally get rid of Jo from the Police and it was a great privilege to do so.'

'Well, I have spent the evening with your number one fan. I might also add that she has a maturity well above her age. And I even spoke to her about the possibility of working with me as a solicitor's clerk, essentially working as my assistant but with a clear career structure if she wished. She's more than capable of it and has more than the usual experience of the legal system behind her. Anyway I mentioned it and I am sure she will either reject it or want to discuss it with you and Jo.'

'That's amazing,' said Alice.

'It might take a while to be set up, but Katia is very special and I would like to work with her, because there's so much I think I might learn from her.'

'Isn't it meant to be what she might learn from you?'

'Most of that comes from books; her knowledge comes from life.'

'I think you've had quite a bit yourself,' said Jodie, putting her arm around Maddy.

'I rather suspect we all have,' added Dani.

'Katia makes her own mind up about everything, so when she's ready, she'll let you know,' said Alice.

Alice went home, Jodie and Maddy to bed, leaving Jo and Dani sitting together on the sofa.

'Ok, out with it,' said Jo.

'Don't be ridiculous Jo, you know it all anyway.'

'Are we talking about your possible appointment as Her Majesty's Inspector of Police Cells, for which the Justice Minister asked my advice at the suggestion of the Home Secretary?'

'Good heavens, no. Where did you get that idea from? I was being asked if I would be willing to be the goalie for the retired police officers team in the annual match against the inmates of Dartmoor nick.'

'God, you're sexy when you're being sarcastic!' said Jo with a grin.

'Just be careful, you. When I'm Her Majesty's Inspector of Prison Cells and I find you in one, I shall insist you are chained up.'

'Gosh, I never knew you were into bondage!'

'Well, actually, my lovely Jo, I'm not, and the other thing I haven't told you is that there is a new person in my life.'

'Oh, Dani, what wonderful news. Tell me more.'

'She's called Louise and she's the manager of the Refectory in Norwich Cathedral. I sometimes pop in there for my lunch and had noticed her and then one day she came into Waterstones and I approached her and said that I recognised her and could I help if she was looking for something special. She smiled at me and said that perhaps she had found it. She then said she had followed me from the Refectory to see where I worked but promised she wasn't a stalker. I told her I wouldn't have minded if she was and that was where it all began, about three months ago.

'When she had picked herself up off the ground after learning my previous occupation, she said she wants me to move in with her – at my age. All I can say is she reaches the parts that only you have drawn near. I was going to discuss with you how your mum and dad would feel if I moved out and then this job has arisen. I need to discuss it with Louise of course, as we would need to move but I think she will be more than ready to leave the job behind.'

'Would you like the job?'

'Only if Louise is included in the package.'

'You know that mum and dad have loved having you, but there is no way they would ever get in the way of your fulfilment, even at the grand old age of, what is it ...76?'

'I'm 52 and Louise 43.'

'Dani, I am simply thrilled for you. Let me kiss you.'

They did so properly and with feeling.

'I can tell you've been in practice,' said Jo, as their mouths parted.

'And I hope you will be too,' said Dani.

Jodie was the first to set off after an early breakfast. Maddy received a call from Katia to say that Alice and Henry would like her to join them for breakfast across the road. Dani was still in bed as Jo headed off with Josie and Ollie and announced en route that there were a couple of things she wanted to mention.

'Are you still happy sharing a bedroom? I wondered whether you might prefer a bedroom each.'

'Why?' said Josie.

'It's just that as you are getting older, I wondered whether you might want a degree of privacy.'

'You mean dressing and undressing?'

'Well, yes.'

'I don't see the problem. We both know what the other looks like with no clothes on and so accustomed, we just get on without being concerned about it. Isn't that right, Ollie?'

'The thing is mum, we've both grown up and changed together. I know my sister is attractive and I know why, but to me she is Josie and we have the great link that through mum who died, we look alike and can remember her even though we know how extremely badly she behaved to you and a lot of other people. But you are the best mum in the world.'

'Yes, you are,' said Josie. 'So what's the other thing you want to mention, as if I can't guess?'

'Go on then, guess.'

'It's not a guess, is it Ollie?'

'No. A little bird called Katia said it wasn't fair just dropping it on us, so she told us, and explained that when we get in from school today there'll be someone else living here.'

'We know the name of this person and just so relieved that the world's slowest lover has finally seen the sense that everybody, and I mean everybody else, has known about for ages and ages. We will therefore welcome this person to our house and lives, but most especially we welcome her to your life.'

'You haven't said her name.'

'But we have to each other, time and again. Jude is a lovely person, generous and kind, but this person you love and we know she loves you. I am referring of course to Kelly.'

'Kelly!!??'

The pair of them giggled.

'Or perhaps we mean Darcey, yes I think we do, mum.'

Giggling gave way to laughter by the three of them.

When Dani rose her first act was to telephone Norwich Cathedral and make sure a table could be booked for dinner later. Jo arrived back from the school run and they sat chatting about Dani's new job, which having thought about it in the waking hours of the night, she decided she would like to have a go at.

'That's really good news, Dani.

'Well, being the manager of a bookshop is interesting, but not *that* interesting. I'm still young enough to be doing an important piece of work and this is important.'

'It certainly is. We've both locked people up in facilities we had doubts about. But tell me more about Louise.'

'There's not much to tell. She comes from Drayton, and is Norfolk born and bred – she even has a slight accent which is very endearing.'

'And her surname?'

'Well, you'll laugh, given where she works. It's Kitchen.'

The hairs on the back of Jo's head were standing.
'You're not laughing, Jo.'
'"Kitchen"! Are you sure?'
'Ah. You can take Jo Enright out of the police, but you can't take the police out of Jo Enright. I'm sorry my darling; I'm winding you up. The new lady in my life is called Louise Sarkar of an Anglo-Indian background, and looks not unlike Aisling who used to work for you. Yes, I know who the total bastard Kenneth Kitchen is, and you put him away. Don't ever think I don't always watch my back. I had Louise checked out and I also told her after I got the all clear. She understood why.

'Do you remember the first time you spent a night under my roof?'
'Yes, I had just come from Hereford and that horrible chicken head murder.'
'Which you and you alone had solved. I failed that night, and I've never forgiven myself for it because I did not do what I should have done which is to have come to you in your bed. That would have been a turning point. I shall strive to learn to love Louise, but there will only ever be one love in my life.'

Jo came to her and put her arms around Dani.
'Life is complicated, Dani.'
'I'm glad you've noticed,' she said and kissed Jo.

Across the road Maddy sat at the table with Henry whilst Katia and Alice were preparing the plates each containing a full English breakfast.

'In the presence of those two,' said Maddy to Henry, 'I feel only awe, when I consider what they've come through, and yet both seem so well-balanced and, dare I say it, normal.'

'You know Katia is hoping to tell the story in book form.'
'Yes, and though I'm not a libel lawyer, I have offered her my legal advice.'
Alice and Katia entered bearing an amazing breakfast. As they tucked in, Alice said: 'What actually is a Solicitor's Clerk?'

'It is an assistant to the solicitor who will often sit in at meetings with clients, do research and most important of all, make me Full English breakfasts.'

They all laughed.

'But it can also be a way into becoming a solicitor. That would involve working part-time for the Open University Law Degree but I have no doubts that Katia would manage that without much difficulty. At first, as there would only be me and her, my clerk would be involved in everything I do, including the drawing up of documents. Katia would not be a dogsbody – far from it, and in addition together we could work on the book, to which I feel a great commitment too, though it will be Katia's and only Katia's.'

'Hello,' said Katia, 'you two do know I'm here, don't you?'
'You told me,' said Alice, 'you'd already accepted Maddy's offer crossing the road, so I'm just trying to find out what might be involved. You know I would never get in the way of what you had made your mind up to do, because I trust your mind totally.'

'I feel the same and I'm hoping Katia and I can take a closer look at Bury today and see where we might set up in business.'

Dani watched in silent fascination as Jo ran through the pre-flight checks and spoke to ATC. On a Tuesday there was more military traffic so they had to climb much higher to allow flights to land and take-off from Mildenhall and Lakenheath. It was a short flight and there were no gliders around on a Tuesday morning. Soon Jo was given clearance to descend, and she landed on the grass runway. Jo taxied to where Dani's car was parked.

'Forgive me for teasing and testing you earlier.'

'You know I would never knowingly leave you unprotected. Let me know when the new job begins and no doubt I'll hear from mum and dad when you move out. Parting from you is always ghastly. I'll never stop loving you.'

Dani had tears rolling down her cheeks. Through her tears she said: 'You'd never think we were once two of the most senior police officers in the land.'

Minutes later Jo was back in the air giving her total concentration to the task in hand, and knowing what lay ahead, and it filled her with joy.

19

With Josie and Ollie at school, Katia drove Maddy into Bury St Edmunds. On their feet, they found two firms of solicitors and another called property lawyers. Neither of the two firms gave any indication of being woman-friendly, and Maddy thought that would be their best bet as they sought to be established. Especially in matters of divorce, women usually preferred a female solicitor.

'I can't imagine you would need to seek their permission to set up,' said Katia.

'As a courtesy I will have to let them know, but how you and I do things after that is up to us.'

They walked the streets and noted two vacant properties of which they needed to make further enquiries.

'I can't say exactly when we can get up and running, Katia, as we shall have to furnish and decorate, and then install computers and the like, but I'm keen for us to work together, and Jodie is hoping we might be able to work for the SCU with legal advice and guidance. In the meantime, if you wish, I'd like you to register with the OU. Ignore me completely if you see things otherwise, but I believe you would make a very good solicitor, not least representing those who have been arrested by the fascist police.'

'You mean like Jodie, the woman you love.'

'Exactly.'

They both laughed so loudly, people turned to look at them.

'And is there someone special in your life?' asked Maddy.

'Not one person in particular though I have a number of close and intimate friends. When I consider someone like my hero Jo, she has gone through trials and tribulations to arrive at today. She and Darcey have loved each other passionately for years and, as far as I know, never given physical expression to it. They've both been married, Jo catastrophically and Belinda unhappily, and all the time the one they wanted was the other. I've got a long way to catch up with them so I don't worry. I have a lot of fun and laughter to catch up on before anything serious, and as far as I know, lesbians don't get pregnant without the intervention of medicine, and I stay well away from that.'

'Do you visit lesbian clubs?'

'In Saxmundham?' said Katia with a giggle. 'Sometimes. There's a place in Ipswich but I prefer the AAA Club in Cambridge, which Jude recommended. She used to go there when she was a vicar. There are lots of students, of my age, in term time.'

'You make me feel jealous.'

'Don't be, Maddy. Most of the girls there are confused and uncertain about their identity and my feeling is that they could quite easily be hurt. You have Jodie and boy, have you chosen well. She is everything many women and men, would die for: she is brave, highly intelligent and gorgeous, but you don't need me to tell you.'

'Yes, I was devastated that she had that dinner last night without me because she looked stunning, and it was all wasted on four Chief Constables. But I'm completely stunned by everything that has happened – that Jodie could love me of all people, when I was associated with criminals and my face smashed in.'

'I agree. How could she? Unless it was the only thing that matters, by which I mean love. Though I think you're also pretty gorgeous yourself. If it helps and even if it doesn't, I fancy you.'

Maddy stopped in the street and gave Katia a hug and a kiss.

'Thank you, Katia. When we open the business you will be in charge as manager. Between you and me there is no choice.'

"Who is going to be manager in the house?" thought Jo as she drove up the road and parked in such a way as to allow the removal van to continue unloading. To be fair there wasn't that much furniture as Darcey and Belinda had lived in furnished property, but Jo was excited by the sight of things being taken in. Despite asking herself that question, she already knew the answer. Darcey had been a more than capable leader of the Armed Response Unit in Norfolk, work which required rapid detailed planning where lives were at stake and speed of reaction. Jo knew Darcey had never discharged her firearm in Armed Response but that she had let others under her do so when necessary, incapacitating rather than killing, and so decided that if Darcey insisted on furniture removal she would let her have her way! And if her hopes for farming came to pass, it would be Darcey and not herself who would have the shotgun licence. Jo walked in.

Darcey was sitting on the sofa, reading something or other. Or was it Darcey? She had a new haircut in which almost all of her hair had been shaved. She turned towards Jo and smiled.

'O my God,' said Jo, 'your hair is more than simply wonderful, it is heavenly' and she came to her and held her head in her hands prior to a prolonged kiss.'

'Thank you my darling,' replied Darcey. 'About three years ago I was with you and we saw a woman with hair like this, and I remember you saying that as far as you were concerned it was perfection and the most erotic haircut imaginable. So I thought I would try it.'

'And have you got 30 days to change your mind?'

Darcey laughed.

'Well, don't you dare change your mind. You look amazing all over. That tee shirt does terrible things to me too.'

'It's meant to.'

One of the men carrying small items of furniture came in with a stool, interrupting Jo and Darcey about to wrap themselves around one another.

'Er, excuse me, where do you want this?'

All they could do was laugh as Darcey pointed.

'We're going out for dinner tonight, my darling, and guess what? We don't need to take our phones any more. No more being on call.'

'Would you like a cup of tea?'

'I could murder for one.'

'That's nothing to do with me anymore.'

'Nor me, but I'll drink it all the same. It's a good job you didn't say "What's your poison?"'

'Jo, people think you're so clever, but really you're an idiot.'

'Oh thank you, and I love you too. In fact I love and always have loved you beyond the capacity of words to describe.'

Once again the removal man had entered, carrying a small item and overheard the conversation.

'Are you two rehearsing for a play?'

'There have been lots of rehearsals,' said Darcey, 'but at long last, the curtain's up.'

The man remained standing, staring.

'So are you what are called lisbins.'

'Something like that, said Darcey.'

The man shook his head.

'What a waste and where should I put this bag?'

For Jo and Darcey, these were to be repeated many times in days to come accompanied by guffaws of laughter: "What a waste and where should I put this bag?"

'What time do we need to collect Josie and Ollie from school?' asked Darcey.

'Katia is doing that and it'll give us time to put your things where you want them, and your clothes away in our room. Did you hear that, Darcey, my own Darcey, *our* bedroom?'

'It's two words I have longed to hear for a very long time.'

'Me too, unless of course you snore.'

'Cheeky sod. I don't have to be nice to you any more.'

'You never were before.'

'My Jo,' said Darcey taking hold of her hand, 'that's because I love and adore you, and know that I can say and do anything, and that I'm wholly secure in your love.'

Voices approached as Ollie and Josie rushed in, followed by Katia carrying school bags and coats.

'Darcey!' was the shout as the two of them clung to her. Instinctively knowing her to have long been Jo's favourite, Ollie and Josie felt exactly the same way. Together they had assumed she would have come once their mum had left for America, and although they liked Jude, they were disappointed that it wasn't Darcey who had come then.

The three of them chatted for ages, taking up from exactly where they had left off the last time they had met. Darcey noticed changes. For his age Ollie was remarkably intelligent in his thinking and expression, whilst Josie was rapidly growing up into the beautiful young woman her mother had been. Jo admitted to Darcey that sometimes and in a certain light he could swear it was Marie.

The combination of television and supper allowed Darcey an escape and she prepared to get ready for dinner, until that was, Katia came and sat on the bed as she changed.'

'Are you child-minding this evening?'

'No. My mum and Henry are coming over. I've got a date, though at the moment she doesn't know it's a date and probably thinks it's for a group of us.'

'Katia, that's terrible.'

'I know, but it's my only chance to get her by herself and I didn't lie, just allowed her to infer, and it's not as if I live with a police officer anymore.'

Darcey smiled and shook her head.

'Can I ask you something? Josie's just told me that she and Ollie still share a bedroom, and they are happy with that. But surely you've noticed that Josie is burgeoning into a woman, whereas Ollie is still a boy.'

'And yet whenever Jo asks them if want a room each, they always say no. They say that they belong together as brother and sister and that this saved them when Marie committed suicide and that although they know that one day they will go their separate ways, being together until then is most important.'

'But what about dressing and undressing?'

'I've asked them both individually if that's a problem and both more or less said the same: "Don't be silly, we're brother and sister".

'I don't think I'd want to take my clothes off in front of my brother,'

'I didn't know you had a brother.'

'I don't'

'And do you like sex in the dark or with the lights on?'

'Katia! You're very direct!'

'Just asking. I prefer to see what I'm doing and always to see my partner's face. But I'll leave you to get dressed.' Katia grinned. 'I don't want to embarrass you.'

On the way to the restaurant, Jo turned briefly to Darcey.

'We got married in a car doing obs. Do you remember?'

'How could I ever forget, my darling Jo? It was my birthday.'

'Your birthday? I didn't realise that.'

'Not that sort of birthday. My coming to birth day, my true arrival in the world of meaning, joy and love.'

'It's a good job all obs duties are not like that.'

Darcey giggled.

'It would be something of a surprise to Warren and Ahmed doing obs together if it were.'

'But it wasn't to me. It was what I had been hoping for, for a very long time.'

'I was surprised to discover from Ollie and Josie that they still share a bedroom even though Josie is now an attractive young woman.'

'I've had words with her about it but she simply doesn't see it as a problem. The thing is, Marie's suicide has brought them so very close together and they've shared a room for years, and neither of them sees it as a sexual thing. In Josie's presence, only a couple of weeks ago, Ollie said to me "Mum, Josie's got really pretty breasts, I'm so proud of her".'

'On that occasion Josie turned to Ollie and said, "Thank you, Ollie, that's really kind," and went on with her reading. It may change and perhaps one day Josie will go off to uni, but provided we can keep our ears open to anything that implies a change is required, I'm leaving well alone. They're a very special pair.'

The restaurant was well known, not least for its two Michelin stars. The maitre d' greeted them at the door.

'Dame Joanne, how wonderful to see you, and Madame Enright,' and having kissed both their hands, added, 'What beauty you bring among us this evening.' He led them to their table and unfolded their napkins and laid them across their laps, before offering them their menus.

'There are no prices on mine,' said Darcey.

'Nor mine,' responded Jo. 'If you eat here you don't worry about such things.'

'I suppose at some stage we need to think about money and about whether we have a joint or two single accounts. Land is expensive, and livestock too.'

'I've told no one at all, not even my mum and dad, but in addition to my police pension, which is not enough to live on, I have received a lump sum in lieu of a monthly pension from both the RAF and USAF (though that is set aside for the children), the latter of which was $½ million. However I have also been making use of the services of an attorney in LA who successfully charged USAF with serious neglect in that Marie was seduced by the base physician and then that the information about being grounded was mishandled, both of which contributed to her suicide. For that I was awarded $10.4 million, which makes you and me, my darling, very wealthy indeed.'

'Jo, that's wholly yours, not mine.'

'From the day that our wedding occurs, it will be legally yours too, though as far as I'm concerned we are already married, already one. So have anything you fancy tonight.'

'I know what I do fancy.'

'Me too, but they might lose one of their Michelin stars if it happened now!'

On their way home after a quite unforgettable meal of tastes and textures, Darcey asked Jo how she was hoping to set about buying land and farming.

'Is that what we're going to do?' asked Jo.

'It's what I thought you said.'

'Perhaps I did, but that was when I was just me. I'm not just me any more, am I? I'm half of us. Such things are now decided by us together. I'm not the senior officer any more. We are equal in every way and what we decide about the future will be ours.'

The night belonged to them both – with the lights on!

They were awakened just after 7:00am, still tightly wrapped around one another, by the appearance of Katia with cups of tea.

'Thank you,' said Jo, 'and don't worry about the school run this morning. Darcey wants to be able to do it as well as you and me, so unless you have a pressing need to go into Ipswich, you can take it easy.'

'That's fine by me, Jo.'

'Did you have a good time last night?' asked Darcey.

Katia laughed.

'Not quite. She's really lovely and as we spoke initially I thought I might be in with a chance. Then she stunned me by saying that on 1 December she is entering a convent as a postulant and hoping in time to become a professed nun.'

Jo and Darcey both laughed.

'It's not funny. Just imagine what might have happened had I kissed her. Still, it's all part of life's rich tapestry.'

'Indeed,' said Darcey, 'and sometimes we drop a stitch.'

'Can you drop a stitch in a tapestry?' asked Jo.

'I don't know,' replied Darcey.

'Nor me,' said Katia.

'What is the name of your date – your dropped stitch?' asked Darcey.

'Chloe Battersby, and two things I did learn about her were that she works on her dad's farm, and that she can drink most of the young farmers under the table.'

'Is there any chance that you might persuade her to come and have some supper with us as I would like to meet her' said Jo.

Katia looked puzzled.

'Are you serious?' she asked.

'Yes, we are,' said Darcey.

'That won't be a problem. Don't let your tea get cold,' said Katia as she closed the door.

'That leaves us about 15 minutes,' said Jo.
'For drinking the tea you mean?'
'Darcey, shut up!'

Another couple in bed drinking early morning tea, were Jodie and Anna. Life had undergone a massive change for both and at present they were living together in Anna's house. They had also exercised great daring and looked on the internet at how lesbians might perform together. They we so happy together but there were anxieties that a defence counsel for Aleksandrov could call Anna as a witness for the defence, regard her as hostile and force a not guilty verdict, and the same might well be true of his henchmen. Here at least Jodie could argue she was protecting Anna against further assault, but the two corrupt offices Hendry and Bowlby might to attempt to evade justice in the same way.

Today, Jodie, Anna and Frankie were to meet Counsel from London to discuss these matters. Anna had once instructed Toby Armitage QC and they had related well in securing a successful prosecution, which made it easy to hear his opinion

'You have sufficient evidence to secure a conviction in all instances without evidence from Anna, and it would be as well not to call you as a Prosecution Witness. As I'm sure you will be well aware, it becomes complex if the Defence Counsel calls you as a witness and begins by alerting the jury to the fact that you are now living with the Detective Chief Superintendent of the force that arrested the defendants. They will enjoy informing the jury that this is a same sex union, not because it proves anything but is an insinuation that you are being motivated by odd sexual preference that they hope some of the jury will disapprove of. Counsel for the Prosecution will object to this and the Defence will withdraw it but it will have registered in the ears of the jury.

'In substantive terms there is nothing in any Interview with the police that indicates anything more than the matters on which your former clients have been recorded, nor that you failed to do your duty to the best of your ability. Defence Counsel will embarrass you, but will be able to do nothing more. As I said earlier, you have enough evidence as it is and your best support comes from Dame Joanne who took on the Foreign Office and won. It will therefore be high profile and the people will not wish to see the baddies getting off.'

'Thank you Toby,' said Anna.

They chatted for a while. Just as Toby was about to take his leave he drew Anna aside.

'Defence counsel will be led by Ellie Adamson QC. She's good, even very good, and I imagine you've come across her before. The etiquette of court means that Counsel do not make use of material about their opposite number and judges will endeavour to stop witnesses doing so, unless the witness acts quickly to say something such as "But you, Ellie, are in the Cambridge Lesbian Club regularly", or 'You use coke regularly, so it's not surprising you defend your chief supplier". Don't mention this to Andy Cousins QC, who's prosecuting, whatever you do, or he will stop you, and of course I didn't tell you.'

'Thanks, Toby.'

'My pleasure. Am I allowed to say how much I fancy Jodie.'

'You can say anything you like, Toby!'

20

On the Monday morning, Jo had to go on a two hour lesson on teaching others to fly. As when she was learning herself, the RAF had offered to train her to teach others and she was more than happy to take up their offer.

Once back from the school run, and with Jo away at the airbase, Darcey was joined by Katia.

'How do you spend your days?' asked Darcey.

'I'm writing the story of my mum's, and later my, exile from decent society for the crimes she didn't commit, so I usually cross the road in the course of the day for conversation with her and Henry. Soon things may change as I'm looking to do an OU course with a possible view to becoming a solicitor and being employed by Anna as a Solicitor's Clerk. Given my involvement with the law I should have a flying start.'

'That's such a good thing to be aiming at'.

'What about you?'

'Hey, I only just stopped on Friday, but I may soon need the services of you and Anna for my divorce.'

'Oh Darcey, however much we all know you and Jo are made for each other, and I know you do too, it must be painful too.'

'Of course, and I shall always love Belinda but I could never do so in the way I love Jo, and have loved her ever since I stood before her in police college.'

'But when I see you, Darcey, I see the wonderful person who worked closely with Jo as you released us from hell, and for which I will never be able to thank you adequately.'

'But Katia, perhaps the time has come to stop.'

'To stop? What do you mean?'

'I mean it's over, it's done, and now what matters is what is to come. Neither Jo nor I want to be thanked any more, because we both love you here and now. We shall not mind even if you never mention it again, in fact we would prefer you never to do so, because if you do it shows that in some way you are still held captive by all that happened and you're not. You're free.'

'What you've just said is strangely liberating because I don't want to be someone with a past any more. Jo has been more than wonderful in allowing me to live in the flat here. I am somewhat anxious about what might happen if she and you move to the other end of the earth. Her dad said had been exploring the possibility of Scotland.'

'Nothing at all has been decided, and that includes dreams of living in a croft. We shall be giving thought to our future together of course, but post in our thinking are your needs, and those of schooling for Josie and Ollie, but I don't think it is likely that our plans will include selling this house, so please, Katia, don't trouble yourself unnecessarily.'

'Oh thanks Darcey, that's taken a great weight off my mind, but have you any thoughts as to what and where you might go?'

'Given that I've been here less than 48 hours and we haven't spoken a word about it, no, though it's also true that I really don't care as long as I'm with Jo.'

'Oh, by the way I called the future Sister Chloe earlier and invited her to come and meet you and Jo tomorrow night to have supper, which I'll cook, unless you have something already arranged.'

'That will be great. I'm looking forward to meeting her and to learning about keeping farm animals, because wherever we go, I think's Jo's still harbouring thoughts about farming when we get there. Of course perhaps she will convince Jo and me to become nuns!'

On her return, Jo told Darcey she had seen an advert for a parcel of land not far to the north of Saxmundham which was due to be auctioned on site on the following morning, and wondered if they might attend. They telephoned the vendor and he told them it would be at 9:30.

They attended early to look over the land which consisted of 1½ hectares of rough grazing land but were present only to see how the auction was done and the prices being paid. Oddly there were no other vehicles or pedestrians present and when a rundown landrover arrived from which an even more rundown farmer emerged they were rather puzzled, and even more suspicious, and by habit Darcey noted the number plate.

'We're here for the auction,' said Jo,' but I presume it's been cancelled.'

'No. You're the only ones showing interest. £19,000 and it's yours.'

'It's poor land,' said Jo.

'And that's why it's only 19k.'

'And how do we do the deal between us?'

'We shake hands and return this afternoon at 3:00. You pay me in cash please – I'm a farmer – and I'll get the land ownership documents ready and at 3-30 it will be yours.'

'What about the land registry?'

'It can be done online.'

'Well, I didn't realise how easy it could be.'

The man was back in his landrover and soon away.

'I think we'll stay awhile,' said Jo.

'I thought you might say that!'

About ten minutes later another car arrived containing a young couple who exited their vehicle and quickly approached the fence overlooking the land. The young man turned towards Darcey.

'Are you here for the auction at 10:00? I thought there might be quite a bit of interest, but it appears not.'

'Darcey,' said Jo, 'When does your resignation take effect?'

'The 31st of the month. Next week. And yours?'

'The same.'

'Let me explain something,' said Jo to the couple. 'Until the 31st we're both police officers and I think we've uncovered a scam. We were due here half an hour before you and invited to part with £19,000 in return for a landownership document. Whatever you do, don't hand over any money but agree to return this afternoon to pay then, but do not. We will arrange for him to be arrested. I'm sorry about this but if you're willing to play the part in just a few minutes' time, we can get him in the midst of his crime.'

'Of course,' said the man. 'Do we just stay until he comes?'

'It would be helpful, but so would recording it on your phone.'

'No problem,' said the woman.

Darcey showed them her warrant card to confirm.

'We'll go and park just back up the road and then come back and join you.'

This was repeated twice more before Jo suggested Darcey ring her friend, Sgt Netherhead, inform her of what was happening and get her to come with a couple of cars to arrest the man and find out all about him.

'How did you come across him, Darcey?' said the sergeant.

'Jo and I wanted to see how an auction happened and to judge the prices.'

Darcey gave the number plate and short while after received the information that it belonged to a blue mini.

'Ok, Darcey, I'll come up to where you are with a couple of gentlemen in uniform and bring him here. Because none of you potential buyers are handing over money the only thing we'll be able to do him for is the landrover with false plates but we'll make it clear we know what he's been doing, find out where he lives and then warn the locals what he's been trying on. He's wasted the time of people but that's not yet an offence.'

'Thanks, Hils.'

'I was sorry to hear about you and Belinda.'

'Thanks, but don't be too sorry At long last I'm where I've wanted to be for aeons and Belinda is meant for bigger things and better things than me. I still love her and want the best for her. She's not a natural detective but she is a leader..'

'And will you be having children?'

'We've been together less than three days, so we don't yet know what sort of breakfasts we each like. Of other matters we know nothing.'

'As you know, Darcey, I'm definitely heterosexual, as my Steve would confirm were he here, but I can understand why you are attracted to Jo. She's not a dolly bird or anything like, but she embodies all that's wonderful about being a woman. In fact the last time Steve and I saw her in Cambridge, she was plainly dressed, her hair nothing special and no make, yet as we walked on Steve suddenly said, "God, I didn't half fancy that woman".

'He's obviously got special taste: you and Jo.'
'H'm. I think it means he's got weird tastes.'
'Hey, Hils, don't call yourself weird, 'cos I can tell you, Jo doesn't'
'Too much information!'
'Happy arresting, sergeant!'

'Is Katia a good cook,' asked Darcey as she broke all the police driving rules and held Jo's hand as she drove home.

'She is. I would go further and say that Katia is good in so many ways, as also is her mum and I very much like Henry too. He caught sight of me on the newspapers day, and you need to remember he was a civil servant at the Home Office, and came over, congratulating me on my stand against idiots in the Foreign Office. It meant a great deal. But going back to Katia's cooking, you won't be disappointed, at least by the food. I'm sure how we'll get on with a potential nun after my recent experience of a former vicar.'

'Though potential nuns probably don't visit clubs of a certain variety – or we may be in for an evening that's far more interesting that we might imagine.'

'O God, I hope not. What I want hear about is her family farm and whether they have any alpacas. I would love to have alpacas.'

'O wow, so would I.'

Jo had played football on the lawn with Ollie, a rare event, but all the more enjoyed by both for that. She had then sat with Josie as shut put together a scrap book with photos of Nathan, his mother Karen, her beloved Grannie, and of course Marie.'

'You don't mind, do you?' she asked Jo.

'Of course I don't. I love or loved them all, Karen most of all, but I loved Marie enormously and only wish I had been enough for her. But I have no bad thoughts in my heart towards her, none whatsoever. She was extraordinarily clever on the ground and in the air, but so beautiful, and you my darling are going to be just as beautiful.'

Josie cuddled up to Jo.

'Thank you for saying all that, mum.'

Darcey was having a shower prior to the arrival of Chloe, allowing Jo the unusual opportunity to read a book for sheer enjoyment, something she had not done for some time. She had turned to R S Surtees, and her favourite, Handley Cross, which told of Mr John Jorrocks's own hunt and the sheer love of hound work she recalled from her days out hunting with her dad. The animals rights lobby these days would want her blood, so she had spoken of it so very little, but first thing on a clear October morning when she could sense that the scent would be breast-high, she would give a great deal to be with her dad, him hunting the pack with the wisdom and experience that mostly allowed the hounds to do the work; what could be better? On the other hand there was an aroma emerging from the kitchen that was pretty enticing too, though she very much hoped it was wasn't roast fox!

Coming from the kitchen Katia looked quite lovely even if slightly provocative, as if this might be her last chance to save Chloe from the snares of religion. On the other hand, when Darcey emerged from the bedroom, it might very well be her making the attempt to save Chloe's soul by looking simply stunning. Darcey then told Jo she needed to go and change and she did exactly that.

'I suppose there has to be a first time for everything,' said Josie, observing, 'she actually did what you said in the matter of clothes. Darcey, you just worked a miracle.'

If there had been an identification parade in a police station, done electronically as they are now with video, and Darcey had been asked from eight young women to choose the one most likely to become a nun, there was simply no way she would have chosen Chloe. The blond ringlets first of all would have led her astray (and perhaps in more ways than one, she thought), but it would have been her relaxed but total femininity. Jo, coming out to meet her felt much the same. It was little wonder that Katia felt about her as she did.

Chloe made conversation easily and was also interesting to listen to – although as far as the main course was course, nothing to do with religion or farming as yet. But it couldn't last. With the table cleared and syllabub due to arrive, Jo asked Chloe, 'Where is the convent you are planning to enter, Chloe?'

'In Oxford. They're called the Sisters of the Love of God. It's an enclosed community given over mostly to the work of prayer which is the mainstay of their life. They were the last community to abandon the night office, but still get up early, though I'm used to that when it's my turn to milk the cows on the farm.'

'Do they have any at the convent?'

'Not in the centre of Oxford,' she laughed.

'What sort of farm does your dad have?'

'Mixed. Mostly arable: rape, barley and winter wheat, plus 200 sheep, mainly Suffolk, appropriate I suppose but really ugly, some rare breed pigs, chickens and 45 Hosltein-Friesians which when they're not dry need milking twice a day.'

'No alpacas?' asked Darcey.

'There's more than enough for my dad to manage without pretty things that spit at you.'

Everyone laughed, and the syllabub arrived, which turned out to be quite wonderful.

'How did you decide to become a religious sister?' asked Jo, 'but you can tell me to mind my own business.'

'That's astonishing. You didn't say the word "nun", which just about everyone else does. I think your question is important and I'll try and give you an answer, if you wish.'

'I don't want to intrude on your personal space, Chloe, but I would genuinely be interested to understand something I really don't.'

'Well, as with all things, it is not one thing but a number of quite different elements. It might be said to be happening at this time because my dad wants to get out of farming, and that means there is nothing to keep me. I might have wished to inherit the farm but it is in fact a tenancy – it belongs to someone else.'

'Then there is the whole question of *Theos.*'

'You'll have to explain that.'

'There is a word which must be the most overused and abused word in the English language and it is the word "God", a word I neither use nor think of, save when explaining as I do now. *Theos* is the Greek word for God. It is not a swear word nor used in just about every sentence young and old alike utter. It has become totally devoid of meaning.

'I belong in the countryside and it was in woods that I thought about a year ago that I was being encountered by *Theos*. No lights in the sky or anything like that, just a bit like it is in the story of Elijah, a gentle breath. I was confused and wondered where help could be found. I didn't go to church but one day I saw the vicar and asked if he knew someone I might talk to. Humbly, he directed me to Oxford and the sisters and they interpreted what had happened along the lines of being a mystical experience and even suggested that my dad's retirement would free me to consider testing my vocation with them.'

'Isn't that quite a leap from a breeze to a convent?'

'Put like that, I suppose it is,' Chloe laughed.

'And if your dad were not retiring?'

'He is though,'

'Of course. Well thank you for trusting us with your story which is really moving.'

Darcey brought in coffee and the conversation lightened, but Jo's mind was working overtime (and not for the first time).

Conversation had turned to the world of music and the new album by Adele though Darcey and Jo looked at one another as if the others were speaking a different language, which of course they were. Jo was intrigued how songs written for a child explaining their parents divorce could be anything other than mawkish.

As Chloe was preparing to leave, Jo approached her.

'Chloe, who owns the land on which your dad farms?'

'The Ministry of Defence. They have a full-time land management department because most of the land they own goes back to the war'

'Do they ever sell?'

'I don't know as dad was never in a position to ask them, but the rent is considerable and making farming sustainable is getting harder and harder.'

'I can imagine. Chloe, it has been so good to have you here this evening. As you may know, Katia is a very special person and having her living in the flat is tremendous. Have you got a date when you will become a Postulant?'

'I'm due to go there on November 30 but you don't become a Postulant right away. You share in the life as an aspirant and if and when you and the community judge you're ready, that's when you become a postulant.'

'It's very much like the police! Well, let's hope we can tempt you to come here again before you leave.'

'Yes, I hope so too. What a cook!'

Lying in bed together later, wrapped around each another and full of joy and wonder, Darcey asked Jo what she was thinking about a future in farming for the pair of them.'

'It's quite simple, my beloved, I won't think anything about farming if you don't want to go ahead with it 100%. I told you before that what we decide our future is to be, must be owned by us equally, whatever it might be, with the exception that we are not becoming nuns.'

Darcey started to laugh.

'You're not taking me seriously,' said Jo.

'Oh, I am, my darling, and I love you, love you, love you.'

'Old Macdonald had a farm...' Jo began singing.

Moments later Darcey's delightfully placed hand stopped the caterwaul and the choirs of angels began!

21

Jo would be leaving straight after breakfast for a further lesson for teaching others to fly, but as they sat together, before Darcey was due to take the children to school, Darcey took hold of Jo's hand.

'Is there any chance of getting some alpacas?'

Jo smiled.

'You see Jo, I don't care what we do, as long as we do it together. My life has now begun and so has my love. If you want me to learn to farm, then I will happily and joyfully do it, as long as we do it together, do it as one.'

'Oh Darcey, please forgive all the wasted days, months and years until that moment in a car when we married one other. I imagine Chloe would say that I should reserve these words only for what she calls *Theos*, but I worship you, my darling.'

'Are you already married?' protested Ollie. 'Why weren't we able to be there?'

'It wasn't a public wedding and that will follow in time, and of course you will be there, Ollie. It was more of a promise made to each other which we both intend to keep.'

'Is that what they call getting engaged?'

'Yes, that is exactly what it was,' said Darcey.

'In which case you need a ring, both of you.'

'Yes,' said Jo. 'That is exactly what we need and must get.'

'But before then, it is school run time.'

With Darcey, Josie and Ollie on their way to school in Ipswich, Jo was joined by Katia.

'What did you think of Chloe?'

'I think she is a lovely and special person, whom the world will lose, when it cannot afford to do so, if she enters an enclosed religious order. I have little doubt that such places are important in their own way, but we, you and me and everyone else need Chloe and her *Theos* out here.'

'I know I do,' said Katia, 'but do you think there is anything we can do to help bring this about. You're the miracle worker, Jo.'

'By which you mean the death of Ellie, the betrayal and death of Marie and the disaster with Jude. Some miracle worker, Katia.'

'I'm sorry, Jo. That was stupid of me, but I meant the one mum and I know most about.'

'I know, but I do have an idea but whether or not there is the time to bring it off remains to be seen. When Darcey gets back from school, the three of us can have a chat, but first I need to make a couple of phone calls.

Jo had a direct number for the Commander of the base at Lakenheath though had never made use of the privilege, and wasn't altogether sure whether this was a legitimate use.

'Good morning, Roy, it's Jo Enright here.'

'Jo, it's been much too long since I saw you, and now you have retired. At what age, may I ask?'

'I shall be 40 next time.'

'Lucky you, and congratulations for taking on the cretins at the Foreign Office who prefer political expediency to morals. You won fair and square, and everyone who has mentioned it to me agrees wholeheartedly, and now I have been told you will soon be equipped to teach others to fly, following in the footsteps of Marie.'

'She would be highly amused, but I am calling to ask your advice. I gather the MOD owns a great deal of land, left over from the war.'

'Yes. A whole department is given over to it. Most land has tenants as few farmers could afford to buy the land and the MOD is under strict instruction to make proper financial use of it, which means not giving it to anyone at a knockdown price which might later be sold at great profit.'

'USAF have paid me a considerable compensation for Marie's death, and I mean considerable, and I am giving serious thought to a future in farming, and I've learned that a local farmer is soon to abandon his tenancy.'

'There will be a lot of people putting in bids, Jo – tenancies are in short supply.'

'I understand that, but I do not wish a tenancy, Roy. I want to buy.'

'You might be talking about millions.'

'I am talking about millions, Roy, and it would be our intention of keeping the present farm staff and the livestock on.'

'Haha, this must be Dame Joanne Enright I am talking to. It's why we here love you so much. Have you a pen and paper? I will text you a number and only speak to Commander Trevor Fraser, who is the head of the land management department. Tell him you and I have spoken and that I will support your application, and Jo, make sure you are *Dame* Joanne Enright, when you call. Finally, you will need a runway – don't overlook that.'

'Roy, as always you are so kind and generous.'

'As you have always been to us. But a word of warning. Farming is a perilous business to be going into and fraught with the possibilities of financial calamity, not to mention the vegan idiots.'

'Roy, I will only do what is well thought out just as I never fail to do all the pre-flight checks before I get to the end of the runway.'
'Received.'
Jo laughed.

It was a very windy day and her instructor rang to cancel the lesson, enabling Jo to wait for Darcey to return so that they could discuss the possibility she spread out before them, and they decided to bring Katia in.

'I am hoping to train as a solicitor, not a farmer,' said Katia, 'working with Anna Groom, not milking cows, just milking clients of their money.'

Jo and Darcey laughed and both got up and kissed her cheeks.

'Well, that's blown that,' said Darcey. 'Who else is there to milk the cows and shovel the muck away afterwards – it seemed made for you, Katia.'

'Gee thanks. Milk and muck – yes, I can see why you thought that,' she said with a broad grin.

'No, Katia. We want you here because you're a key person as will become clear. This morning I spoke first to the Commander at the base about how their land is handled by the MOD and he directed me to a number in Whitehall. The senior office I spoke to unhealthily grovelled when speaking to a Dame, and especially one who had stood up to the government in public. So I began at an advantage and then he was amazed when, with the support of the Commander of the air base at Lakenheath, I said I was interested in Fiona's dad's farm. He replied that soon there was an opportunity for bids to go in for the tenancy and that we would send me the papers necessary. And he was even more surprised when I said I had no interest in a tenancy and that I wished to buy the land and continue to farm it as it has in the past few years.

'He laughed, and I told him that patronising me because I am woman could be dealt with under the law with regard to hate crimes, and that Superintendent Francesca Wawszyczk would be more than willing to investigate and he at once apologised. He then said that at the last valuation, to purchase the land with no intended change of use it would cost just over £3 million. Yes, I said, that was what I was assuming and that therefore I wished to purchase from the MOD when the tenancy is complete at the end of November.'

'Jesus, Jo. That is a huge amount of money' said Katia.

'Yes, well, I am sure Jo won't tell you, but once we robbed a bank, covered it up and arrested innocent people,' said Darcey.

'I've always thought that might be the case,' laughed Katia.

'The answer, Katia, is that I have been awarded compensation payments by the USAF for Marie's suicide and with which I can afford this. However a big part of this possibility depends on you. You see we want to appoint Chloe as senior farm manager of what would be her father's farm. Going into a convent because she is being forced to leave her father's farm seems to so wrong to me. If she will stay and take complete charge, Darcey and I will be the novices. If she is still set on Oxford and the sisters, then there would be little point in our buying the farm, because Darcey and I don't know one end of a cow from the other and we would have think again. But might it be possible for us to meet Chloe and put it to her?'

'I'll give her a call to see if she might meet to discuss a serious proposition from the Dame!'

'Thanks, Katia. I've got to meet Jude today. She's coming to meet with Diane to work on their book together and asked if we could meet. I said yes because we haven't spoken since she left.'

'Of course,' said Darcey. 'I'll be pleased to see her again, if you think she won't punch me in the face for usurping her.'

'According to my calendar, you and I remain police officers until midnight tonight, so if she does we can still arrest her.'

Jo was sitting drinking coffee with Alice and Henry and saw Jude's car arrive at Diane's house, and watched as she walked the short distance to her own house, almost immediately opposite the house owned by Alice and Henry.

'Jude's just arrived, Jo', said Henry.

'I'll finish my coffee and then go over. Darcey will let her in. She's very good at potentially awkward situations.'

'I saw Katia drive out earlier,' said Alice.

'Me too,' said Jo laughing. 'She keeps me as well informed as she does her mother, and why should she? She may well be meeting Anna to discuss arrangements for buying property in Bury.'

'Tell me, Jo,' continued Alice, 'is Katia wise to go in with her?'

'Anna was highly regarded in the East End of London where she operated. But as sometimes happens that can work against a solicitor in that undesirables can seek her out to take up their cause, and it happened to her. She might tell you that taking someone as a client is not an endorsement even though it can look like it. For the police, dealing with suspects in the Interview Room, the solicitor is part of the opposition who can be a real pain, but that's what they are there for. She represented some unpleasant people but certainly is not unpleasant herself and I know how well she did her job, and trust me when I say she would not be living with Jodie were it otherwise, and in the end the nasties beat her up so badly she needed surgery, showing that she was on the side of the goodies.

'Moving to Bury makes sense because if you give a dog a bad name because of some of her clients means it might be better to begin again somewhere else. I think Katia will be fine with her, might indeed flourish, and if I had doubts I would share them with her, but I have none.'

'Thank you, Jo. Perhaps I will never get through my life totally free of suspicion.'

'You're doing fine, Alice, and I will never let you down.'

'Jo, there's nothing I can say, but you know it anyway.'

There was a small teashop which would close for the winter at the end of the following half-term week and it was somewhat out of the way so took Katia a little while to find it. When she finally entered she could see Chloe in what were obviously her farming clothes, not quite what she had been wearing when she came for supper. Katia was please when Chloe stood and gave her a hug.

'What would you like,' Chloe said. 'After that amazing meal it will be rather inadequate.'

'No, it won't, Chloe,' said a voice belonging to an emerging body behind the counter.

They all smiled at one another.

'Toasted teacake and a cup of tea please.'

Chloe paid whilst Katia went and sat down, and was soon joined by her friend.

'I can't stay too long at this time on a working morning.'

'I take it you'll need to get back into your working clothes.'

'Have you made a study of rudeness or is it just natural?'

'Look Chloe, I'm going to tell you something which is almost unbelievable but is quite true so bear with me.

'Jo's wife, Marie, who was allegedly an outstanding aircraft pilot, first of all with the RAF and then in the US as a test pilot, by means of bad treatment at the hands of people in the United States Air Force, took her own life at a base in Los Angeles.'

'Are you serious?'

'Oh it's been even worse for Jo, but I'll miss that for now. The Air Force have admitted liability and paid compensation. Now she and Darcey have retired, they have one hope for their future and that is that they learn farming and want to obtain a farm where there will be those who can teach them and manage the farm.'

'Without experience and knowledge they won't stand a chance of getting a tenancy. Someone seeking hobby farming just won't be able to compete with those who have already been farming for quite some time. Farming looks fun on television but you have to know a great deal without absolutely everything going pear-shaped.'

'You know all this, of course.'

'I know a great deal as I was born on the farm and have been farming ever since, but I also depend on the others we have on the farm.'

'What's going to happen to these others when your dad leaves?'

'Well, sadly, they're out of work from then on, but might hope that the next tenant will offer them a job.'

'And of course it's forcing you into a very different life which will negate all your life experience, but if it wasn't happening would you be doing that?'

'It's a hypothetical question, Katia. It *is* happening and often it is circumstance which teaches us what we should do.'

'No. That's simply not true and if you knew what happened to my mum and then to me you would know it wasn't true. When she was ten my mum was sent to prison for the murder of two babies in Nottingham. Even as a girl she was put into adult women's prisons and when she was eventually released, she was persecuted constantly, not least by the police. She had to change her name again and again and received no support from the social services. She had a relationship with a man, which produced me, but when he found out about her past, he disappeared. I went to school after school, and was equally hounded by the Press. In time we moved to Saxmundham and mum had a part-time job in a café where she met one of our neighbours, Detective Chief Superintendent, Dame Jo Enright. From their first conversation and mum's description of what had happened Jo know that mum's account had been drilled into her but could not be not true.

'Jo and Darcey spent hours in Nottingham digging in libraries and police archives. One of Jo's friends, a journalist also investigating the same history, was murdered in Cambridge, and that brought about the breakthrough. By superb detective work and typical Enright courage she was able to arrest the same woman for the murder of the babies and that of her friend.'

'That's incredible. And is that why she is a Dame?'

'No. She's not allowed to say what she got that for, but the official mention said, "courage beyond the call of duty", which makes it all the more wretched that she has known such personal sadness.'

'You must value and appreciate her enormously.'

'Mum and I owe her just about everything, and Darcey too, because she was the only one of her colleagues that Jo worked closely with as she strove to unravel the deliberately tight knot of the past. And I'll you something else about Jo that will amaze you. She still regularly visits in prison the person who committed those murders, because as well as being a top police officer she is essentially a person of enormous compassion. Understandably, I have ambivalent feelings about her doing that, but it is Jo.

'One other thing before you rush back to the farm and on to the convent, Jo lets no one down and is always true to her word. She wants you to take over your dad's farm and those who work with you, the only condition for which would be that you teach her and Darcey about farming so they can share it with you.'

Chloe sat deep in thought.

'I would need to meet them again, very soon.'

'Tonight?'

'Are you cooking?'

Katia laughed.

'For you, anything.'

'Anything?'

'Yes, Chloe, for you, anything.'

They smiled at each other.

It had been in a tea shop that her mum and Jo had met and experienced the transformation of her life, and as she drove back to Saxmundham having already alerted Darcey that Chloe was returning for supper, listening to a CD of Pink, Katia wondered just what change of circumstance she had begun. If it was what she increasingly hoped it might be, it would mean a change of life but maybe she was ready for an end to sex with partner after partner, picked up in the clubs she visited. She had always been amazed that Jo had said nothing about her lifestyle of which she must have been aware, but she had only two rules: no drugs and no smoking, and on one occasion, of which she was very proud, Katia threw out a girl who broke both!

Despite the tea shop meeting with Chloe, which she thought wonderful, Katia had a slight uneasiness within. Jo never pretended anything other, but Katia knew it was also the day she visited Nikki Hampton in prison, the woman who had actually been the one to murder the two babies and allow her mother, Alice, to take the blame for many years, and who would have got away with it had it not been for Jo. Katia knew from the trial that the young Nikki had been raped by Alice's (Ella, as she was then) step father and forced to have an abortion, and who then took her revenge by murdering the two babies and allowing Ella to take the blame, condemning her and Katia to many years of hell. She then murdered a journalist friend of Jo's, Andie Bolam. It was difficult for Katia to understand just why Jo kept in touch with this horrible woman.

Jo opened the front door quietly and could hear Josie, Ollie (both on half-term), Darcey and Jude all chatting happily and felt somewhat guilty arriving like the spectre at a feast, but everyone turned towards her with smiles, not least from Jude who was looking much better than she had the last time Jo had seen her following the operation.

Jude got up and gave Jo a warm hug.

'How are things in your tummy?' asked Jo.

'The staples and plastic cover are gone which makes life a little more comfortable and I now have a full-time nurse to make sure the recovery continues.'

'Have you brought Abby? I would love to meet her, and both of you will always be welcome here.'

'That's such a typically generous offer, Jo. I'm hoping she's fast asleep as she's on nights still, though hoping to move to days soon. But tell me, how is retirement?'

'I prefer resignation given that I'm still not 40, and I'm hoping that soon I may be allowed to train people to fly.'

'You'll love doing that. I fear I wasn't the best flyer in the world.'

'Perhaps you could be my first learner.'

'And then again, perhaps not, though Abby is game for most things and would love to do so. What about you, Darcey?'

'When I have my own resident pilot? I think not. Josie wants to learn and before too long so will Ollie, I'm sure.'

'For both of you that will be a wonderful tribute to Marie, but now I must make my way to spend some time with Dianne as we work on the book.'

'How is it coming on?' asked Jo.

'Slowly, but definitely,' she said a laugh. 'But before I leave may I just say to you, Darcey, that this was always meant to be where you belong. All those who know you both have long since been aware of this. I kept the nest warm for you, but it's yours.'

Darcey came and hugged Jude, unable to speak. Jo led Jude to the door.

'What a wonderful thing to say, Jude. I will always love you and I mean it when I say you can come here whenever you wish to, but next time bring your nurse.'

'I will.'

They kissed.

22

Jo had not informed the prison officials that she was no longer a police officer, so apart from the compulsory metal and drug tests, it did not take her long to get inside. By arrangement they met in the Chaplain's room which meant armchairs.

'I've sneaked in lots of coke,' said Jo, and they waited. That no one rushed in meant that no one was listening. Nikki smiled.

'And are you now a civilian?' asked Nikki.

'From midnight.'

'And does it feel good?'

'I'm still waiting to find out. My car still has all its fittings, but nasty Russian villains are not my concern any more.'

'I imagine they've told you that I'm on the pathway to release. Next week they're moving me to Askham Grange, just outside York, and provided I keep my nose clean I'm up for parole in a couple of months. Jo, did you have anything to do with this? And if you did I can't think why. At my trial you spoke movingly about what happened all those years ago, and no one doubts that it helped, but I murdered your friend Andie Bolam, and there could be no reason for me to expect anything but contempt and hatred from you.'

'I hope, Nikki, that I feel those things for no one and I don't for you. As it happens Andie was never my friend, but my stalker. As with many journalists there was a fine line in what she said between truth and convenient lies. She wanted lesbian sex with me because she wanted to write the story in the papers and would have enjoyed the glory of her by line and cared nothing for what it might do to me. Yours was a totally defensive action, protecting the horror of the past coming to the light of day. If I am asked to speak at your parole hearing, that is what I shall say. And why do I do these things, when I do not do them for others, and especially when I live across the road from the woman you caused such pain and unhappiness to, is because there was once a little girl who's life could have been so very different, but who also lived in a prison for years and years and for whom being here is simply the continuity of being imprisoned ever since that bastard raped you. I shall want to stay in touch, Nikki, if you will let me.'

Nikki couldn't reply for her tears. Eventually she summoned up the courage to say, 'I love you, Jo, I hope you know that. You are the only person in my life who has shown love to me.'

'I'm not going to stop, Nikki and I might fly up to see you in Yorkshire.'

'O God, Jo, you are such a show-off.'

Jo stood by the huge doors until they opened and share a joke with one of the officers she often saw when visiting Nikki. She walked towards her car and that was when she spotted them: two large and unpleasant men she had seen in Chelmsford, men who almost certainly were part of the retinue of Ivan Alexandrov. They were walking towards her with menace written on their faces.

Jo kept her car keys in her hand and was grateful the car had not yet been de-policed. She turned towards them.

'Ah, lesbian bitch, not so mighty without your girlies around you, are you? And especially now you have left the police and without access to help. Do you remember the face of Anna Groom? Well, in a very short time, yours will look just like that, and not be so pretty for your fellow lesbian cows to enjoy ever again.'

Jo knew she needed just a little time longer.

'Tell me,' she said, what is it that so terrifies you about female sexuality? Is it because you fear that women will not want what you have between your legs which you feel is so wonderful, and we don't, and can manage without. So you are left forcefully screwing Alexandrov's whores to try to prove something to yourself, if not them, that your penis is not redundant. Because there must be a reason why you are terrified of women as a whole, and hate them, and lesbians especially.'

'Shut your fucking face, bitch and now we're going to change it for ever.'

And hugely to Jo's relief, that was the precise moment when two police cars with blue lights pulled into the prison car park. The two men ran for their vehicle but were rammed in by the two cars, and the two were quickly handcuffed and placed one each in the two police vehicles.

The sergeant came towards Jo which a huge smile on his face.

'I believe I can call you Jo from today, but you're off to a bad start back in civilian life. How come you still have your police emergency key fob?'

'They haven't taken it off me yet and I feared it might not still work but it did, I'm pleased to say. Thank you so very much for responding so quickly. I imagine you'll be wanting a statement.'

'Probably not. We've been on the look out for this couple of bastards. Will you be wanting to claim a reward?'

Jo laughed.

'No, but I'm intrigued to know how they knew I would be here today and I shall ask the SCU to try and find out. The other thing I want from you, sergeant, is your permission to give you a kiss. I'm a great admirer of the police service and it's my way of thanking you. And who knows, perhaps it's your first ever kiss from a lesbian.'

Jo stepped up to the sergeant and kissed him firmly on the lips. The other officers were stunned to see it.

'Wait 'til I tell my wife,' he said.

'Wait 'til I tell mine!' said Jo.

As she drove home, Jo called Frankie.

'Sorry, but you can't have your job back and I knew it wouldn't be long before we heard from you begging for it.'

'Thanks for those encouraging words, Superintendent, but I want to report a crime.'

Jo told Frankie what had happened, who grasped its significance immediately.

'Changing the subject completely, Jo, I ought to call an old friend, Kelly Jones, and see how she's doing.'

'What a great idea, Frankie. Give her my love.'

'Of course. I'll give you a ring some time.'

Thanks. Bye.'

Katia excelled herself on the cookery front, amazing Chloe with wonderful tastes, even with something as apparently simple as sausage and mash. During the meal nothing was said about the farm, but once they left the table and were sitting comfortably, they began. Chloe had brought the farm books and had them by her side.

'There are those in farming who say that in practical terms you'd be better off simply using your money as fuel on a fire, that farming is in trouble in so many ways that you will lose money every day, and that farming is getting so very little support from government. Before Brexit farms received EU subsidies based on acreage, but the payments of the interim period have already been cut from between 5% and 25% before they are cut completely over the next five years. Then In future, there will be payments of "public money for public goods" – that is, farmers taking measures to restore nature, nurture the soil, improve air and water quality, and provide habitats for wildlife, in return for taxpayer-funded support under a system of environmental land management contracts, or ELMs. Interestingly, the only animals referred to are not cows, sheep or pigs, milk and meat, but wildlife.

'Things have been getting worse for some time. Supermarket prices for milk give us no profit, and what a difference even 1p would assist. It costs more to shear than to sell wool. More and more farmers are getting out and everyone is being forced to diversify. We haven't done because my dad felt he couldn't and that's why he wants out.'

'And did you have thoughts about or even plans for diversification?' asked Jo.

'I had one or two ideas but all of them require capital investment and I am not a financial wizard or even a financial novice. I drive a tractor, a combine harvester, milk cows and look after sheep and pigs, and they're all things I love, but we now have difficulties when it comes to selling our animals. At the two main livestock markets in in Norwich and Colchester, which we use, vegan protesters block the road forcing vehicles to stop and drivers are photographed and have abuse hurled at them, and the police apparently have to allow them to do this as the law says they have a right to protest.'

'So, Jo, why on earth would you want to do this? You'd be better off coming to a convent with me.'

'As I told Darcey on the phone shortly before I got home this afternoon after what had been a very eventful day, the MOD have given approval to my offer of £2.8 million, and would seek to make your dad an offer in excess of what he hopes for in the animals and equipment sale meaning it would cancelled. I gather most such sales are often disappointing in the capital raised.'

'Always, because the purchasers know the seller will take what is offered and therefore do not offer much.'

'If I was to offer double what he might hope to make, how much would that amount to?'

'But why would you do that?'

'Because I want desperately to convince his daughter that Darcey and I are completely in earnest about this, in the hope that she will remain as farm manager, in total control not just of what is, but might also be in terms of diversification. So how much is your dad hoping for at the sale?'

'He will be pleased to get £25,000.'

'Darcey and I will offer him £50,000.'

'Do you have limitless funds, Jo?' asked Chloe.

'No, you can't have a new pair of shoes.'

Everyone laughed.

'No, of course not, but enough for this investment for our future and for that of Josie and Ollie and any others that might come. I suffered for this money but I never sought it. It was what I was paid for the humiliations and pains brought upon me by my former wife and it gives Darcey and I the future together we both crave and which has taken a long time to arrive.'

'When do you have to let the MOD know?'

'When the farm manager says yes.'

'And if she doesn't?'

'Then we shall have to start again.'

'I bet that when they saw you coming to interview them, criminals tried to hide under the table!'

'When my darling Jo was interviewing I used to hide under the table as well. It could quite crowded!'

Chloe stood and gathered her books.

'Do you want me to leave these so you can terrify yourselves?'

'Once you have made up your mind, Chloe, I might ask an accountant to frighten me further, but we already trust you so much that I doubt even then we shall need anything more than your direction. And we both hope you will be willing to teach us what is necessary.'

'I may remind you of those words during lambing when you will work very hard ending each shift filthy, smelly and knackered.'

'Sounds like a night shift as a PC on the streets of Norwich,' said Darcey with feeling, causing them all to laugh.

'I've got your coat in my flat,' said Katia, who led Chloe away, causing Darcey and Jo to give the other a knowing look and smile. They went into the kitchen and loaded the dishwasher.

'I don't understand why sausages and mash when I make them, don't turn out like Katia's,' said Darcey.

'Ah but there are things we make together that cannot be surpassed anywhere.'

Chloe and Katia sat together on her bed.

'Is Jo always quite so persuasive?'

'She couldn't persuade her great love Ellie to live, nor to prevent Marie from being a traitor and liar as she set out to destroy Jo, but I know no other person so wise except in the matters of her own heart. People easily fall in love with her. But those of us who know the pair of them know that Darcey and Jo were made for each other - a match made in heaven.'

'And you want to stop me getting to heaven as a nun.'

'You know, I'm sure, that I am in love with you. I can't help it and I can't stop it. Since meeting you I have been unable to stop thinking of you. You know enough of me to know I'm wounded by my past, but Chloe, I love you and believe you can make me whole.'

'I've never had a boyfriend or girlfriend. On a farm, caring for dad, it has just not been possible, and who wants to go out with a stinky farm girl anyway? That means I've never heard those three words before, but if what I have been feeling inside since meeting you is anything to by, whereby I can't stop thinking about you, and all I want is to be with you, and if that is love, and remember Katia, I'm a real beginner, then I'm shocked, amazed and delighted to say I love you too.'

Darcey was first up and the children slept on with their week off school. She looked out of the window at the side of the house. Fiona's car had gone, as she had expected, but so had Katia's, which was most unusual. She shrugged, made some tea for her and Jo and returned to bed wearing nothing at all.

'I heard Chloe leave,' said Jo, 'shortly after we came to bed. She has to be up for milking, but I didn't hear Katia's car leave but no doubt she'll be back sometime.'

'You've had the chance to sleep on it, Jo. What thoughts are you having?'

'The best thing was that she didn't spare us the negatives. In fact she didn't bring much other than the negatives. And I'm glad about that. We need to know those things though even a little about the joys would have been welcome.'

'Yeah, but we've had a lifetime like that, Jo.'

'True, my lovely darling. Now, wrap yourself round me so your's and my body are one.'

An hour or so later, their door opened and Ollie came in, pulled back their duvet and got in, the first time Darcey had experienced Ollie's apparent ability not to notice she and his mum were naked, as if he simply expected it.

'What are we doing today, mum?'

'What do you fancy?'

'Josie fancies a couple of days staying with her dad so she can visit the shops. I'm happy to go with her, if that's alright with you, but is there any chance we can fly?'

It will mean three calls. First to Nathan to see if he can have you, second to Jude, to see if she can meet the plane and take you to Nathan's, and third to Plaistows Airfield to see if they will have have me. But I'll give it a try.'

As she got out out of bed and put on her dressing gown, she heard Katia's car arrive back, and before making her calls waited for Katia, who when she came in looked surprisingly alert.'

'You're either up early or very late to bed,' said Jo.

'It's the former. I woke at about 5:00 and went to the beach at Aldeburgh to see the sun rise.'

'It's overcast, Katia.'

'Yes. But it still rose even if it did so invisibly.'

'She's a delight, isn't she? Chloe I mean. And she does not compromise with the truth. I don't know what you spoke about after you left last night but I can guarantee that whatever she might have said, she meant it. I can see too that she is attracted to the religious life of a covent because, presumably, it's a place where the truth is told at all times, unlike in this naughty world as some religious book describes it. I remember the effect of having to ask questions in a Greek Orthodox Community in a place called Tolleshunt Knights in Essex had on one of my officers, and mostly for that reason.'

There was the sound of a vehicle pulling up outside.

'It says on the side its a Police Mechanics Vehicle and there's a woman coming to the front door,' said Katia, just before the bell rang.

At the door was a nice young woman in a blue police overall.

'Good morning.'

'Hello, you're bright and early.'

'I stayed overnight in a hotel nearby once before, so I could make an early start.'

She lifted her piece of paper.

'Are you former Detective Chief Superintendent Dame Joanne Enright?'

'You can call me Jo, if you like.'

'I am ...'

'Marlene! Yes I know who you are. The night you stayed in the hotel was spent with Ed, one of my team, though seeing you I can see why he might have risked everything.'

'He was such a gentle and considerate lover. Does he still work in the your team?'

Jo grinned.

'Nice try, Marlene. Actually he left the Force and is now training to be a doctor and has a very lovely fiancée.'

'Shame. Ok, let's consider your car. It seems that yesterday some horrid people knew where you were when it had not been made public, so I've been sent to have a look at your vehicle and see if there's a clue. I've also been sent to dismantle your blue lights, siren and police radio, and that of former DCI Bussell.

'The most likely way someone can know where you are is by a tracker attached to the vehicle by a powerful magnet and most likely underneath. I'll get out my Floor Jack and take a look.'

'I need to go and put some clothes on.'

'I won't object if you don't.'

'I'll take that as a compliment, Marlene, but once you've found what you're looking for, bring it and show me, and you can meet my partner.'

Marlene rang the door bell about 20 minutes later and was greeted by Darcey.

'Ah, Ed's mysterious lover! Come in.'

'Did he get into trouble?'

'Well, the love bite didn't help!'

'Oops.'

'If we had needed you as expert witness he would have been in considerable trouble in court, but I do recall him saying to me when I asked what you were like, "Oh definitely expert".

'Bless!'

'Coffee?'

'White, no sugar, please.'

'So did you find anything,' said Jo, now decently dressed, coming out of their bedroom.'

'Here it is,' said Marlene, holding up a box.

'But that's a box we use.'

'Isn't it just. And there's a reason for that, it's one of our trackers. I gather you were attacked, or almost so, then you need to consider the possibility that it was a police officer or officers who set you up. I have already called someone called Frankie to let her know.'

'Thank you for that.'

'She also instructed me not to remove your blue lights and siren, nor anything else – at least for now, so you might be seeing me again, but should you see Ed again do invite him!'

'Marlene, you are terrible!'

'That's not what Ed said!'

Jo called Frankie.
'Hi Jo. I take it you've heard from Marlene,'
'I've heard all sorts of things from her. She's quite a character.'
'So I gather. Anyway, I spoke to a friend of mine in London who set about a search of earth, sea and sky and found nothing. It may be that the two men in custody might come up with something but they haven't yet, so Ahmed is going over to Peterborough to have a chat with them later, but as Marlene has found a tracker under your car she's on her way to examine their vehicle to see if there's anything to be learned from how it was tracked. In the meantime feel free to use the emergency radio, lights and siren if you need them. We'll keep you informed, Jo, but should you be flying, double check everything before take off.'

Jo pondered her options which seemed to be fewer than when she was in bed. She decided to phone the airbase and seek the help of Roy, to whom she told the story and the warning she had received.

'Oh Jo, what a pain, the last thing you need. I'll send two guys over straight away to give it a close examination. I'd be much happier, Jo, is you kept the kite here, safe from anyone interfering. I'm sure you remember the time someone was in the back of Marie's plane and hijacked her. That couldn't have happened here. So are you happy for one of them to fly it here.'

'Certainly, Roy. I'll go and meet your men.'

'Men? That's very sexist of you, Jo. Be careful you don't get arrested. You know what the police are like!'

'Thank you, Roy!'

Jo put the phone down.

23

Darcey saved the day by agreeing to take Josie and Ollie swimming, and Jo promised that if all was well with the aeroplane, she would fly them to St Albans on the following day. Just before she was ready to leave for the aerodrome, another car pulled up outside. It was Chloe, a quite unexpected visitor.

'I'm on my way to collect some feed and I found my car bringing me here.'

'Does Katia know you were coming?.

'Of course and she understands why I said to her that you and I need to talk business and farming a little more. I will see her on my way back.'

'I have to go to the aerodrome.'

'So I understand. I'd love to see your plane.'

'I can't take you up today as the engineers are coming from Lakenheath to make sure it's safe, but I'd be happy to let you see your farm from the air, if you wish.'

'Thank you. Please let me drive.'

They set off and Chloe began to speak.

'I must first of all apologise for being so completely negative last night. I think I have listened not just to my dad but other farmers at NFU meetings going on about how impossible the future is, that I'm afraid I have caught their mood when thinking about how any of us on the land go forwards. It's easy to forget those feelings of exhilaration that can come in the lambing shed or when the August sun rises over the wheat, or even....' she laughed ... 'The day the milk cheque arrives.'

'I admired you, Chloe, because you didn't go in for the soft sell. You described the worst case scenario and we needed to hear it.'

'What I didn't tell you are the ways in which there could be changes which might make a difference, the sort of things my dad has resisted every time I have mentioned them.

'First and probably hardest for him, is to get rid of our entire dairy herd. The return on milk, thanks to the supermarkets is more or less nil and wholly disproportionate to the work that has to go into them. It's sad because I like the girls, but we can't keep them. It's as simple as that.

'What I do like is Darcey's wish for alpacas and with capital investment we could even diversify into an alpaca visitor's area which I assure could be a good earner.'

'What sort of capital investment are you thinking of?'

'Fencing, a café and loos for visitors, staff to manage visitors and someone on the gate to take money. And of course, to make it work and worthwhile for people to come, the real investment would be in the animals themselves.'

'I also think we would need an area for rewilding if we are to obtain government subsidy and make it accessible to the public. There is an area not suitable for arable and without dairy we could rewild those grazing fields though what an irony that is, having for years sought to make the wild become useful, we now have to reverse it. I was too young to vote in the referendum but I could never have voted to leave EU subsidies.'

'Was it the goose that lays the golden egg?'

'No, but some who have now abandoned farming might still be doing so, not that the government are the biggest opponents of farmers. It is the idiot animal lobby, vegans and other brainless adolescents.'

'Is that the farmer or the would-be aspirant speaking?'

'As they say in Parliament: "I need notice of that question".'

They laughed together.

'Chloe, are you saying to me that you think with your ideas the farm might be sustainable, even taking into consideration the extra labour costs of a visitor centre?'

'A visitor centre and farmshop is what I have in mind, transforming half the current farm house. So to answer your question: yes, I think it can be done, because if you are the owner, and not merely the tenant, you can more or less do what you want.'

Jo thought for a while.

'Suppose I say yes, there is another matter to be resolved first. Darcey and I are quite clear that the only way we could do this would be for you to be the farm manager. We could not countenance anyone else doing it. Now if that is too much pressure and I fully understand that it might be, I truly don't want to place an obstacle between you and a vocation which these days people often regard as utterly bizarre but which I don't. If I am preventing what you believe to be true and right, Darcey and I will begin to look again, possibly at a croft in Scotland, and not feel anything but sadness at losing you, and not the farm.'

'That's not fair, Jo. I'm driving and I want to cry.'

Jo directed her to the aerodrome and showed her where to park. A short while later an aircraft of the RAF trainer flight came into land and once parked, two people, a man and a woman emerged and walked towards the hangar.

'Good morning,' said the woman. 'Compliments of the Base Commander and he says I have to point out that I am woman, as well you know!'

'Good morning, Hanne. Do let him know I will get my own back. How are you?'

'Pregnant again. For some reason despite having four degrees between us, my husband and I still haven't managed to discover how contraception works – I'm pleased to say.'

'And this will be number ...?'

'Four.'

'Congratulations. This is my friend Chloe with whom I'm hoping to work in the future now I've left the police.'

'Hi there. I taught Jo to fly and now she's learning how to teach others. Passing on the baton.'

'Hello. You have an unusual name.'

'Swedish.'

'It goes with your lovely blonde hair.'

'Yours is not so bad.'

'Thank you.

The other airman was already doing a close external check on the Pipistrel and the three walked towards him.

'I shouldn't come any nearer if I were you – just in case. There's nothing external and the door doesn't look as if it's been interfered with but I will be able to tell you better when I have the keys, Jo!'

She threw them to him. Ten minutes later he was able to say that it was all clear, but that just in case he would let Hanne fly it back to Lakenheath!

'You're a real gentleman, Justin,' she said as she caught the keys he threw to her.

'The boss asked me to give you this,' said Hanne to Jo, as she handed her a car sticker and some papers for entry to the base when she was intending to fly.'

'Thank you, and thank you, Justin, for coming. It was a security matter following my resignation.'

'Well, you take good care, Jo,' said Hanne.

'And you and number four.'

Chloe took the wheel again as they returned to Saxmundham.

'On the return journey you can tell me about the other matter.'

'The other matter?'

'I spent many hours interviewing those who didn't tell me everything, and they didn't realise I could tell when that was the case. I always knew when something was being held back, and yet very often when it was out in the open things felt a lot better. I've long been a reader of Sigmund Freud who taught me how to be a detective and also a human being. So, Chloe, my darling, tell me about the other matter, but only if you want to, though I'm not sure there's anyone else for you to talk to about it.'

'Ah well you're right about that. I couldn't speak to my dad. I thought telling him I was to enter the convent was difficult.'

Jo smiled and nodded.

'I've never had a relationship before. Running a large farm doesn't allow boyfriends, especially as when I was at school I had to get home in time to help milk the cows or to do my shift in lambing often to midnight. But you see I didn't mind, because ... well, put simply, I didn't like boys. I hated the way they boasted or made up their sexual exploits and the way they way they spoke about women and girls. There was one occasion when we were changing after gym when some entered our changing room waving their penises around, and I remember laughing and saying that compared with a bull they were nothing. So I've neither missed nor wanted a boyfriend.

'I can understand that, Chloe, from my time with male prisoners and male police officers. Some years back in the West Midlands we arrested a whole host of sex offenders including the Police and Crime Commissioner who thought rape was nothing getting worked up about as it was only a woman proving hard to get. He's currently serving ten years and reminds me of what comes out of your cows, and I don't mean milk.'

Chloe laughed.

'In a way I thought myself asexual and assumed a convent might be appropriate after my experience of *Theos*. And then I met Katia Watts. I had not been long with her when I felt my nipples harden and my vagina tingled. The former happened when I was out in the cold, but the latter had never happened. Last night, Jo, I wanted to stay the night with her, I wanted to explore every nook and cranny of her beautiful body and I longed for the same.'

'Yet, you didn't.'

'I knew that if I stayed I would never want to leave, and I had the cows to milk. I told her how much I loved her and how much I wanted to make love, and without laughing at me, but with me, she also knew why I had to get back. I discovered the meaning of the word "reluctantly".

'There are two reasons why I have needed to tell you this somewhat intimate story – the first being that I was desperate to tell someone about something wonderful. The second is more serious in terms of plans for farming. I cannot go to a convent because I have met and fallen totally in love with Katia so whatever happens I want to be with her, and I have told her that. But, Jo, I do not think you should buy the farm. In fact I genuinely feel it would be completely wrong for you to do so, a waste of you and Darcey.'

'You are happy to let the farm go at auction?'

'Not happy because it has been my home and life since I was born, but the right thing to do.'

'Are you sure, Chloe, you're not just interested in Katia for her cooking?'

'Oh no, however did you guess?'

'Because that sausage and mash last night was one of the best meals I have ever had.'

'How did she learn?'

'When she and Alice, her mum, were being hounded from pillar to post, she acquired a recipe book. As you will discover, Katia is one of the strongest people I have known, and also one of the gentlest, with depths of compassion

In The End, Love

and love you are just beginning to discover.'

'She told me last night that she loves me.'

'Do you know, Chloe, I think you should believe her. But you've not yet told me what I should be doing instead of spending £2.8 million on your farm.'

Suddenly, she put on the breaks as if in an emergency stop.

'Oh, no. I forgot.'

'Forgot what?'

'As I was coming this morning I had to stop to get some petrol. On my way back to the car, a man approached me and warmly asked if I was on my way to see Katie. I told him it was Katia and he laughed an apology. He handed me a small rucksack and said it was hers and could I give it to her. He said s he had left it when she had stayed over with him and that I should say that it came with love from Marvin.'

'Have you opened it?'

'No, and I forgot because we left almost immediately.'

'Did you recognise this man?'

'No. Never seen him before.'

'Ok, lets get out of the car and I'll make a phone call.'

Jo called Darcey who reported that shortly after they had gone two police vehicles had called wanting to speak to Katia.

'They were from the Ipswich Drug Squad and had received a tip off that Katia had a significant stash of drugs. They wanted to look round the flat and I stuck to them like limpets before they departed.'

'How is Katia?'

'She's had a lot of experience dealing with the police so she's perfectly fine.'

'I think you should call Frankie or Jodie, or both. The stash of drugs is in the back of Chloe's car and I'll let Ipswich know, and the circumstances in which they got there. This, as you well know, my love, is not aimed at Katia, but at me.'

'I realise that, but it's not for you or me to iy, but the SCU. What are you going to do now?'

We're only about a mile away and once I've spoken to Ipswich. Chloe will drive us home.'

He rang the drug squad who said they would pick up the drugs.

Jo climbed back into the car and Chloe set off.

'Where were we? Oh yes, you were going to tell me the alternative to buying your farm.'

'Oh, what a shame I haven't time and I need to get back to the farm.'

'Chloe ..!'

'Don't get impatient. I need first to talk with Katia. Oh look, here she is by the door. What good luck. Perhaps we can talk again later.'

She rushed out of the car, gave a big and knowing smile to Jo, and disappeared into the house and, presumably, into the flat. It was now the turn of Darcey, newly returned from the swimming pool, to wait by the door as Jo made her thoughtful way into the house with her.

'I had to wear a swimming cap, would you believe it,' complained Darcey.

'But you've got no hair.'

'That's what I tried to tell them but they insisted that being a female I would have to wear a cap.'

'Josie and Ollie stood up for me but to avail.'

'It still looks simply incredible to me.'

'Thank you, my darling. I know I can always rely on you.'

'But from now I shall demand you wear a swimming cap in bed!'

'Of course, what else.'

'Oh nothing else, please!'

After telling again the story of the drugs on the back seat, and Darcey repeating the story of the drugs squad, Jo began to tell Darcey about Chloe's's thoughts about their hopes for farming.

'Oh Jo, that must have been very disappointing for you.'

'In a way, though there's more to come from Chloe when she and Katia have done some talking or whatever it is that the young do at this time of day.'

'Did she give you a clue?'

'No. And anyway it's you and I who have to make the decision, not her, no matter how wise her words. The more I hear and read about farming makes me wonder whether we shouldn't forget this altogether and consider other possibilities, although at the present time I must confess I have no idea what they might be.'

'We could possibly open a swimming pool in which ladies are allowed to swim without a cap.'

'I think that, even then, some busybody from a government department will come along and prosecute us. For now I need a cup of tea.'

'I'll make you one. By the way, Frankie's on her way and that reminds me, there's some post for you on the dining table.'

Jo waited for the tea to come, and then she picked up one of the letters which was a thick plain white envelope, and tore it open, only to find another white envelope inside, bearing the legend on the rear: "From the Prime Minister".

'Oh, shit,' said Jo. 'There's no way I want to open this', and handed it to Darcey. 'It has to be opened but I can't do it. Please.'

Darcey tore open the flap and unfolded the letter, and quickly read it.'

'It's ok, my love, it's not important. You have been nominated to a crossbench seat in the House of Lords to be announced in the New Years Honors List. You have to return the accompanying letter accepting and deciding on the place of your title. As I say, it's not important.'

Jo had gone white.

'But this can't be, my darling. They will want me to be a working peer and I don't want any kind of public role. All I want is to live with you, Josie and Ollie. I don't want to be a politician of any kind.'

'Don't you fancy being Baroness Enright of Saxmundham and appearing on the television?'

'I certainly don't. O God, what a bloody nuisance.'

'Jo, it's only a nuisance if you feel you have to accept. Otherwise all you need to do is to reply politely and say No. I know you will wonder whether duty should come first and see what it is the government might want of you, which is most likely to be on some sort on commission on matters relating to your expertise, which is life in the police force. You might even, and almost probably, will be asked to chair such a commission, and at the end of the work you will produce a report which will be received by parliament, and like most other such reports, be well spoken of and then forgotten. Surely that's all that's left for the House of Lords to do.

'And there's another point. To be a member of the House of Lords demands spending a great deal of time in London to attend the House, and that will demand a flat, and that's before you begin to travel and meet others on a commission. And wouldn't there be a great irony if you found yourself serving as the parliamentary mouth for Belinda's new commission, seeing a great deal more of her than you would of me? But I think that this is the work of Dani Thomas, whose spokesperson you would be in the Lords. I think it is she who almost certainly nominated you to the Home Office, who in turn informed Downing St. She may have a new girlfriend, but it has always been you she wants.'

'Darcey, may I remind you that you are not a detective any more and just because you have solved this in record quick time, it doesn't mean you can look quite so smug. And, there's another thing. Why did you even think for a moment that I would choose to do anything in which I would be separated from you. I've waited years for us to be together and I'm not going to chuck it over for something as utterly unappealing as this, Dani or no Dani. You, and you alone, are my life now, and to prove it I might even go out this afternoon and buy you a bathing cap!'

She turned round and at that moment caught sight of Chloe and Katia staring at them.'

'Oh hello,' said Jo.

'Tell me,' said Katia, 'are bathing caps what you buy to show your love? Can you get them in a shop or do they only come from Amazon?'

'How much have you heard?' asked Jo.

'Hardly anything,' replied Katia, 'apart from the invitation to go the House of Lords as a Baroness, probably at the behest of Dani Thomas who is clearly still dreaming up ways to get you for herself, and your telling Darcey to stop being a detective, which would be like telling Chloe to stop being a farmer, and then speaking of your love that almost moved me to tears, which was then utterly lost in some rubbish about a swimming cap which Darcey needs like a bull needs milking. Apart from that we heard nothing, did we.'

'Nothing,' said Chloe, suppressing laughter unsuccessfully, and all four caught it.

'Come and look at the letter "dictated by the Prime Minister and signed in his absence". I think I will have it framed and mounted in a cowshed, so they can enjoy looking at it when they they are being milked.'

'There may be problems there, Jo. Katia and I have been talking and we have quite different plans for you to consider and then accept..

'Surely we consider and then decide?'

'Of course, how silly of me. It's just that these plans are a little like the three-card trick. Consider alternatives by all means, but there is only one you will choose. Unfortunately I haven't time now, so it will have to wait. Bye, bye my love,' she said to Katia and kissed her.

'Sorry, Chloe. That's not possible. A police officer called Superintendent Wawszyczk will be here very soon and she will need a statement from you about the person who gave you the drugs. She won't take long so come and have a cup of tea with a potential Baroness.

24

Frankie was gentle with Chloe and was able to let her go.

'Someone's after you, Jo. Marlene the engineer reported that your police tracker had been followed by police equipment in the car by the men who came to Peterborough. I'm doing a search of cars from all over that who might have lost theirs, whether through theft or following a collision. Our new administrator is good, but but not quite as fast as Kelly was, so it may take a little while for us to find this out. Then we have two stages of what has happened today. How many people know that Katia lives here, and secondly how many know she's in a relationship with Chloe? And is there anything else I ought to know?'

'You might be interested in this,' said Jo handing Frankie her important letter. Frankie read it through and smiled.

'You know it's bogus,' she said.

'Of course. Since when have Honours been spelled without a "u"?'

'But it might well have been aimed at making you look stupid, not least after your recent brush with the Foreign Office.'

'Do you think, Frankie, that these three incidents might be related, and somehow a consequence of my minor disagreement with that particular arm of government?'

'If they are, and I have to keep an open mind, I understand you have some friends who might be able to root out what's going on. There are other possibilities, of course, as there always are for police officers, notably some of those we've put away wanting some revenge, but this doesn't have that sort of feel.'

'You're right. Changing the subject completely, I haven't spoken to Sharon and Kim for ages. I should call them and see how they are getting on.'

'Do let me know how they are,' said Frankie.

Jo smiled at Frankie.

'I'm afraid you're not up to your usual standard, Frankie. More often that not when you come to Saxmundham you arrest someone, and usually the vicar.

'Promotion's made me soft!'

* * *

With Frankie departed, once again talk returned to the question of what Chloe had in mind farm-wise.

'All I know', said Katia, 'is that she is totally opposed to you buying her dad's farm because she feels it will be a case of throwing good money after bad and that she has a much better idea she wants you to think about and then agree to.'

'Yes, I managed to get that much.'

'It's still farming, but even as she was describing it to me I was lost, but in case you hadn't realised this before now, she's quite a special lady and I think it will be worth weighing her words.'

'And I know,' said Jo, 'doing what she says.'

'And you haven't long. Remember she's due to enter a convent before long, so we have to get it sorted.'

'Sorted?' said Darcey, 'Don't you mean we have to agree?'

'Same thing. You're going to have to trust her big time, but her judgement is reliable.'

'You mean we can see that by her having fallen in love with you.'

'Oh Darcey, I've never had you down as a cynic.'

Josie and Ollie came to join them.

'Is there anything to eat, mum? asked Josie, allowing the conversation to de dominated by thoughts about food, and arrangements for the trip to St Albans on the following day.

Anna had gone into Chelmsford to do some shopping and was delighted to meet Dorn as fellow members of the smashed-in face club.

'You're looking good,' said Anna.

'Well, so are you. What a wonderful lady that surgeon is. I've often seen photos of before and after plastic surgeons have been at work and it truly is wonderful, little thinking that it might happen to me one day. And I owe a great deal to that detective woman, Darcey.'

'She's left the police now.'

'You're kidding?'

'No. It's rather wonderful really. For a very long time, Darcey had been in love with the detective at the head of the team, Chief Superintendent Enright, and it was mutual, even though both made things extremely difficult by marrying others, even though everyone in the team knew the reality of their intense love for each other. Now at last it's happened.'

'I shall be in tears in a minute.'

'The more I've learned about it, tears of joy seem appropriate. But tell me, Dorn, at least that is if you wish to, how it was you ended up working for Alexandrov as you did?'

'As a whore in Chelmsford, you mean? Well, it wasn't always like that... There was time when I was not engaged in the oldest profession but a different profession altogether. I went to Reading University, where I read

History, after which I became Secretary to one of my professors, one of my tasks being to prepare manuscripts for publication. Then came the big mistake. He was writing about the Russian misadventure in Chechnya and invited me to come and make notes at his meeting with Alexandrov. I will admit to being flattered by the Russian's interest, and ended up in his bed, and then the beds of two of his scum men. It was a short but terrible journey to what the police call being a "tom". I decided to put an end to it and you know how warmly that was received which, like you, it took the skills of Miss Dawson to correct.'

'Have you any idea what you might do next?'

'None at all.'

'Have you thought of the Criminal Injuries Compensation Authority? I would be willing to represent you and although it can take up to 18months, you would receive a considerable amount.'

'But wouldn't what I was doing count against me?'

'It would have nothing to do with it.'

'Are you doing the same for yourself?'

'It's more complicated if it is a solicitor applying. Dorn, would you interested in a job working with me and another young woman, in Bury St Edmunds or, possibly also, in Cambridge? I am having to transfer my practice away from London and ideally I would like two branches. We will find you a flat and you would be one of my two solicitor's clerks, working with Katia. I'm not ready to get going just yet, but I'm hoping to start in a couple of weeks' time. Might you be interested?

'Why would you do this for me?'

'Why not? Look at what we have both been through, though it's nothing compared with what Katia has endured. That gives all of us unique experience. I want to make our practice especially women-friendly. It's important women can go to a solicitor and know they're not up against it because they're having to deal with a man. We won't turn men away, but I would hope most of our clients will be woman. You will be bringing a great deal of sometimes unusual experience. Interested?'

Frankie pulled into the garage and parked, but not near the pumps. She looked around as saw what she hoped to see. She entered the shop.

'Good afternoon,' said the young girl attendant. 'Can I help you.'

Frankie produced her warrant card.

'I'm Detective Superintendent Frankie Wawszyczk. I would like to see your CCTV tapes from early this morning.'

'Today's will still be running, I'm afraid.'

'Then stop it.'

'I can't do that.'

'Can't or won't.'

'Don't you need a warrant or something to do that?'

'Obstructing a police officer in the performance of her duties is a serious offence and would make we wonder what you might be hiding.'

'Nothing, I'm hiding nothing.'

'Then take me to the recording machine and I will stop it.'

Once there she stopped and removed the tape, and immediately replaced it with one still to be used.

'There you are, it's recording again, so you can go back to your work, though I have a question. What time did you begin work this morning?'

'Half past seven.'

'Did you serve a woman farmer?'

'Chloe? Yes. I've known her all my life, and if you're going to accuse her of anything, don't, because she's one of the best people you could ever meet.'

'I agree. I'm more concerned with a vehicle that might have come in at the same time, the driver of which you might have seen give her a small bag.'

'I saw it all, though I'm not convinced she was all that happy about taking it from him.'

'Can you describe him?'

'He was wearing a smart suit and in his 40's, dark hair.'

'And his car?'

'Very nice BMW, dark.'

'Did he get petrol?'

'Only after Chloe had gone. Paid with a £50 note. I'd never seen one before.'

'I don't suppose you were able to get his registration number.'

'Course I did.'

She showed Frankie where she had written it down, and although not much given to smiling, looking at the name badge of the attendant, for once smiled broadly.

'I'm not joking when I say this, Sophie, but I would like you to give consideration to becoming a police officer. As an observer and witness you are superb. This is my card, and when you've decided we can talk about it. I'm taking the tape but I hardly need it having listened to you.'

'How ever do you pronounce your name?'

'Don't you speak Polish?' asked Frankie wickedly.

'Look, I have trouble enough with English.'

Unlikely though it was, Frankie smiled a second time.

'Vuffchek.'

'Yeah, I thought it probably was!'

Even more unlikely, Frankie laughed, and left.

The two ne'er-do-wells who had threatened Jo were, singly, facing Ahmed and Tommy, who towered over them. The preliminaries over, Ahmed addressed the first.

'Tell me.'

'Tell you what?'

Ahmed sighed audibly and briefly closed his eyes.

'We are trying to work various things out with regard to you and your mate and as yet we haven't decided. Intimidation and threatening behaviour towards our former senior officer and driving an illegal vehicle. Linked to the name of your former employer and his other thugs who will be away for a while, I suspect you will be joining them.

'The alternative in return for something simple would do away with all that both for you and for me. You wouldn't credit how much is involved in getting you charged and off to the magistrates and then to prison, so you'd be doing me a favour too. Really simple, and you'll be on your way home in a very short time.'

'What's simple then?'

'The name of who it was asked you to visit Peterborough and where you collected the car from.'

'And if I give you the answer I can go home?'

'Please excuse my rudeness, but it's not you we're interested in, and trust me, whoever it was will never know.'

'How can I trust you?'

'Look, I'm not doing a deal with Mr Big, am I?'

'He was a politician, I think. He said the copper was a danger to the country but that they couldn't use the army to get at her but in addition to what he wanted us to do, other things might be done to make sure she would be keeping her mouth shut in future. He added that being a lesbian she was a pervert and it was time that real men fought back.'

'How much?'

'250 each.'

'Not bad ... Name!'

'Victor.'

'Victor who?'

'No idea.'

'You are going to have to try harder, very much harder,' said Ahmed.

'I'll take him to the cells,' said Tommy, standing.

'Now hang on a minute, 'I've given you the name; you said I could walk if I did that.'

'And when you give me the name, you can.'

The man was evidently thinking hard.

'Victor Lewin, and he gave me a mobile number to use when we'd done the job.'

'I assume you weren't able to call. Write the number down.'

'One final question. When he made contact where did he meet you?'

The refreshments café in St James' Park.'

'Ok, on your way.'

The second mostly confirmed all that the earlier man had said but was able to give a description of Victor Lewin. When reported back to Frankie it was almost identical to that on the VHS from the garage, and before the man was let go, he was shown the tape and confirmed the identity. Frankie decided to wait until both were at home before calling Kelly though she made a point of inviting Sally, Kelly's replacement to join her for some supper, and then get her to do the competing that Kelly suggested.

Kelly directed Sally to a data bank for all those working at the Foreign Office which contained photographs of all staff other than ministers. He was called Martin Dewberry and low-grade, working in Belo-Russian department, and when looked up on the DVLA website, he had used his own car when he had approached Chloe, so hardly a professional.

Frankie called Jodie and shared the findings of the day.

'In view of the fact that he was handing such a weight of drugs we should do what we would for any other and arrange an early morning raid and bring him up to base for questioning. Do you want me to arrange that or will you?'

'I'll do it boss and I'll attend. It's not so far – Brentwood.'

'Would you like me to sit in when we interview him.'

'That would be good. By the way Sally's here with me and checking FO links between him and his superiors to see if any stick out like a sore thumb.'

'Is that legal, Superintendent?'

'Wishing you and Anna a good night, ma'am!'

Jodie moaned. Frankie was showing all the signs of being a second Jo!'

Once Sally had gone, Frankie decided to call Jo. 'Your two friends have provided us with useful information and because they didn't actually assault you, in return we have released them. I did however get CCTV pictures of Chloe and the man who gave her the package of drugs, and we know who he is, some minor nobody in the Foreign Office. Using her ingenuity, with a little nudge from her predecessor, Sally has found links to a more senior official whom, we think, might be the originator of the plot against you and yours.'

'That sounds to me like very good work, Frankie, though that's what I would expect of you. Are you going for an early morning alarm call?'

'For the lesser of the two to see what he reveals and he handled enough drugs to Chloe to put him away for a long time, but of course you and we want the man at the top.'

'Forgive me if I'm teaching granny to suck eggs, but wear your uniform. In that way the other officers will know you're not just a nosy passer by.'

'Somebody called Enright taught me that some time ago, and I always follower her advice.'

'Oh well, there's little hope for you.'

Sadly for both Katia and Jo, Chloe was unable to come this evening as there was an important meeting of the NFU she had to attend, but Katia had turned up the papers about the croft in Scotland that Jo's dad had received.

'There would be an enormous amount of sorting things out, if we followed this, Jo' said Darcey. 'What would we do about the house and schooling, for example, and how on earth would we manage without the guiding hand of

Chloe?'

'I think I'd rather forgotten that romantic possibility, not least because every time I listen to Chloe I think we should take up something quite different from farming.'

'I know what you mean, but I also know, my dearest darling, that anything you put your mind to, you could achieve.'

Early in the morning, dressed in her uniform, Frankie drove to Brentwood and left her car some 150 metres from the target house. The team made light work of collecting the target and putting him in a van for transportation to a holding cell in Cambridge, where he would later be interviewed. Before she left she went into the house, where officers discovered a significant amount of drugs, which would be handed over to the Essex drug squad. His computer was disconnected, bagged with his mobile and taken by Frankie for Sally to work on.

Sadly had worked for Northumbria Police before responding to Jo's invitation to join and the team as their technical expert. Although not having been in prison as had Kelly, and therefore lacking a certain unspecified something she acquired there, and not quite as fast as her predecessor she was clearly superb at what she did. Knowing that Frankie would be in early, she set herself ready to work on what her boss would bring to her.

It proved to be straightforward: a PC running Windows 10 with next to no safeguards other than the password which Sally made light work of. The important emails he had deleted were of course just waiting for her to discover. Some were to do with consignments of drugs which he was delegated to pass on to others, but some to do with the attempt to bring about injury to Jo and her good name, as the response to her treating the FO with contempt, a humiliation they were determined to avenge. Sally chose to ignore the porn she found there. A cursory glance revealed nothing illegal and in any case their concern in the present was with more pressing matters.

Sally printed out the emails and then set about finding who the interlocutor was. It was not a government IP, so presumably the messages were sent from a PC in the home, but neither receiver nor sender seemed to have the first idea of security, and Sally rapidly had the IP of the sender, and a little while longer knew where the machine could be found and the name of the sender.

Before they drove out to Cambridge, Frankie and Jodie discussed how they should handle the arrest of Sir Norman Williams, an under Secretary at the Foreign, Commonwealth, and Development Office Sally's computer discovery.

'To arrest him at work might be difficult and cause something of a scene,' said Frankie.

'Yes, you're right, which is why that is what we should do. It's about defending the integrity not just of Jo, but of the law which government itself must abide by.'

'You've been listening to your resident law officer Anna.'

'What an outrageous statement, Superintendent. Anna is now our legal advisor, and she said that what I am suggesting is not against the law and may indeed enhance it.'

'That's excellent news.'

Steph was back in harness and glad to be. It gave Frankie and Jodie the opportunity to see how she and Ahmed could work together. Steph would lead and Ahmed take over if necessary.

Before her maternity leave, Steph had learned from Jo, the art of the disarming smile, and following the naming of those present she decided to reveal it. It was often possible to see the effect it had on those being questioned as they softened slightly.

'Mr Dewberry,' said Steph, 'may I call you Martin?'

'Please do. I've never liked the name myself but perhaps many of us don't like what our parents inflict on is.'

Steph smiled, and understandably so as she had already won the competition – he was talking.'

'In a way, Martin, what we are doing here today is to engage in a matter of confirmation. Most of the evidence we need to put together in order to wake you this morning is straightforward. For example the photographs from the CCTV at the garage when you approached Chloe and asked her to hand over to Katia Wallis a parcel containing drugs. Equally the two thugs you instructed to beat up Dame Joanne Enright but were prevented from doing so, and the bogus letter from Downing St on your computer, and you were also identified from your Foreign Office mug shot accessible on line. So we know we are dealing with the right person.

'However, there are things we still need to know, and which, if you are able to help us, will serve to advance your course when you are in court.'

'In court? Do you really think it will come to that?'

'Yes, but that does not automatically mean prison if we come to see that you were the instrument of another. So tell me the precise nature of your relationship with Sir Norman Williams.'

Martin froze for a moment or two.

'In terms of life in the FO there was no relationship. He functions at a much higher level than me. Outside we are both keen supporters of Saracens Rugby Football Club and that is how we came to know one another, buying drinks in one of the bars. After a while he offered to come pick me up and we would would chat about all sorts of things apart from matters to do with work – we were both strict about that. He admitted to being ambitious, not just for himself though he was that, but for the FO which he believed to be the finest branch of government.

'One Saturday I indicated that I could not come again as I had foolishly got myself into serious gambling debts. It was in the same week that the detective woman took on the FO and won which apparently outraged the upper echelons and gave Sir Norman a chance to advance his own cause and defend the honour of the FO. To him £15,000 didn't seem as great an amount as it did to me, and so he offered to pay off the debts if I would be willing to help the FO right a very definite wrong.

'Just three things would be required. The first was to make contact with the two men of the Alexandrov gang who had escaped when their boss was taken and inform them that a beating was required, especially of the face, and that they were to pick up a car which contained a police tracker mechanism and follow a tracker attached to the car of the woman they needed to deal with a lesbian former copper who had put their boss away.'

'Where was the car?'

'In a lay-by in Chipping Ongar, the keys on the rear offside wheel.'

'But you used your own car to hand over the drugs to Chloe at the garage between Woodbridge and Saxmundham.'

'I'm more used to my own car, though perhaps that was a mistake.'

'Perhaps you're just not cut out for a life of crime, Martin! How did you know the lady in question would need to stop for petrol?'

'I didn't. That was just good fortune, though in the light of the CCTV camera, bad luck. I had been told to bump into the back of her vehicle and make the transfer then.'

'And when the transfer was made ?'

'I returned home and my gambling debts were paid off.'

Steph looked at Ahmed and they both looked at the solicitor.

'As a result of a legal search of your house, illegal drugs were found.'

'But only for my own use. I would never sell them to others.

'Until Sir Norman Williams made his offer. We shall be making further enquiries as to whether you provided drugs to others in order to earn enough money to pay off your debts. And who gave you the consignment you sought to get to Katia Wallis?'

'No one as such. I found them in the well of my car leaving work. I assumed they came from Sir Norman as he was the one who gave me my instructions.'

'You have been extremely co-operative in providing us with information and that will be greatly to your advantage. However, I shall be recommending to my superior officers that in speaking to the Crown Prosecution Service you will be charged with various offences which will require that you appear before magistrates at a date to be agreed. Once this is agreed you will be released under the terms of what is known as post-charge police bail, full details of which will be made known to you.

'The interview is now terminated.'

Rod Hacking

25

They were now in early November, with the darkness following the change of clocks, and still no decision had been made, and it was proving difficult to get Chloe to come and reveal her thoughts about their future. Chloe had not announced any changes to her own intentions to enter the Convent on 1st December, either to Katia or Jo and Darcey. And to add to the confusion, now they had survived what increasingly seemed to be a revenge assault on them by someone in government, later today Dani and her new partner, Louise were coming to to stay, but first Jo was due to take Josie and Ollie to St Albans, via her new hangar at the airbase. Darcey was coming too, leaving Katia at home in the hope that Chloe would come soon.

It was s short flight and Jo soon would have to undergo her tests before she could advertise flying lessons, but she was looking forward to that though it might all end if Chloe suddenly decided they buy a farm on Orkney!

Jude and a quite exotic lady were waiting for them. Jo knew that Abby was a nurse at the maternity hospital, but she certainly didn't look like it. Her hair was astonishing, not as sexy, she thought, as Darcey's, no! Not anywhere near as sexy as Darcey's but she was impressed or appalled by how much flesh Abby was showing on a cold November day, but Jo could see just how proud she was to be with Abby, and Abby could barely keep her hands off Jude.

'I know it's silly,' said Darcey, as they were up to 3,000 ft on the return journey, 'But I felt such joy for Abby and Jude, that they have found one another. The wicked me however, hopes that Jude will go back into the Church and take Abby with her, dressed as she is.'

'Did you fancy her?'

'No. I think she will have to get past the immediate period of being "out", though I understand why it is like that for her, but the real problem is that if she stays undressed like that she will be dead by Spring. Oh, how wonderful for her to discover and celebrate.'

'It wasn't like that for us though,' said Jo, after responding to ATC instructions before making her approach.'

'That's because we never knew anything different. No change was required..'

'True, though I've never told you but following an inspection at Police College when I shared the women's changing room rather using the officer's rooms, I had already noticed you and made sure I could see you as we changed, and nearly died of ecstasy when I saw you in your bra and pants. It was deeply troubling, because at that time I was still married to Marie and although everyone knew she was supposed to be a stunning beauty. I knew that the person I wanted was you'

'Sorry, Willow23,' said the ATC, 'I didn't catch all that. Can you repeat?'

'In your dreams. Over.'

'I heard enough to give me dreams. Willow23, descend to 1,000 feet and begin your approach, though I doubt whether you need my advice. Out.

Jo and Darcey laughed as Jo struggled to keep her line of approach.

'Lakenheath Approach, Willow23, 1,000 ft on western approach, permission to land.'

Once on the ground Jo took the plane to its hangar and then completed the post-flight external checks. One of the officers Jo knew came over to see them.

'Jo, would you like me to show you how to turn off the transmit button in the plane?' and burst into fits of laughter.'

'O God,' said Jo. 'Am I ever going to live it down?'

'The point is, Jo, everyone on this base loves and admires you, but for us to see the human simply adds to our love for you, and although none of us have seen Darcey as you did, we all wish we had.'

'Thank you, captain,' said Darcey, 'compliments are always welcome but I'm pleased to say I'm taken.'

Jo and Darcey arrived home to find mot Dani and Louise, but Chloe, sitting on the sofa with Katia holding hands and watching something on the big tv screen.

'I've brought some sandwiches,' said Chloe. 'It struck me that you might need some nourishment after your journey to St Albans.'

'Did you meet Abby?' asked Katia eagerly.

'We did and isn't she amazing?' said Darcey. 'Perhaps they keep her on the labour ward to scare the mothers to be to get on with it, though not's fair. We both thought she was really lovely if a little over the top in her choice of lack of clothes, but we could see how enchanted Jude is with her, and I could understand why.'

'Coming out has simply transformed her existence, enabling her no longer to be just a timid girl but a woman truly herself. I guess her mum and dad are a little surprised..

'The journeys towards the discovery of our sexuality and our true existence are many and varied,' said Jo. 'We are unusual in that all four of us never thought we are were anything else but for most the process was gradual and often quite traumatic. I don't think one is more valid than another.'

'Sandwiches?' said Chloe.

'And words of wisdom?' asked Jo.

Chloe gave her an enigmatic smile.

Darcey made drinks and they sat together.

'Ok, the time has gone to let you into my thinking and to say that if you choose utterly to reject it, I shall not take it personally. I shall simply take the veil and never be seen again.'

'No pressure, then,' said Jo.

'I've spent quite some time on the telephone to my cousin Jerry who farms dairy, beef and sheep in Eskdalemuir, in the South West of Scotland. One of his best farming friends is called Rhona, the farm manager whom Jerry says is outstanding, on a mixed farm near Galashiels in the Borders. The owner of the farm is her close friend but her husband is recovering from cancer and they need to move to the south and a gentler climate. Until recently Rhona had an experienced colleague, Andrew, but he has inherited a small holding of his own and inevitably wants to leave and work there. There's a former academic called Adam who's had a lot of trauma in his life and is married to a former member of French Intelligence, and he helps out when he can.

'That's the backstory. Now the suggestion and I regret to say there is not a lot of time to get this sorted. I have already spoken to Anne-Marie who owns the farm about my dad's farm. Like you, she would be interested in buying it outright, stock included. Her present farm has two houses, in one of which Rhona lived, and shared it with Andrew. The other house is a good sized family house probably in need of a measure of modernisation. Anne-Marie dreads having to get rid of Rhona with the farm but cannot see an alternative. She confirms Jerry's view that she is outstanding. So, and this is what I have had to keep you waiting for, is that you purchase Anne-Marie's farm and both become apprentices to Rhona, as well as her boss.

Katia and I will go further than this and suggest you keep this house enabling us to ensure Josie and Ollie can complete their schooling, and I said us because Katia has succeeded in persuading me that the reality of *Theos* can be pursued properly by me without having to become a nun or at least I should give it a try, and when I am not meant to be providing her with drugs we get on well enough.

'As I've said you will need to act quickly and, presumably, fly up to see for yourself.'

'Will it be possible for me to speak to both Anne-Marie and Rhona before I endeavour to visit. There are aren't a lot of airfields around there, other than Edinburgh airport of course, but if we go and see, we'll manage. Our pipistrel is used to taking off and landing with far bigger planes that come and go from Edinburgh, so it won't feel even slightly intimidated.'

The doorbell rang, announcing the arrival of Dani and Louise. After welcoming them and letting Darcey get them a drink, Jo withdrew for a short while with Chloe into her bedroom.

'People will talk, Jo!'

'Oh, I'm used to that. I just want to thank you for what you have done. I will phone Anne-Marie and Rhona later today and say that whilst Darcey and I will need to come and see, we are very interested indeed. You also will be pleased to know that the man who unloaded drugs on to you and tried to arrange for my face to be amended and offered me a seat in the House of Lords, has been charged and will be up for the magistrates. My former colleagues are looking forward to arresting the man behind it all. I might just make the tv news again tomorrow.'

'That's so good.'

'But Chloe, my darling, you are not just good but the best and you deserve only the best in what is to come, and Katia is that. I think the world of her, so care for each other as best you can.'

Chloe had been waiting for this moment when Jo kissed her full on the lips and held her there. It was not a disappointment. They returned to the sitting room.

'Everyone, this is Chloe and allow me to meet Louise.'

Chloe greeted everyone and then left with Katia to the pub where they were having some lunch before Chloe inevitably had to get back to the farm.

'All those old people,' joked Katia.

'Yes. If they were animals I'd send them all to the abattoir.'

Katia smiled.

'In her job, Jo got pretty close to that, and I know I'm biased for obvious reasons but she's exceptional and I very much hope this farm in Scotland comes off. I would always want the best for her. My mum and I worship the ground she stands on.'

Chloe drew nearer and kissed Katia.

'I'm doing all I can to bring it about.'

'Oh Chloe, I do love you.'

Anna, Jodie and Frankie were giving thought as to the best way of arresting Sir Norman Williams. Jodie and Frankie both wanted it to be in Whitehall at his workplace in full view of his department.

'No,' said Anna firmly. 'As your legal advisor I cannot sanction that, as I am sure you both know. You would be acting solely on the basis of revenge which is no basis at all. You both know how it has to be done, with the minimum of fuss and in accordance with normal practice. I doubt that Sir Norman is sitting upon an arsenal of weapons, so just our team should be able to pull it off in such a way as even the neighbours won't know.'

'It's people like you who stop us having fun,' said Jodie.

Anna pursed her lips and jauntily raised her eyebrows.

'Really?'

Jodie blushed.

Frankie drew them back to order and the decision was made to pick him up at 6:00 on the following morning, all the team apart from Steph and Sally to be present. The arresting officers would be Frankie supported by Warren Rolle with everyone else in backup, with Frankie and Warren taking him to

Cambridge.

The afternoon and evening with Dani and Louise went well and they all got on well together. Louise had indicated that she would like to cook them all a meal as a thank you for making her feel so welcome, and the meal was worth it, not perhaps in Katia's style but very tasty. They also enjoyed some good wine brought from Norwich..

Whilst the table was being cleared, with Darcey's consent, Jo slipped into her office to telephone Anne-Marie.

'First and most important, how is your husband following his illness?'

'It was touch and go because of his extremely rare blood type until we experienced a miracle in the form of Charlotte who lived and worked on the farm and was a perfect match. He's not 100% yet and that's why we need to move south to get away from the cold that hurts him to breathe, but I'm still wanting to farm. I'm wanting to buy outright. Chloe's farm would be ideal but would be dependent on realising the necessary capital for here.'

'How much are you needing to make it viable, Anne-Marie?'

'£1½ million.'

'And preferably?'

'To do what Chloe suggests, I would think £2 million.'

'Bank of Scotland or Bank of England money?'

Anne-Marie laughed.

'I suppose we each need to see,' said Jo.

'Ah well, you see, I've seen. Chloe, who should be a land agent, invited me down because she didn't to raise your hopes until I had seen. I did and I liked what I saw. Would you like to come and see here. You will like it, I know, because I adore it.'

The only airfield I can use is Edinburgh airport and I'm willing to pay the astronomical fee they will charge me to land. If someone you know has a private airstrip you can let me know. I have a partner, in every sense of the word, called Darcey and she will be with me. How about early afternoon tomorrow? Oh, I should mention however, that there is a condition.'

Darcey and I are beginners but we want to learn. Rhona must agree to teach us.'

'She will so enjoy that and laugh at you when appropriate.'

The arrest went smoothly, as Jodie thought it would. The Civil Servant was civil throughout and bizarrely indicated the officers should take with them his PC as it contained material they would wish to see, He also invited them to look around and discover there were no drugs and that those passed on to his accomplice (a word they were all amused by) was the sum total of what he had obtained for £2,000!

It was, they all later admitted, the oddest arrest they had ever made, almost circumventing the need for interview under caution, but only almost. After breakfast, it was Jodie and Frankie who sat opposite him and his lawyer, with

Warren present to deal with the mechanics and introductions.

'Sir Norman, a couple of things I need to clarify,' began Jodie. 'The first is that you are still under caution, and the second is that whilst under caution earlier, you made certain statements about your involvement in a number of illegal activities that I would like you to repeat here even though they were written down at the time of your arrest.

'Three stand out. The first concerns drugs which you maintain cost you £2,000, and which you then passed on to your alleged accomplice. And when you passed this on, what was your intention?'

'I asked him to intercept a vehicle being driven by a young farmer of her way way to visit a friend with the intention of her taking it into the house and leaving there for the police to find.'

'Had you been spying out the comings and goings of that house, such as that you knew the young farmer would be likely to make.'

'Yes, otherwise how could I have known?'

'Let us consider for a moment your accomplice. What is his name and how do you know him?'

'Am I not supposed to say now that I am not a grass and leave you all cross and flummoxed?'

'Congratulations on your use of the correct word but as we already know the name of Martin Newberry, you need not fear the terrible recriminations of the underworld, but why him?'

'In the main because we are both supporters of Saracens and he foolishly had acquired gambling debts and I saw him as the way I could accomplish this.'

'Accomplish what?' said Frankie.

'The humbling of that interfering Chief Superintendent Enright with her ludicrous title, who had made the FO look stupid and placed herself above the elected government.

'And exactly where were you elected, Sir Norman and for what did you acquire your knighthood?'

'I received a knighthood for faithful service of the government, which is more than she did. One who overturns the government's will as she did is a traitor to my mind.'

'You cannot of course know what Dame Joanne's DBE was for because it is an official secret. What you can know is that she awarded it not in the ordinary fashion but at a closed ceremony for military awards, most of which have to remain secret but which deal with men and women who have engaged in outstanding courage and bravery. Yours was for being a time-server.'

He said nothing.

'Did you or the idiot accomplice place the tracker under Dame Joanne's car?'

'He did'.

How did you obtain the service of the two blockheads you wanted to follow her car?'

'I made contact with someone at the Alexandrov house who told me about them. I told them I was putting together a way of getting their boss out of prison, and together with money they were keen. I told Martin that he would give instructions when I was ready.'

'And the car with police equipment still on board? Not easy for a knight of the realm and true servant of the government to get hold of?'

'For the right amount it proved easier than you might think. I visited five or six wreckers and with the right sort of cash they came up with the goods.'

'I shall need to know who they were.'

'G R & Sons in Colchester.'

What instructions did you give?'

'We agreed the car would be left in Chipping Ongar and I told Martin to let the Alexandrov boys what they had to do, which was to trace, follow and scare.'

'As we understand it, the rubrics were to beat her face, and if you feel you have to deny that, it will be up to the jury to decide.'

'You know as well as I this will never come to court, and at the end of the day what have I actually done apart from being ludicrously munificent with my money. No one got hurt, no one took drugs, and basically, nothing happened other than the police decided to have another attack upon the Foreign Office echoing the attack already made by the former Chief Superintendent which itself should be referred to the Home Office for an official enquiry.'

'Norman Williams,' began Jodie before being interrupted.

'*Sir* Norman,' he said.

'Norman Williams, I shall be making immediate contact with the Crown Prosecution Service, informing them that you on beings on charges of pushing drugs and seeking illegally to plant them on another, of making use of an illegal tracking device, of hiring two men and giving instructions that the target should receive considerable injury, and other offences, seeking their agreement to charge you with them. We shall then arrange for you to appear before the magistrates and recommend that as a dangerous offender you should be transferred to prison.'

'You can't do this to me. I am a knight of the realm.'

'I suspect you won't be much longer. Recording terminated. Constable, please conduct Sir Norman to the cells.'

Anna and the other members of the team were in the AV Room.

'I expect you know that he's probably right about none of this coming to trial,' said Anna.

'Of course, but just to subject him to a tiny part of the penal process will be worth it. And we must do everything we can to keep this from the press, mustn't we, everyone, because a leak might be very embarrassing to the Foreign Office and I would find it hard to sleep at night if that were the case.'

'Don't worry, Detective Chief Superintendent, I'll do my best to help you,' said Anna with an innocent face that fooled no one!

26

As Jo made her final approach to Edinburgh from the North East, Darcey could see a number of large jets returning holidaymakers into the rain of home, but Jo was totally at ease and simply obeyed what the Edinburgh ATC told her to. After landing the Ground controller took her at least 100 miles from the airport building before letting her stop.

The Ground Controller apologised about the parking but said as she was an official government visitor there would be no landing fee and laughed when Jo informed him that her home base was Lakenheath.

Darcey noticed as Jo was doing her post-flight inspection that a far from clean green landrover had pulled up on the other side of the fence and that a jolly-looking driver was waving to her.

'Darcey?' shouted the woman as she left the vehicle.

'Yes.'

'I'm the official government welcoming party, so welcome.'

Immediately Darcey loved the accent.

'Jo's just putting the plane to bed but will be here in a moment or two.'

'You'll need me to get you out, at the gate down there on the left.'

By the time Jo came with their overnight bag and her flight bag, the other had disappeared, only to emerge when Jo and Darcey approached the gate which was opened for them.

'Hi, there, I'm Anne-Marie.'

'It's great to meet you, and I'm so pleased the Scottish government have to such lengths to wash and polish the official transport.'

This *is* washed and polished,' she replied. You should have seen it beforehand.'

Jo fell in love with the farm and the land at once, and both her and Darcey hit it off with Rhona who gave them an enthusiastic trip around the place, speaking of the cattle as her "ladies" and the many sheep as her girls.

'There is a terrible downside,' said Rhona, and led them to a different area which was fenced off"

'Look,' she said, 'the curse of my life – miniature Chinese pigs, beloved of Anne-Marie, and always escaping.'

To Darcey and Jo they seemed quite wonderful;.

'How would you feel about getting rid of them and replacing them with alpacas?'

'I would feel great about that,' said Darcey.

'But how do you get rid of Chinese pigs? Surely no other farm are going to want them.'

'You're right, but the Chinese takeaways do.'

'Oh,' said Darcey.

'Livestock going to slaughter is a given. You'll get used to it. Now some tea before milking. Adam will be here to milk with us. You'll like him and he has it in common with you, Jo, that his first wife took her own life. His wife Anaïs, used to work for French Intelligence and sadly for the rest of us she is extremely beautiful. They will be eating with us later at Anne-Marie's.'

'You mean next door to you?'

'Oh yes, so I do.

Over tea Jo asked Rhoda important financial questions about the viability of the business.

'I won't pretend it's a quick way to get rich and so much is against us, but I wouldn't exchange it for anything else. It brings me such happiness.'

'Do people ever lie in wait to shoot you or plot to beat you up or lie just for the hell of it?'

'Not yet.'

'In which case, Rhoda I'm sold. Darcey?'

'Jo, you know that being with and alongside you is all I want in my life, but to be here, learning the sheer volume Rhona has to teach us will be very heaven.'

'Can I remind of that on a bitterly cold winter's morning when I send up the hill to break the ice of the sheep to drink?

Jo and Darcey laughed but with due hesitation.

'Now,' said Rhona, 'we mustn't keep the ladies waiting. I've just seen Adam pass the window so I've put out some things for you to wear instead of what you've got on and then you can have your first milking lesson.'

In the milking parlour there was music – Mozart.

'Mozart is their favourite,' said Rhona.

'Does it increase yield?' asked Jo.

'I'm not sure how we could measure that,' laughed Rhona, 'but the ladies and Adam seem to like it.'

Jo worked with Adam, and Darcey with Rhona and it was obvious both were enjoying themselves doing so, and the end they were actually attaching the cups.

'There are some not coming in,' said Jo to Adam.

'Yes, they're in calf so won't be milking again for a little while. We keep a rota so that all get a dry period in calf, otherwise there would be no milk at all.'

Once all the ladies departed it was necessary to hose and shit-shift, as

In The End, Love

Rhona described it, taking it all over to the slurry where there were dire warnings about its dangers and the story of how a young man fell in some years ago and died.

'Always take extra care. Not long ago in Ireland a farmer fell in and his two rugby-playing sons jumped in to save him, and all three died.'

Jo and Darcey looked at one another.

'There are seasons when spreading slurry is allowed and when it is not, which have to be observed rigorously, but it marvellous fertiliser.'

The went back into the parlour and up towards the door at the end where they found Adam dressed only in his underwear and Rhona following suit.

'We have to change completely to enter the dairy but you need not do so today. We are preparing the milk to be collected first of all by being cooled and the stored milk safeguarded from any infection – hence we change out of the dirty clothes into these white uniforms, not unlike what you both must be used to wearing at the site of a crime though I expect you wore them over your clothes. We can't do that for obvious reasons. Now why don'y you go back into the house and change, and I'll be with you soon. Make yourself a drink.'

'I didn't have doubts before we set off,' said Darcey, but if I had they would be gone now. Doing that milking with Rhoda was simply glorious.'

'I totally agree. I have to do some negotiating with Anne-Marie later but I'm not even thinking of saying No.'

Jo and Darcey had been senior police officers sometimes facing great dangers at all times of the day and night – and one experience of milking a herd of ladies and both fell fast asleep in Rhona's sitting room. When the lady of the house entered and found them she laughed and woke them both up.

'I hope you both come because I think you've got the potential but sometimes the hours are long and probably demanding in a different way to those you are used to, but well done today, you've made a good start.'

She then to their complete amazement removed all her clothes and put them into the washing machine.

'Very busy apparatus this. I'll go and get a shower and then we can get ready to out for dinner with the posh people next door.'

'I can't deny it was a very pleasant sight,' said Darcey.

'You're right and yet totally unselfconscious. It wouldn't surprise me if she did the same if it was a mixed group.'

Jo and Darcey also changed and the three of them sat down for a chat together before the meal.

'I'm sure you know there is an enormous amount to learn in farming, and some of it somewhat unpleasant, such as digging maggots out of the rear end of a sheep in summer, but I truly believe it is a wonderful life. Some years back there was pressure applied to get me to train as a vet, mainly because when vets are puzzled by a large animal I can usually suggest a way forward, and of course, vets get paid well and enjoy a status farmworkers don't, but why would I want to leave this life for six years with adolescents who would mostly know far less than me, and swap this life for castrating dogs. So here I am.

'Anne-Marie recruited me when I was at Agricultural College in Cirencester and now I not only know all the farmers in the community, I know all the cattle, their mums and grandmas and ever further back, and it's the same with the sheep. This is not a plea to you to keep me on if you take over, but I promise, Chinese pigs notwithstanding, to continue to give of my best because doing my best is what makes me happiest.'

'I think, my darling Rhona,' said Jo, 'that however much we might learn and work hard, we shall never be able to match your knowledge and experience. I can only promise that, Chinese pigs included, if we come and I hope we will, you will be in total charge.'

'I hope so too, but at supper, it might be best not to mention the pigs!'

The meal was superb and the company just as good. Anaïs was as gorgeous as Jo and Darcey had been told, and her husband Adam did not resemble even slightly the fellow milker of two hours earlier. Ed was apparently much better from his cancer and expected to make an eventual full recovery, but still did not look anything anywhere near 100% well. Anne-Marie on the other hand seemed full of life and keen to get on with moving to a new life. But then came a shock.'

'Did you know you were on the six o'clock news, Jo? said Anaïs.

'What?'

'Yes. It has emerged that there was a plot by two people in the Foreign Office, both now in custody. Apparently they paid two thugs to attack you but they were caught, and an attempt was made to offload a stash of drugs in your house, followed by the arrival of the drug squad, but apparently you were one step ahead. The Foreign Secretary was asked questions in the House about it and he paid great tribute to you.'

Jo laughed.

'None of this came from me and of course it wouldn't have come from the Foreign Office. It's accurate in the sort of way the Press wouldn't have known anything about, so it must have been leaked by my former team, and I imagine it's because getting those charged through a court would have been difficult or worse, so all the team would have been told that under no circumstances was this to be leaked, and told in such a way that it meant the exact opposite, and everyone would have understood. So thank you, guys.'

Everyone laughed.

Anne-Marie left the coffee making to Ed, and she and Jo went through to her office.

'Chloe was so lovely when I went to see the farm and very honest about how things are, but has a splendid set of ideas for diversity which should enable the farm break even. She told me that she had been thinking of becoming a nun in an enclosed community until she met someone you know

In The End, Love

very well indeed, having worked some kind of miracle through an investigation 34 years old, for this person and her mother. I gather her name if Katia and you are thinking of letting live in your house if you can be persuaded to come here.

'I hope you can, primarily for the sake of my husband Ed. It was a strange miracle that means he is still with us, but we need to be away from the bitterly cold north-eastern winds. I think Suffolk would be ideal, but no pressure, Jo.'

Jo burst into fits of laughter.

'No negotiation is required, Anne-Marie. I am happy to agree to what I mentioned on the phone, that's £3 million. Are you happy with that?'

'Yes, Jo. Thank you. I suppose we ought to get solicitors to make some money at our expense.'

'Yes, but I'm more than happy to shake on it here and now Anne-Marie, if you are. Tonight's news is a reminder that I have to leave down there. There are things to sort out but I would like to move in here by early-December.'

'I totally agree. The Ministry of Defence want us to move in by then too to assure continuity on the farm, though I think we can rely on Chloe for the time being. Oh and before I forget, I've managed to find you a landing strip, and I'll give you the full details in the morning.'

'That's great, thank you.'

'Before we go back, please allow me to say two things. The first is that although you have been highly regarded as a detective and risen to the top, and are even a Dame, though she said you are not allowed to say why, you have also en route known more than a little personal tragedy and pain, but she also told me of the love story, if they are the right words, of you and Darcey. I can only say that she is a joy to be with and is what Scots call a truly bonny lass.'

'I love and adore her, Anne-Marie, and have done ever since I first set eyes on her when I was doing an inspection at the Police College, but never more so than when I glimpsed her setting-to with Rhona in the parlour. As for the rest, Chloe's right about it all, but it's wonderful now to be away from the world of crime.'

'Until you take some sheep to market and get considerably less than you know they're worth. That's called daylight robbery!'

They laughed and returned to the others.

'We can go through the books after breakfast,' said Ed. 'They're relatively straightforward and I'm sure Rhona will tell you everything you need to know.'

'What we all need to know,' said Rhona, 'is that milking starts at 5:00am, and therefore bed should start now. Do you two want to have another go in the parlour?'

'We'd better get into practice,' replied Darcey. 'Are you with us in the morning?' she said to Adam.

'Oh no,' replied Anaïs. 'He's all mine at that time.'

'It's me,' said Anne-Marie. 'Sleep well.'

***

As Jo and Darcey cuddled up close together in bed, Jo asked Darcey what she thought of it all.

'If I was to give my true answer, I think you'd be shocked.'

'Oh!' said Jo. 'Don't tell me you want to throw me over for Rhona or Anaïs, though isn't she lovely and so French with it?'

'They're both lovely women, my darling, but not a patch on you. You are my life – utterly.'

'So what's going to shock me?'

'We haven't long to accomplish all this moving business, and you have a great deal to get sorted, not least in flying to St Albans tomorrow for Josie and Ollie, and then in deciding their futures. You need to talk with your mum and dad, Katia and Chloe, and make decisions about the house and cars. You need to see your solicitor, and in all this I am going to be a useless extra, so my thought is to get a head start in the learning process by asking Rhona and Anne-Marie if I can stay. It might also be an incentive to you to complete everything as quickly as possible.'

'It's a terrible idea, my beloved, first of all because however can I bear the thought of sleeping without you, but much more important, by the time I get here in a couple of weeks' time you will be so much better at milking than me.'

'And shit-shifting!'

'We've both had plenty of that in our time, my love, so it should be second nature. And of course you're right. I think it's very sensible and I'm only a bit shocked. Now come closer and closer until we are one.

There was a wonderful urgency about their first love-making in Scotland.

27

The landrover pulled into the yard and stopped outside the house.
'You've mastered this quickly,' said Jo.
'That's nothing. You should see me milking.'
Ollie and Josie had been so excited about arriving in their new home, and out of the door of the house emerged Chloe who with Katia had driven Jo's car up yesterday.'
'Hello,' she said. 'This place is smashing. I've been milking by myself for ages back in Suffolk so to be able to share it with Rhona and Darcey has been a total treat, and Katia is now the queen of the shit shifters. Meanwhile Darcey has taken to the alpacas like a duck to water.'
'What happened to the Chinese pigs?' asked Jo.
'Very tasty I thought,' said Rhona. 'I felt it would make life easier if they disappeared on the day that Anne-Marie did too, and I bought four alpacas at the insistence of Darcey. However one of your first tasks as far-owner is to reply to an email from Anne-Marie asking us to arrange transportation for her pigs down to Suffolk!'
'Ah! I'm not at all surprised,' said Jo. 'Well with Christmas coming I guess that what remains of them will have to be wrapped in blankets! A new departure for the ship but with the same captain.'
'I'm very excited, Jo. It's nearly Christmas which I love, though it's still a 5:00 am start and again in the afternoon. We have to spread slurry after Christmas. Then we've got Hogmanay, winter snow and the earliest calving, and then lambing, which will sort out the sheep from the goats. Is everyone coming to live here? If they are it's going to get pretty packed with your mum and dad staying too.'
'No. Once New Year comes and goes I shall fly Josie and Ollie back for school. Chloe and Katia are returning by train tomorrow as Chloe has to return to the farm to work for Anne-Marie. My friend, Dani, former Chief Constable of Greater Manchester is going to live in our house with Louise her partner, with Katia and Chloe in the flat, and between them they will do the school runs each day, though it's possible Josie will go to live with her dad in St Albans, and if so Ollie will go with her though of course I hope they might

come here. They are unbelievably close; some might say unhealthily close, but what unites them is their mother, Marie.'

'But I thought you were Ollie's mum.'

'I carried him for 9 months, so of course I'm his mum, but he was not mine biologically. The fertilised egg was Marie's, which is why they look alike. Sadly, Marie could never be their mother and as far as they and I are concerned I am their mum, but I cannot object to what they regard as holding them so closely together.'

'We have the same here on the farm.'

'What do you mean?'

'AI – Artificial Insemination for our ladies, not Artificial Intelligence. I went on a course to learn how to do it, and I'm responsible for getting them pregnant, not just here but on local farms too. That's more or less the same as IVF, isn't it? If you and Darcey are considering it, just let me know. I'm not expensive, though it will be cold in the barn when we do it, but you can't have everything.'

'Rhona, do remember I'm your boss now and would expect it for free.'

'Oh God, I knew this would happen: a boss who would exploit me. It's the beginning of the end.'

By now the three of them were rocking with laughter.

At that moment a marked police car pulled into the yard behind the landrover, from which an officer emerged from the back seat, readjusted his hat and came towards him. Darcey and Jo knew his rank from his shoulder insignia.

'Good afternoon,' he said. 'Where can I find Dame Joanne Enright?'

The three of them looked round at each other as if the name was completely new.

'She could be milking,' said Darcey, 'talking to the alpacas, or it could be this remarkable woman on my left.'

The Chief looked at Jo.

'Ok guv, I'll come quietly, it's me,' she said with a huge smile, 'but to you I'm Jo, please.'

'Jo it is, and I'm Frank.'

After shaking hands, Jo led him into the farmhouse whilst Rhona and Darcey, joined by Chloe, made their way to the milking parlour.

'Our furniture only arrived yesterday so we are a little upside down and I only arrived just before you, but please find somewhere to perch.'

'I won't get in your way. I just wanted to welcome you to Scotland, and to bring greetings from the First Minister who knows this house well. Her former head of the civil service, Ed, lived here and she often called to see him.

'Police Scotland functions from a castle between Stirling and Dunfermline and we have a Police College close by. Perhaps at some stage when you're settled in, you might come and talk to the lads and lasses about being a detective.'

'I'd be happy to do that, Frank, once, that is, I've learned some of the rudiments of animal husbandry.'

"Ok, so we'll see you in about three years' time!'

Jo laughed.

'Thanks for the vote of confidence, but a genuine thank you for coming today. Some will think I'm mad, and I have been offered opportunities to rise to your illustrious level but I knew I needed an end to my days hunting down criminals and crime. Unexpectedly, an opportunity arose and here we are. But I'm always available for anyone in Police Scotland who would welcome chewing something over.'

'That's very generous of you.'

'I owe the police service a great deal.'

'Well, you've certainly given a lot, and when you've got sorted in the house, I take it you'll be at work in the milking parlour. '

'Oh yes, and we begin at 5:00 am, taking me back to my days as a constable in Boston, although I have to say that despite an utterly misogynist boss, I look back on those years with considerable affection, because that was where and when I learned to be a detective, to which I added my regular reading of Freud.'

'I wish I could stay and hear the whole story but of course I have a meeting I must attend, so all the best, Jo.'

'And you, Frank, and when it comes, have a happy Christmas and Hogmanay.'

Frank left and Jo sat down by herself, reflecting the oddity that now having left the police, her first visitor should be a Chief Constable! Josie and Ollie were watching television and making plans for Christmas. The door opened and in came Darcey.

'I just wanted to pop in and tell you, Jo, how much I love you.'

'And I you – forever. Now get back to work, you reprobate!'

They kissed long and hard before Darcey did as she was told, but made her way back via the alpacas.

Further Reading

Many more novels by Rod Hacking can be seen at

Salisburywriter.com

and are available from the Rod Hacking page on Amazon

Printed in Great Britain
by Amazon